MW01133984

Other books by Barry B. Powell

- *Composition by Theme in the Odyssey*, Beiträge zur klassichen Philologie, 1974
- *Homer and the Origin of the Greek Alphabet*, Cambridge University Press, 1991
- *A New Companion to Homer* (with Ian Morris), E. J. Brill, 1995
- *A Short Introduction to Classical Myth*, Pearson, 2000
- *Writing and the Origins of Greek Literature*, Cambridge University Press, 2003
- *Rooms Containing Falcons*, poetry, Pegasus Books, 2006
- *The War at Troy: A True History*, Mock-epic, Pegasus Books, 2006
- *Ramses in Nighttown*, autobiography, Bascom Hill Books, 2006
- *Homer*, second edition, Wiley-Blackwell, 2007
- *Writing: Theory and History of the Technology of Civilization*, Wiley-Blackwell, 2009
- *The Greeks: History, Culture, Society* (with Ian Morris), second edition, Pearson, 2009
- *Ilias, Odysseia*, Greek text with translation of Alexander Pope, Chester River Press, 2009
- *World Myth*, Pearson, 2013
- *The Iliad*, Oxford University Press, 2013
- *The Odyssey*, Oxford University Press, 2014
- *Classical Myth*, eighth edition, Pearson, 2014
- *Homer's* Iliad *and* Odyssey: The Essential Books, Oxford University Press, 2014
- *Vergil's* Aeneid, Oxford University Press, 2015
- *Vergil's* Aeneid: The Essential Books, Oxford University Press, 2015
- *The Berkeley Plan: A Novel of the Sixties*, Orion Books, 2016
- *The House of Odysseus, and Other Short Fictions*, Orion Books, 2016
- *The Poems of Hesiod: Theogony, Works and Days, Shield of Herakles*, University of California Press, 2017
- *Take Five: A Story of Jazz in the Fifties* (with Sanford Dorbin), Telestar Books, 2017
- *Tales of the Trojan War, with illustrations from European art*, Amazon Publications, 2017

A LAND OF SLAVES

a novel of the American university

Barry B. Powell

A LAND OF SLAVES

a novel of the American university

Orion Books
New York

Orion Books
New York City, New York

Library of Congress Cataloguing-in-Publication Data
Powell, Barry B., author
Land of Slaves/Barry B. Powell

ISBN 9781466378230

You have the Pyrrhic dance as yet,
    Where is the Pyrrhic phalanx gone?
Of two such lessons, why forget
    The nobler and the manlier one?
You have the letters Cadmus gave—
    Think ye he meant them for a slave?

—from *Don Juan*, Lord Byron

1. *How things began*

Fat, hungry, Professor Wally Wills sat on the crowded sundrenched terrace. It was the spring semester, 1991. Wally Wills was one of the five leading experts in the world on Greek black-figured vases from the sixth century BC. Everything about Wally was huge, and his round face with bulbous too-red nose and full black beard made him look like Falstaff, or a medieval bon vivant.

He sat with his good friend and rival, the lanky, handsome, but too thin Professor Raymond Birch, a scholar known even in Germany. Wills held his cigarette like a Russian count, poised between thumb and middle finger while Birch wore Doug McArthur dark glasses and smoked like a punk from Chicago, which in a way he felt himself to be.

"You've gone completely out of your mind," said Wills under his voice.

"Things were better before, in the old days," Birch replied.

"Things are not so bad," Wills grunted.

"For one thing, I could blow smoke rings then, in the old days!" Birch puffed like a dragon but could not make the rings. "Too much wind, I suppose. I think that this encroaching email thing is a big part of it. With email, you're never free."

A tame sparrow alighted on the wire-mesh table and picked

at a crumb.

"Watch out, Birch! You're in danger," Wills said, suddenly ominous, crushing out his cigarette beneath his Greek sandal.

"What do you mean I'm in danger?" said Birch. "How do you know?"

"A little bird told me," said Wills.

Below them the clean well-dressed young couples with ruddy faces and their children in sun-bonnets fed eager mallards at the edge of the water. The beautiful lake stretched before them at the foot of the sloping terrace where the two men were sitting. In the far distance, on the other side of the lake, you could just make out the State Mental Hospital where the famous cannibal and murderer Ed Geen had died after decades of incarceration. But you needed to know where to look to see the hospital.

"You know I love these Midwest milk slobbering types," Wally was saying. "They're dumb as cows, sure ... but very sweet, and I'd take them any day over, well ... "

"Over the cool and the beautiful, you mean?"

"Would you mind smoking somewhere else?" an obese woman shouted from several tables away. "You're polluting our air!"

Birch and Wills guffawed in unison. They crushed out their cigarettes on the bottom of the wire-mesh table.

"Hey Wills, know any good Geeners?" Birch asked suddenly, changing the subject, inspired by the thought of the State Mental Hospital. A Geener was a joke based on the career of Ed Geen, in fact the state's most famous criminal. Now *there* was a cannibal and necrophile, the inspiration for Hitchcock's *Psycho*.

"OK, why does Ed Geen keep the temperature turned up to seventy degrees?" said Birch.

"So the lampshades won't get goose pimples?" replied Wally Wills.

They both laughed together again. They'd heard it a thousand times. Birch lit another cigarette, and so did Wills.

"What kind of danger, if I might ask?" Birch asked.

Wills patted Birch on the back of his hand, saying nothing.

White sails scudded in the distance over the deep blue placid water that sparkled and flashed under the brilliant sun. The balmy air was scented with something warm. The professors wore jeans, their shirts open.

Hundreds of students crowded the tables above and below them and around them, drinking beer, laughing, having a very good time. They all looked the same in their cut-off jeans, T-shirts, baseball caps turned backwards, the boys with close-cropped hair and the women clean as a whistle in shorts with jumper tops.

"Is this a dream, or are we living in a film?" Birch asked. "I keep thinking that I am living in a film."

Birch and Wills were being watched all right, and they lowered their voices.

"Once we were great, Wills. But now we are shit."

"You naughty boy." Wally dragged on his cigarette and inhaled the smoke deep into his lungs with unashamed pleasure. "You live like a prince."

"Like a divorced prince!"

"Well, the way you were carrying on … You're lucky you weren't sacked," said Wally Wills.

Birch's adulteries meant little to Birch. They simply seemed the thing to do. When he thought about it now, a wave of revulsion swept over him, pushing him down into a dark place where there was a ringing in his ears, and far away, a blinding light. Was this just the temper of the times?

"You know I've been having these thoughts," Birch said. "I'm thinking that this planet is some kind of experiment. Like somebody is running an experiment."

Wills took another deep drag.

"There, there, dear boy," he said.

Birch poured out the rest of the lukewarm beer into his Dixie cup. The moaning and licking, the usual oaths, a lifetime of unhappiness. Where would it all end?

"The point is, Wills, a long time ago, these space guys came down to this planet. I know it sounds wild, but this is what happened. 'And the Sons of God saw the daughters of men, how they were fair. And they went into them.' I am quoting the fucking Bible to you, Wills."

"You're insane, Birch!" Wally mocked and rubbed his grizzled chin. He gave Birch the eye while Birch sipped at the crumbling cup.

"I've never felt better," said Professor Birch. "Now that I've given up the life of the body. That's what I'm trying to tell you. Now I live in the pure white light of the spirit."

Wills pretended to swallow his beer and cigarette smoke at the same time. He shot the mixture straight out through his ears.

"Some advice, my dear Wills," said Birch. "The only way to survive is to live like Job. To remember that, in the end, after all our horrid pain, we will be justified."

Birch thought of his grown daughter, who had rejected him for his immorality. Tears came to his eyes. She had said it was only her duty as a woman.

"Yes, Wally, thanks for the warning," Birch said, subdued. "I'll be careful. Of course now that I live in the pure white light of the spirit ... well, these things matter less to me. Do you see what I mean?"

"Of course, dear boy. You are so dear to me!"

2. The pure white light of the spirit

Birch adjusted his orange colored dark glasses that gave him a brighter view of the world and leaned back in the metal chair with the springy seat. His eyes searched the crowds, but he recognized no one. Birch was a recluse now and almost unknown outside the classroom and, of course, the obligatory violent hateful department meetings. Today, however, he had made an exception, expressly to drink beer with his old pal Wally Wills.

A mallard duck landed at Birch's feet and looked up at him in a puzzled way. The bird appeared to be smiling. The duck waddled under a railing and tugged at a French fry lodged in the dirt. The two friends, Birch and Wally, had fallen into silence, exhausted by the topic. A Medivac helicopter hovered above, VROOOOOM, low in the distance over the lake.

"You should never have hired that little prick Jack Devries," Wills said at last.

"And don't forget Olivet Oil," said Birch.

A boy undergraduate slouched past them.

"Hi professor Wills," he said, beaming with strong upper arms and a curl of blonde hair and a bulge down there.

"Hi there—do sit *down*," Wally encouraged, looking up. "Sit down, dear boy!"

"I can't Professor Wills. I have to go to class."

The boy swallowed and adjusted his eyes.

"But come out to the house some time, dear boy. As soon as you can. Come out!"

Everybody wanted to go out to Wally's cushy pad on the lake. That's where the action was. "I will," he said, and disappeared into the crowd

"Who was that?" Birch asked.

"That is ... *Tom*. Good old *Tom*."

"He's a bit young, don't you think?"

A ray of sun caught the ruby pinkie ring that Wally wore on his left hand, an emblem of his great personal, even baronial, wealth, his freedom from daily want, from the fear of impoverishment that gripped academicians, terrifying its inhabitants. But mostly they were a gang of losers and wannabees from the provinces, their heads filled with shit—at least in Birch's opinion. They made so little money because they contributed so little to society, that was pretty obvious.

But Wally was truly a breath of fresh air, a Boston Brahmin from the Cherry Hill neighborhood, whose family owned a twenty-six room house on Cape Cod and kept a yacht in Greece. Fat, bald, cocksucking Wally Wills only did this teaching stuff for fun, and because he so loved the topic. He was a real scholar, though in a small way. He knew the rules all right. He always had everything, sucking the milky white fluid of life from the great mother of family and wealth. The pinkie ring was the symbol of his status and freedom. Birch exalted in their friendship.

Yes, Wills was too careless with his money, and his vices were famous, but you knew he'd be there when the toss was down, that in the crunch he'd throw you the line you needed to survive.

Birch lit another cigarette and drew down on it.

"You know, taking all this bullshit on a broader front, we are really talking about the evils of democracy," Birch said, "if I may put it that way. I mean they put power into the hands of the people—who are hysterical, consumed by fear, godless except in sentimental ways, anxious to die for nothing, and unwilling to arrest all Muslims at airports. Give power to the people, and you take it from us, Professor Wills!"

Wally Wills laughed heartily.

"Democracy!" he said.

"Without it you'd be nothing, Wally!"

Wills laughed again.

"By the way, Wally, give me ten thou, would you? I'm a little short."

"You're going to need more than that before this is over," Wally cooed and blew a stream of smoke into the air.

A band was setting up on the podium twenty feet away from where Birch and Wally sat. That night the place would rock with loud groovy tunes.

"OK, so Jack Devries looks shaky, you're right," Birch agreed. "But you know I got into this mess because I believed in the old days, in the poets, in the guys with the common vibe, in the revolution of the spirit and in the triumph of truth."

"That's where you made your mistake," Wally scoffed.

"And that's why I have chosen to abandon the fight and to live in the pure white light of the spirit. That's what I've been telling you, Wills. Are you listening to me?"

Wally laughed so loud he nearly fell out of his chair.

"You are mad, Birch, mad! Devries is a pimp. I used to suck his dick."

"Some distinction!" Birch crushed out his butt on the underside of the table, raining sparks everywhere. "How was I to see he was going to team up with Angela Bellamy and proceed from there to the Great Moogah? I thought Devries would build bridges. I really did! I thought he would heal old wounds. What a fool I was."

Angela Bellamy scarcely spoke to Birch any more, but she and Wally were forever *tête a tête* it seemed, every time Birch saw them together. It amazed Birch how Wills was able to carry on close relationships with people Wills feared or mistrusted. That certainly wasn't Birch's style. He let them have it, right between the eyes, KAPOW! Get out of my way. Now it looked like they were going to return the favor.

"The fact is, it's a miracle you've survived so long," Wally sighed.

"Oh, very poetic." Birch lit another cigarette. "Just like that hotshot little *poet* with the frizzy piled hair and German manner, our friend Jack Devries!"

3. He wouldn't listen

Suddenly Birch felt like he was going to faint.

"See, you know, I wanted Devries to come into the big myth course, but he wouldn't do it. He told me to go fuck myself," Birch said sourly.

"Sure, you had your chance," said Wills.

"He thinks that Bellamy can protect him from anything, that she is out to get me and if he pitches in that will increase his influence with her," said Birch bitterly.

"You could be fired *for cause*," Wally said in a low voice. He rubbed a new cigarette beneath his nose like a cigar.

"Not very likely. Too much noise."

Birch didn't care if they did fire him. He was sick to death of the whole thing. He would like to escape, to get away.

"I could of course just take my life," Birch said sardonically. "I thought Devries would fit in so well. He's a *feminist*, for God's sake!"

"A *feminist*!" Wally laughed so hard that people sitting on the higher ground, under a magnificent spreading oak, turned to see.

"Let them spread their wings and fly, I thought!" said Birch.

"You've lost your mind, old pal!"

"So the other day I go into Devries's office, see, and I say, 'Hi Jack,' I says, 'how would you like to understudy the big myth course?' "

He saw Jack as in a vision ... on the other side of the desk, his curly blonde high-piled hair-can-do.

"You know Jack Devries is really very cute," Birch said. "While I'm talking to him, I see up on the edge of his shelf—he's got this, you know, this fucking black-figured Greek pot! It used to belong to George MacDoodle, I guess. I saw it in his office once, a pretty nice piece. Somebody was supposed to have picked up this thing, I dunno, at some dig."

"George MacDoodle, that figures," Wally said with contempt. "I know that pot! It should be in the museum!"

"So I says, seeing the pot on the shelf, says 'Nice pot. Where'd you get it?' Devries says, 'George MacDoodle gave it to me as a welcoming present.' "

"Welcoming present!" Wills spewed beer across the table. George MacDoodle was retired and, as an emeritus, was sinking fast into alcoholism and despair, it was rumored.

"MacDoodle doesn't even own that stuff! So I says to Jack Devries, 'Funny, I thought that stuff belonged to the department.' "

"Yeah."

A black Labrador dog was swimming away from the shore, heading for a frisbee someone had thrown into the water.

"And so Jack Devries says, 'Well, *le département—c'est moi*!' "

said Birch.

"*C'est moi!*" Wally hyperventilated.

"He fucking said that. And I says, 'Back to the big myth class, Jack old boy. You know I've been teaching it for twenty years, and we depend on its big enrollment and of course the grad students it supports.' "

"Right."

" 'No,' he says. 'Raymond, I don't think I could do that course for you.' "

"I warned you, Birch!"

"Sure. But I wouldn't listen."

4. The real thing

"**Y**eah, the big myth class. That's what you're asking about, isn't it?" Devries had snarled gently the week before, when Birch faced him off again in Devries' office on the thirteenth floor of the mini skyscraper. This monstrosity was built in the sixties and held all the language departments, a demonic Tower of Babel. The faculty offices ran down either side of the building, but in the windowless middle corridor they put the TAs. Birch could not actually see Devries's face, but his golden hair was framed against the burnished light of the late afternoon sun that filtered across the blue lake far below. Somewhere in the cavernous mini-scraper something was humming, vibrating, as if the building were alive, eager to devour something near.

It occurred to Birch that he might be going insane.

"Just what I say, No, I can't do that," Birch heard Devries say in the distance.

What were they talking about? Surrounded by enemies of every stripe, Birch had started to carry a Smith and Wesson .38, just in case. The pistol nested comfortably in his jacket pocket.

"But Jack, that was the main reason we hired you, to understudy this course, so maybe you and me could switch off. It needs, you know, someone with a popular touch, someone who has, well, a way with words—like you, Jack."

"Oh, I really don't think so," Jack Devries snickered. "I've been talking to Angela Bellamy about my position in the department. She thinks I should keep away from pop courses like that. You've done a pretty good job with them over the years, Ray, and, really, what we need in the humanities today is someone to focus on the hard-core stuff, like George MacDoodle says, *das echtiges Stoff.* I guess I'm George's successor when you get right down to it. People like you and Wally Wills can take care of the front of the store."

Wally Wills now!

"Actually, Jack, I don't see what Wally Wills has to do with any of this," Birch snapped. "I'm chair of this department and I thought that you would be able to help out with this course. These are modern times, mister, and frankly we don't fit in very well. We are going to have to get down and dirty, Jack, get out and fly the flag if we want to come out of this alive. We're up against Her Infinite Potential, Jack, don't you get it? See, Jack, my idea was you could help out—we don't want to give Dean Karla Marsh a reason to realign us, like certain departments I could mention, now do we? Give it some thought, Devries."

"No need for thought," Devries shot back, rocking in his chair and folding his hands in his lap. "Really, I don't have time for that kind of teaching, Ray. Talk to Angela—she'll tell you what's going on."

Birch considered seizing Devries by his curly hair and bringing down his nose CARRUMPH into the desk, breaking the cartilage and the blood vessels into a satisfying mush. Fortunately— for Devries!—Birch now lived in the pure white light of the spirit. There was no need for violence. Devries wasn't such a bad guy. He'd just been getting bad advice.

5. *Good advice*

"**O**h lord, there's Mizz Olive Oyl," Wally groaned on the terrace, jerking with his chin to Wally's colleague in the Art History department, a charmless tall specialist in the gestures of women in sixteenth-century Flemish art. "I hear she's pregnant again!"

Mizz Olive Oyl was certainly dangerous, a personal friend of Dean Karla Marsh, ambitious, ruthless, immoral, and yet with laughing eyes and a good sense of humor. Birch was glad that she was Wally's problem.

"You'll never get rid of her at this rate," Birch agreed. "Let's pretend we don't see her …"

"He called me a popularizer, huh?" Wally Wills whispered as he and Birch rolled their chairs around away from Mizz Olive Oyl to face down along the southern shore of the lake, lined with elegant homes and an expensive hotel just beyond the bounds of the enormous campus.

The campus was built along this lake, went for miles, long but very thin before it broached the town. The university was gradually buying up this property, razing the old houses and building labyrinthine laboratories to study all kinds of things. After thirty years Birch had no idea what they really did in these buildings. He had never entered most of them. He wondered what he was doing here, or whether the problem was with the whole planet on which he did not feel at home. These were not evil people, they were just not his people.

"Devries said as much," said Birch.

"Popularizer!" Wills slammed down his beefy hand on the wire-mesh table. "That little prick!"

"Hey … Olive Oyl is gone. What is her real name, anyway? Sure, popularizer, you know, one of those half-baked types who never made it in the big time, who never came up with the big idea but lived their lives behind glib rephrasings of old clichés posturing as truth. I think you know what I mean. You want some more beer?"

"I've taken care of the beer," said Wally. "It's coming. But listen to this, guy … " Wally said conspiratorially, leaning his shiny red bald pate toward Birch like a Roman battering ram. "I've got something for you, and I'll tell you now," he whispered.

"Oh?"

"Last night I was sitting in the 666 Club and in comes Devries. He sits down, and after a couple of beers I ask him how he's doing. Devries says, 'Oh fine, except I have to jump out of the way every time Ray Birch comes staggering down the hall *coked* to the gills.' "

Birch tried to absorb what Wally was saying.

"Coked to the gills," Birch repeated. "Is this the danger to which you alluded earlier?"

"Not at all. And I says to him, 'Jack, don't let me *ever* hear you—*ever, ever*—say anything like that again. Do you understand me, Devries?' "

"Is he insane?" Birch wondered.

"You don't touch that shit, do you Ray?" said Wally.

"Not since I got tenure," Ray admitted as a chill went through him.

"Right. And that was a long time ago. So then Devries says—'Hey Wally, I don't mind about a little blow once in awhile. Don't be offended. I don't care what you guys do in your spare time.' "

"You're making this up!"

"Not on your life," said Wally Wills.

"We must act. If we wait, he'll build leverage. We must take him now," said Birch.

"We must be stealthy," Wally advised after a pause. "Stealth. These annual renewals are automatic, but they don't have to be … It's a simple matter—committee vote, no hearing, no evidence, no confidence. Then Devries is out. That's how we can get him."

"It never happens."

"It *can* happen. Stealth is the key. You can *make* it happen. You still have enough power," said Wally.

Birch hated it. All this was repugnant to his nature. But Wally was right. Things would only get worse if he didn't act now. The fight would come anyhow. Best to act now. If they waited, the winds would shift.

"We're only protecting ourselves," added Wally.

Thank God Birch had Wally Wills to give him good advice!

6. A certain little matter

"I'd like to remonstrate with you about a certain little matter, Jack," Birch said, forgetting Wally's advice about the need for stealth and stalking into Devries' office on the next day.

"Talk? What about, Ray?"

"Well, I don't think it's a good idea for you to go around saying I use cocaine, for one thing. For another thing, I don't use cocaine and even if I did it's not something you'd talk about. Like you said something in the 666 Club the other day, as I hear on the grapevine."

Today the shades were drawn and against them the white face of Jack Devries turned red like blood. Maybe he would explode.

"Well it's common knowledge that you and Wills and some of the others snort a little blow once in awhile," demurred Jack, "and maybe puff some boo, for all I know ... now don't get me wrong ... I mean I'm OK with that."

Birch fingered the Smith and Wesson revolver, gaining strength from its smoothness, its beauty, its feel of power.

"This is not 1967, Jack Devries. Something you may have read about in a book. This is the other side of winning, brother, and these cocksuckers mean business. The Americans waltz around saying everybody is equal but the Muslims know very well they are superior. Islam is not an equal-opportunity employer, my friend! They wouldn't give you a job if you sucked their dick. You're not going to stop them until you go after them where they live, but because everyone is equal, they are going to shine a light up *your* ass until they find what they are looking for. I am alarmed that you would make such a remark in public! I am the chairman of this department!"

Birch was nearly panting. Maybe he was beside himself.

"Sure, good point—I mean, obviously," Devries replied, alarmed at Birch's manner. "I mean, how do you prove you don't use cocaine? But what's this got to do with the Muslims?"

"How right!"

Birch lingered, thinking Devries might break down, might dampen his hand with hot, repentant tears. But Devries only breathed harder, like a runner slogging up a long, steep hill.

Birch left without saying anything more and went into his own office, leaving the door open. The office was small but sufficient, with an oriental carpet, much worn, on the floor. The walls were lined with books—the Penguin series of translations and textbooks stacked on the floor that he intended to sell to the jobber when he came around, and the hieroglyphic texts from Amarna that he'd luckily found in a local bookstore.

He gazed for a moment through the blinds to the lake beyond. On the shelf beneath the window was an impressionistic clay sculpture, a gray blobbish head with the inscription NIXON. His son had made it for him at school, when he was a little tyke and everyone took it for granted that the future held promise.

On a table along one wall that he used for a desk lay a stack of mail, piles of useless memoranda and solicitations to join some goddam thing, or vote for this or report that activity. He casually glanced at each paper, then slipped them one by one into the trash, as he did every day.

Birch no longer had a computer in his office, which gave it the feeling of a refuge, a place of escape. Sometimes he shut the door and turned off the lights and sat in the dark, hoping no one would know.

He looked up. A female graduate student came into his office and sat down in the chair just inside the door, which she now edged slowly closed with her foot. She had been seen having lunch with Olive Oyl and was probably a follower of Angela Bellamy.

"Hi Ray," she said and smiled to show her teeth.

"How can I help you?"

"Oh Gosh I just got back from the hospital. I had a tubule legation, you know. I mean, Professor Birch, I've had three abortions this year! I mean I use everything, you name it, but I like to boogey and there you are," she laughed. "I'm just too fertile I guess. But not any more. I want to get on with the work, you know. I really have no time for traditional constructions on my sexuality."

Birch saw beyond her, emerging from the gray wall, a shaft of light.

"Would you like me to phone a doctor?" he said.

"That would be silly. I just got back from the doctor!"

The lanky brunette with the forward nose, always striding down the hall with her chest in the air, looked at Birch with contempt and pity as he stroked the revolver in his coat pocket.

"But Ray, what are you doing there?" she asked.

"What can I do for you, Charlotte?"

"It's what I can do for *you*, Raymond. That's why I've come. I just wanted to tell you that Angela—she's got your number. That's all. I think you know what I mean."

"What do you mean?"

"It's useless to pretend. Angela has the goods on you, Ray, and she's prepared to use them. So … a word to the wise."

The woman got up and tossed back a lock of her red-brown wavy hair. She winked and smiled and said "Toodle-oom" and swung open the door.

"Don't be bad now," Birch called after her, letting loose the cold shiny metal and feeling its weight in his clothes.

7. Go slow

It was lucky that Birch now lived in the pure white light of the spirit, because the savage unrelenting winter, cheerless and desperate, challenged every preconception. He was used to it, of course, the walls always holding you in, the little comforts of the electric blanket turned up high, the long hot baths in the marijuana air, the search for meaning. The locals loved the moral dimension of winter. They knew it made them stronger. But for Birch it was a test of his purpose, a challenge to his hopes dashed so thoroughly on the hard stone of reality.

That morning, while upstairs at home in his study, reading email and the sludge of spam and meeting announcements and jokes about blondes, suddenly red and yellow lights flashed across the screen:

GO SLOW JOE BLOW

That caught him by surprise. He didn't like the feeling at all. They were clever, these computer wizards, he thought. They had a lot of power, and somebody was evidently out to get him.

8. Quality, please

Birch nearly knocked down Angela Bellamy as they both came out of their office doors at the same time.

"Sorry, Angela—I've been thinking about Jack Devries,

that's all, and I am quite beside myself, frankly," apologized Birch.

"So what seems to be the problem?"

The short deliberately plain woman with her hair in a bun spoke in a low voice as they walked together down the hall. Bellamy was not a feminist, not at all, but a distinguished poet, though on a very small scale. At least that was in her favor.

The lights in Devries's office were out.

"Well Angela, I'm just wondering who's going to teach the big myth course, our big bread-winner. Since Devries refuses to do it. I thought that's why we hired him," Birch objected.

"Why *you* hired him, Raymond," Angela replied coolly, taking one step back and looking up at him.

"Yes, you know I love to teach it, Angela," said Birch, "but I'm also concerned about the quality of Jack's publications. I mean this has been on my mind. I mean if there *are* any publications, except for maybe a couple of tiny little poems in out of the way places. Not that we're a department of poetry. If I might just run this past you, that issue?"

"O Raymond, I don't think you need to worry about Jack's publications," Angela said patiently. "This is only his first year. I mean—think of your own early record?"

She had him there all right.

"Anyway, Jack and I have been having lunch every week and we've been talking about all sorts of things. He's been showing me his very exciting work on the Augustan poet Perseus. It's very 'post.' I think it's really revolutionary. It's going to make a big impact. You know Jack is quite the thing when it comes to theory."

"Perseus!" Birch laughed. That was the beauty of being cool—you could say any thing you wanted and nobody knew the difference. "Oh, really, Angela, give me a break," Birch said.

"No, I'm serious. He's done a stupendous job explaining the construction of poetic meaning through gender reversal. Brilliant, really."

"Gender reversal!" Birch guffawed. "Excuse my French. Well, I look forward to seeing his *very* exciting work, Angela."

"Oh you will, Raymond, you will."

9. You ain't nothin but a myth

Birch always arrived at the last second to the big myth class, held in a European style auditorium built around 1890, with overhanging balcony and varnished wood, rich with time and odorous from the brain waves of the million students who had sat in this room.

Birch's army of TAs had   prepared the hall in advance, drawing down the shades and lowering the big screen in front and setting up the overhead projector, where he projected his notes. He hurried down the aisle through the thronging masses, everyone talking, newspapers everywhere. The students glanced up at him but he never made eye contact with them—that was far too risky!

Birch put down his pack on the table across the front of the low stage and turned on the overhead projector, which threw a flood of light onto the front screen. He could barely see beyond it, their sea of faces. He didn't talk to them much any more. True, sometimes students came to his office. They were very nice, rather prudish, he thought. But what can you expect? They were young kids, some of them even eager to learn. Birch kept getting older, but they stayed the same age. Their thoughts didn't change. The girls were obsessed about how they looked. The boys loved football and whatever sexual release they could find. Pathetic, really.

"I see you're here bright and early, eager to learn," Birch began in a booming voice, "so let us begin at the beginning."

He stopped and said nothing. His head was spinning. He heard a kind of whining sound. They were waiting, waiting for him to do something, to say something. Birch suddenly felt faint. He looked around for a chair. He espied one behind a portable chalk board. He managed to set it up at the edge of the stage. He sat down.

They all wondered, What was Professor Birch doing now?

"Sorry, folks, I just went to the Bahamas there for a minute ..." he apologized.

The audience laughed. From their energy he felt fine again and stood up. Everything was going to be OK, just OK.

10. *Get 'em up*

Birch came out of the elevator, turned left, then left again down the long sad corridor. He passed swiftly down the hall. Every door was shut. He came out into the seminar room at the end of the hall, with its broad picture windows that overlooked the lake. The Devries hearing would take place here.

Highflying crows oared past the shoddy glass, black ghosts, their beaks parted in caws silent through the glass, enormous and primordial in size and intelligence. In the coldest days of winter, at thirty below zero, they still arced silently from pine to pine, swooping over the reaches of snow and wood. Birch wondered what they ate?

The mailboxes were along one wall. Birch thought he'd flip through his mail in the five minutes before the meeting. But on top and in plain view, as he withdrew the pile from the cubby hole, he immediately saw the photocopy of a letter from a secret file in his office. It was from a woman.

Birch ducked out of the seminar room, found his key with the usual difficulty on the unwieldy ring, got the door open, went in, and swiftly closed it behind him. They must be desperate, to try blackmail, he thought, but what exactly was he going to do?

Birch yanked open the cabinet drawer and reached to the back and pulled out the file THINGS, where he carelessly stored secret correspondence and other stuff hard to categorize. There was the original. It was so easy—a pass key from the office at night … How naive he'd been! They even warned him. All he had to do was get rid of DeVries. But they would expose him anyway.

Birch fell back into his swivel chair and closed his eyes. A forest of tiny dots swam before him, like motes in a sunbeam, dots in the purple darkness. There was a kind of ringing sound there.

Birch opened his eyes. He badly needed a cigarette.

Birch laughed out loud as he walked into the meeting room.

"It's really just a way to be malicious," someone said.

Everyone looked up when he entered.

"Hello, everyone. Everybody here, I see?" said Birch.

Birch glanced around the room, where seven people sat. Devries was in the corner at the back, glowering, pale. Across the room, Angela Bellamy, tired, a flower in frost. Then the grim-faced Lutheran Sven Borgnine, an expert in cult prostitution. Beside him, Giuseppe Randolph, from Pisa, obviously too good for this dump; when he was twenty-five he wrote a book on the poetical writings of Philodemus, fragments of whose works survived from the library of the father-in-law of Julius Caesar in the ruins of Herculaneum, all burned to a crisp. Randolph despised Devries as a modernist and disapproved of his heterosexuality.

Then there was good old Sally Brown, the department medievalist, whose father had been a bishop. Though long an associate dean, she could not complete an English sentence. She was a Christian with a heart of gold, but had no kind feelings for the atheist Angela Bellamy, who hated Sally's prideful Christian virtues.

Birch could not win this without Sally's vote.

Across the table sat Hosea Watt, at seventy years old the oldest member of the department. Forty years before he had written a book on Roman colonies in Spain. Watt was easy to control because he didn't grasp the issues and he didn't care about the outcome. Next to him, Ralph Sneed, who did Greek epigraphy.

There had been no students for eleven years and it was becoming a problem. Luckily, the department had the humungous enrollments in Classical Myth, which Birch had taught for years, to justify the department's existence! Sneed always voted Yes to anything.

The energy crackled around the room, zinging off the ears of the innocent and engraving the walls.

"Sven," Birch said to the expert in cult prostitution, "would you mind calling Helen in, please?"

Helen was the department secretary, a friend and confidante, who kept Birch up to speed and warned him about the enemy's plans, seemingly without choosing sides.

"Why is Helen going to be here?" Angela asked.

"What's that for?" said Jack Devries.

"Oh Jack, only to run over the rules—"

Helen came into the room, holding a telephone and a hank of wire.

"I have to remind you, Jack, that you have the right to be at this meeting, that's true, but not to speak—sorry!"

Without meeting anyone's eyes, Helen hooked up a phone in the middle of the oak rectangular desk. The sun had shifted, gushing through the picture windows, filling the room with golden light.

"What's that for?" said Sven Borgnine.

"Thanks, Helen. Actually, Simon in Athens," Birch announced to the room, "wants to get in on this meeting. So ... I've arranged a conference call. That way the whole department can deliberate, eh?"

Just then a crow darted past the window, reared up, and flew on.

"And so the world reveals to us its mystery," Birch said.

"Can we just get on with this?" Angela said gruffly.

11. Iacta alea est

"It's not so important how you die as how you live," Birch was saying to Professor Sally Brown in response to something, as the meeting wore on. Birch zeroed in on Devries' publications and wondered aloud "where all the camaraderie had gone"—that is, now that Devries was among them.

"Yes, of course," Sally Brown laughed awkwardly, tossing her washed-out blonde-gray hair. Her teeth were covered by a brown and white film because her interest in Roman Catholic virtue did not extend to dental hygiene. After all, she lived the lofty life of the mind. Wally Wills loved diminutive Sally Brown passionately. Birch was never sure why. Wally often said that underneath all her bumbling Sally Brown was "tough as a boiled owl."

Yes, I guess she was, creamy on the outside and tacks and nails beneath. She and Angela Bellamy had been fellow students at Bryn Mawr and were typical products.

"I'd like to bring up Jack's teaching record," Angela was saying.

"Sure," Birch agreed, "so what are the figures?"

"Don't you know, chairman Birch?" said Angela.

"High, huh?"

"Superlative! 3.9 out of a possible 4," said Angela.

"Teaching evaluations, for Heaven's sake, Angela! He just gives them all A's. That is well known. Are the students to make staff decisions, or are we? The very high ratings in fact condemn him—if we believe in standards of quality at this university," said Birch.

Giuseppe Randolph chuckled quietly, enjoying the destruction of the twerp Jack Devries, while Sven Borgnine gazed somberly at the table, arms folded over his thin, muscular chest.

Birch glanced at Devries, who really never should have come to this meeting.

"Anyway, we have to turn to our overseas hookup now,

because we're running up the clock. Can you hear us all right now over there in faraway Athens, professor?" Birch said in a loud voice to the speaker on the table.

"Oh, very well indeed," came the electronic voice. Hofsteder's hostile views on Devries were well known.

"In that case, we should sort of sum this up," Birch said.

"Is this on tape?" someone asked, noticing the Sony recorder on top of the heating register under the plate glass windows amidst the chaos of coffee cups, pizza boxes, and dilapidated dictionaries.

"Yes, Angela had the foresight," said Birch.

Around the table they went, each pronouncing an opinion on the merits of Jack Devries. Devries himself sat impassive. He regarded each speaker with intensity. Angela spoke heatedly about Jack's presence, how the kids adored him, then added, "I know that you and Wally Wills have planned this out ..."

"What do you mean?" Birch snapped. "Wally isn't even a member of this department."

"Oh, do you really think we are so dense?" said Angela. "Don't you think we can see what's going on?"

"Let's move right along now," Birch encouraged. "Let's move on past this, now can we?"

It was Sally Brown's turn to speak.

"In my opinion, Mr. Devries has, well ... of course he's still very young ... but, you know, sometimes, a child is father to the man ..."

"Oh please say what you mean," Angela sighed with contempt.

Devries' mouth was wet, it was shining.

"I mean ... well, really what kind of *mind* do we have on the table anyway, when all is said and done ... ?"

"What kind of mind indeed?" said Dean Karla Marsh, suddenly pushing open the door and entering the conference room. Behind her, in her train, came the extremely tall and angular Professor Olive Oyl. "What do you mean what kind of mind? What are you talking about?" said Dean Karla Marsh.

"Oh no," Birch lamented, speaking to the women who had entered. "Is there some reason for you folks being here?"

"Who's there?" said the electronic voice from the speaker.

Dean Karla Marsh seemed larger than her very large size, larger than her very large reputation in her capacious black print skirt and paisley cotton shirt that hung over her large sagging breasts. Her belly bulged in an aggressive wale beneath them as she sat across two of the chairs along the back wall. She looked the group over from above her clear plastic reading half-glasses. Her gray-blond hair, like Sally's, fell limply around a rough whitened face. Olive Oyl, mouth parted in wonder, stood at her side.

"What was that about a mind or something?" Olive Oyl asked.

"Well, Dean Marsh, what a surprise!" said Birch. "And Ms. Oyl. But why are you two here? I didn't realize you'd be popping in, Dean Marsh. I wonder what Ms. Oyl is doing here, too. Of course with the state's open meeting laws and all!"

"I know this is a closed meeting," Dean Marsh replied without expression, "but I hope that you won't mind my attending. Just trying to see how things are working down at the grass-roots, you see. Ms. Oyl is with me as a kind of witness, you might say. No intrusion intended."

"A witness?" Olive Oyl asked.

"Yes, to the prosecution!" said Birch. "But no intrusion taken. We're glad to have you among us, Karla, democracy in action, the rule of the majority. And why not an impartial witness? And we're also glad on general grounds!"

"My idea, exactly," said Karla Marsh. "So think of us as little flies on the wall." She half-chuckled.

"Well then—little flies you are!"

"Am I a fly too," complained the ghostly voice from the phone speaker. "At least I think I've heard enough about the quality of the young Mr. Devries to pronounce an opinion on this matter."

Dean Karla Marsh stared at the speaker as if a cat had died and from its mouth rolled a tangle of white wiggling worms. Devries was doomed, and even the Great Moogah could not save him.

12. *The university of life*

It was beautiful outside, glorious really, as Birch hastened down the tree-lined path at the bottom of the hill, along the edge of the lake. For some reason Birch thought about his grown daughter who had rejected him. A flush of unhappiness, of hopelessness, swept over him. Yet she probably loved him still—if he ever saw her again. No doubt women were trouble, even if they were your own daughter.

When he got to the 666 Club he would get a stiff drink and calm down. Wally would be there and he would expect a full report about the department meeting.

A crow settled on the path in front of Birch and pulled at something stringy stuck on the ground, then lurched upward nearly into Birch's face, cawing and dropping the meaty thing from its beak.

Birch laughed. What could be more silly that an obsession with crows!

"Perhaps I'm going to die," he said aloud.

How would it come? a blow from behind, a blue screaming blast of light? a twisting and snap of the neck? He was in a small, brightly lit room. Some kind of beings were standing around him, but they were not human.

"What?" said a back-packed student from the other direction, a red baseball cap perched backward.

Birch smiled in a knowing way.

"Sorry," Birch apologized. He had probably said something out loud. This sort of thing happened more and more often, it seemed.

Birch hastened his step on the broad dirt path bordered by the almost sheer and bosky slope crowned by student dormitories built of handsome rough-hewn stones. The kids loved it here. They thought it was paradise. Away from home, in stone dorms, with girls for the boys and boys for the girls. Anything could happen. Were they ever in for a surprise!

The woods ended and Birch followed along the narrow walk that ran over the water, attached to the Limnology lab. The lab was founded by a man who had discovered how salmon smelled the site of their own birth so that they too could spawn in the same place, then die. Birch had known the man before he went blind and died. He was from Utah. One day the man had visited his childhood home in the mountains. As he came around a bend, he smelled something he had completely forgotten, something from his childhood, and that's how he made his discovery about how salmon smell the place of their hatching.

Birch dropped down onto the edgewater dock. The student boating club parked their skiffs here, dozens of yellow fiber-glass hulls stacked in neat rows. In summer everything seemed fine, when the terrors of winter were only a dream.

Birch skirted the prows and ropes of the boats and went down a flight of worn wooden steps onto the broad plaza in front of the student union, just up from the lake. He entered the ground floor of the 1930s student union, built in memory of those who had given their lives in the First World War, that men might be free.

"Freedom!" Birch said aloud as he entered through the ancient, green-painted mullioned doors into the dark low-ceilinged Rathskeller. The buzz-buzz of co-eds in overalls and chesty studs swilling beer filled the room. These kids were nice all right—but they simply didn't understand evil. Its reality was hidden from them, taken away from them. Everything was an accident and nobody was to blame, or so they thought.

He pushed into the thick crowds gathered around the scarred wooden tables. In summer, outside, a rock band blasted the starry skies. That's where he and Wally drank from time to time.

Birch hid behind his dark glasses, anxious not to be recognized, as he crossed the large dark room with soiled paintings of German beer mädchen on the walls, and German slogans on banners, such as WEIN AUF BIER, DAS RAT ICH DIR.

"Drink wine on top of beer, that's OK," Birch said aloud, proud of his German. Birch was always trying to remember that one when he was at some party. SEI WITZIG, DIE WELT IST SPRITZIG. "Be joyful, the world is happy." DES LEBENS SONNENSCHEIN IST TRINKEN, LIEBEN, FRÖHLICH SEIN. "The sunshine of life is drinking, fucking, and being cool."

"Hi professor," said a nice young boy with blond hair and big eyes. Birch had never seen him before in his whole life—but how could he? The boy had probably taken the big myth course or history of civ course that Birch also taught. It was understood that communication went just one way—like being famous, except that you weren't!

"Hi," he said with a smile. "How ya doin?"

"Oh, not too bad, not too bad."

Birch came out of the room into the busy hall, passed the video arcade jammed with players and watchers and the BING-BONG of machines. Then a study room packed with Asians playing chess, punching wooden time clocks. Into the busy hall past the ice-cream stand and the magazine rack.

Sure, Birch needed a cigarette and on an impulse he went up to the glass counter.

"A pack of Camel straights," he asked the clerk.

The brimming co-ed laughed.

"I'm sorry, sir, but the university is a smoke free environment."

"Oh, I see. Leaves more room for the bullshit, does it?" Birch said with a sneer.

The girl was startled. She didn't know what to say. Birch smiled slyly and ducked away like a shadow. She probably hadn't recognized him and, anyway, none of this was her fault. Nothing was anyone's fault—shit just happens!

Birch swung through the heavy swinging oak and glass double doors. He headed down the broad steps, ducked around students huddling on the cement steps in the spring air, hungering for the summer. He crossed the street to the square bordered by the neoclassical State Historical Society on one side and the enormous Memorial Library in German bunker style on the opposite. On the far side stood a pseudo-Gothic church and the red-brick Faculty Club, where Wally Wills always ate lunch.

Birch passed the circular fountain in the center of the square, still covered in its winter cap of heavy aluminum. From fraternity row up the street, at the edge of the lake, came already the boom-boom of heavy metal music.

At the other side of the plaza, he wended through milling crowds onto State Street, which conjoined the administration building on the campus with the state capitol building at its other end. The children of the legislators went to the college and college personnel had a complex of personal relations that bound them to the politicians so that, to some extent, the state budget was always an inside job.

"What can you do? Let's keep a smiley face, that's what counts."

Birch felt himself melt into the white light of the spirit as he strode past beer 'n' brat joints, cut-rate CD outfits, stores that sold hats with feathers and posters of Marilyn Monroe and T-shirts that read TOO DRUNK TO FUCK. He turned right past the student travel office onto a side street, walked along a multi-level car park and, already, although still a half block away, he could smell the sour beer from the 666 Club. From time to time Birch used to come here with his wife to join Wally's crowd, but now that his children were grown, and had perhaps betrayed him, and now that his wife was ... gone gone gone ...

"Wow," Birch sighed to no one in particular and half jumped back when a crow swooped down five feet away from his face and rose up, long legs dangling, to settle on the roof of the liquor store across the street. Birch came down out of the spirit into the real world.

"Someone's going to die. That's for sure," he observed.

Maybe it was Birch himself who would die, catapulted into the pure white light of the spirit that beamed through the prism of the world, at peace, at rest, at last. A certain kind of freedom, no doubt.

13. *The number of the beast*

Birch shook his head to clear it and entered the back door of the club. At first he couldn't see a thing in the yellow haze, only heavy forms slumped around tables. A low cacophonous drone ran around the room like an anaconda in a deep green forest. A neon sign in the front window read THE LAND OF SKY-BLUE WATERS, but the sign was half burned out and hard to see through the dusky windows. The place was Chicago sleaze, including a real tin ceiling and the faded picture of a mountain lake behind the bar and a Dr. Pepper Clock. The air was smoke-filled and the toilets filthy. You wouldn't want to take a shit in here, unless you really had to.

For years the 666 Club had been the only good bar in town, but now the university had bought the property and intended to raze the ancient brick building, probably once a whore house, and build a student laundromat.

"Hey Birch! Fuck you," called a low merry voice from the huddle of dark shapes crammed into the back booth of the long room.

"Is that you, Wally?" Birch peered into the gloom.

"It's always Wally Wills!" said one of the dozen people crowded around the table covered with a forest of empty glasses and three enormous ashtrays overflowing with cigarette butts. Packets of cigarettes spilled out in the melee of torn bags of potato chips and pretzels. Though early in the afternoon, the group had been going at it for a good while.

Birch commandeered a metal and vinyl chair from another table and scooting and scraping he pushed it into a gap between the people gathered around Wally. Wally's crowd was a movable feast with fuzzy edges and sub-groups, including a sporting group that had organized a fishing trip to Montana. They never made it out of the cabin. Wally had missed that trip, somehow. On Friday nights the poker subgroup gathered at Wally's on the lake to play cards, smoke pot, drink hard liquor, and gossip. Birch had played with them a couple of times, but Birch was a serious poker player, an extremely conservative player—he'd played in the card clubs in California. Lo-ball was his game, but these guys liked to get raucous over Pass-the-Shit.

"Hey, you get this boy a beer, would you?" Wills demanded, banging his egg-bald head against the booth partition and rubbing his short grizzled beard. Birch could see better now. Wills was smiling like a pumpkin and very cute. "Get the buzzer, would you, Eddy?" Wills barked to the man at his side.

That would be Eddy Cornel, Wally's newest big heat, a live-in boisterous out-of-control athletic handsome former professor of English, fired for sexual-harassment. Seeing Eddy Cornel only reminded Birch of the probably imminent release of his own private correspondence and the ruin that soon would follow. Right, shit does happen.

"The glory days are over, Wills, for your information," Birch announced. "And the beer won't do you any good."

"Hi Ray," said Eddy Cornel, whom Birch hadn't seen for a while. Eddy reached over Wally's head and punched the buzzer on the green wood partition.

Birch said, "I didn't know you were still in town, Eddy."

"I'm not," said Eddy Cornel.

Wally Wills had shown courage when he took in Eddy after the *scandale*. Poor Wally, he tried to recreate *le grand affaire* he'd had years before with the attractive Sean Stand, with whom he'd owned a pioneer stone-hewn house forty miles outside of town in the woods. Wally was in love with Sean, Birch guessed. He was torn up when they split. Maybe life was good then, and everything different, back in the old days before the computers came. They were flying high in those days.

Eddy Cornel was a pale imitation of the seignior Sean Stand and there was sex, sure, but the passion was gone. In Wally's life the tragic past was relived in comedy. Eddy's job, when he had lived at Wally's on the lake, was to wash out the laundry and take out the garbage and paint the house, in fact to be Wally's boy and slave, grateful that he got to be close to such a famous former colleague. But Eddy rued his fate and didn't like being a slave, for some reason. He became sullen, alcoholic, violent, and several times had beaten the shit out of big Wally Wills.

One morning, early, Wally had phoned Birch and begged him to come out. When Birch got there, "He just keeps coming at me," Wally lamented in a hushed voice, his arm in a cast. "I don't know what to do. I cover up my head, but he just pounds all over me!"

Birch was standing in the front room of Wally's house at the edge of the lake. The brilliant sun flooded the white room. The whole south wall was windows.

"Get rid of this piss-ant, Wally. It's the only way," Birch advised.

"You think so, pal? Get rid of Eddy Cornel, huh?"

"I'm only in town today," Eddy Cornel was saying in the 666 Club, leaning forward into the midst of the merrymakers to speak to Birch. "I live over in Paducah now."

"Yeah, what are you up to?" Birch asked politely around the people between him and Eddy, sitting next to Wally in the corner of the booth. Without asking, Birch shook a Pall Mall from one of the opened packs on the table and put it in his mouth. The man next to him flicked up a Bic gas lighter. "Hey, Harvey Vanderpool—didn't see you," Birch apologized to the man. Harvey Vanderpool was a professional ceramicist who lived in the country and against all odds actually made his living by throwing whimsical ceramic pots, which he sold at art fairs around the country.

"I'm teaching high school now," said Eddy Cornel.

A laugh went around the table.

"Maybe you can get me a job?" said Harvey Vanderpool.

Everybody laughed again.

"And me too ..." Birch said enigmatically.

In the old days Birch and Harvey Vanderpool and Wally Wills were three points in a social triangle, when Birch was married and Wally lived with Sean Stand in the stone house in the country and Harvey Vanderpool was married too, and everybody kept a vegetable garden. In those days they decried the vices of places like the 666 Club. Harvey Vanderpool had rented a beat-up farm-house thirty miles into the rolling countryside not far from Wally's and Sean's pioneer stone house. Vanderpool cut his own wood for the winter and raised a calf or two, grew corn, and sweetened life with an occasional dope deal.

Birch and his ex-wife used to visit Harvey Vanderpool at his place when they felt like getting out of town. They rocked back and forth on wobbly straight-backed chairs around a big wood stove that thundered red. Blue ice hung in jagged sheets from battered curtainless panes. They drank black coffee laced with whisky, in those days.

"Yeah, Eddy has really done well for himself in life," Wally crooned and threw back his head so that it bounced again from the green partition as his massive girth banged against the table's edge. Birch blew out a stream of smoke. The smoke rose in the air across the picture poster of the mountain stream in a forest glen pasted to the wall above the booth. A brown incandescent bulb, up there in the mists, cast a yellow hue.

"Fuck you, Wally," Eddy said.

"Oh yes, words are so cheap."

Everybody laughed uproariously. Obviously they were drunk.

"You're shameless, Wills," Birch complained and wiggled his beat-up metal chair into better position.

"I thought you'd never notice," Wally said.

Wally swallowed an uh-huh and held out his cigarette before him.

"So let's fuck, hey Birch, let's fuck. I'm tired of this hanging around, huh?" he said.

Wills's words brought down the house and made such a stir that patrons all over the crowded bar turned to see what the hell was going on.

14. *Worthless in every way*

"**B**ut really, we're all anxious to hear how the meeting went," said Wally as the hilarity subsided. " ... and by the way, Birch ..."

"What?"

"I don't think you've meant Eddy's new wife, Evelyn."

Birch pretended everything was normal. The woman sitting across the table, brunette with high cheekbones, smiled prettily. She was very nice looking, a really snazzy dame. Birch thought he remembered her, maybe from last summer when he was out at Wally's and Eddy Cornel, kicked out of the house, came by with his new hardbody girlfriend, sweet with rose puckery cheeks, hot, and an intelligent lilting voice. Sure, that was Evelyn all right. In college she majored in percussion, Birch remembered. That was a laugh!

So the rumor was true, that Eddy Cornel, under a woman's influence, had given up drinking and fucking everything that moved and taken on the straight life.

"Hi," Evelyn said to Birch.

"Evelyn and I have tied the knot all right," Eddy said churlishly, taking a deep draft from his beer.

"At least you can do something right," Wally sniped, holding up by implication for the one hundred thousandth time the supposed real and lasting achievements of Sean Stand, a real man who now worked for the Chicago Board of Trade, whatever that was, as against the shame of poor Eddy Cornel, who had never done anything except get fired for sexual harassment. In fact, he was worthless in every way, said Wally!

Wally ran his eyes around the circle of drinkers while

dragging on his cigarette.

"Hey now, where is Birch's beer? Hit that bell again, would you Cornel?"

Birch caught a glimpse, two seats down on the same side of the table, of the disreputable Vergil Rawlins, a petty dope-dealer and hanger-on, who supposedly installed car-radios for a living but who really sold narcotics from his suburban house up the street from Wally's, near the lake. Sometimes Birch would come up on Vergil Rawlins while he was tying up his sailboat at Wally's dock, or tramping across Wally's backyard dragging an armload of sailing gear, heading home.

Once Rawlins's wife, or girlfriend, or whoever she was, was with him, the skinniest woman Birch had ever seen. She was unashamed, wearing a string bikini that showed every bit of her buttocks, her breasts so small there was nothing to hide. Birch had to admit that she was very sexy.

Rawlins and Wills had some understanding about the dock so that Rawlins, who could do things with his hands, put up the dock in the spring, then tore it down in the fall and stored it in the stuffed garage off the parking apron behind Wally's house. In return, Rawlins got to dock his sailboats at Wally's and treat the dock as his own. But when guests came to Wally's, Rawlins had to take them out on the lake to prove how fantastically great it was to live like the very fat and very rich Professor Wally Wills.

Birch nodded to Rawlins while Eddy Cornel lurched up from the table and hit the bell. The bar boy showed up just then. With an arrogant, really contemptuous, manner he took orders for beer all around and one gin collins for Wally.

Here they were, Wally's crowd all around the table—a government worker; a fat pasty woman; an aging hippy with deeply lined face and pony tail; a somber man in the far corner, vaguely familiar; a sadsack who smiled and fawned; a loudmouth who told bar jokes about turtles; the state historian of early weapons; and an obese woman who chain smoked and said fuck every other word—in addition to Harvey Vanderpool, Vergil Rawlins, Eddy Cornel, and his wife Evelyn.

"So cut the shit, Birch, and tell us what happened," Wally

demanded. "You asshole. You know we're waiting."

"At the renewal hearing?"

"No! In La-La Land, you twit!" Wally said. "You really are a wuss! I trust that Devries will no longer be with us."

All eyes turned to Birch.

15. *Leaders in their profession*

"**W**ell, it went more or less as planned, except for the ending, I mean," Birch began. "I brought in the conference call from Hofsteder in Athens, just like you said, Wally, and so I'm thinking, natch, we've got the vote in the bag and Devries is out. It's a cliffhanger, but Hofsteder is going to push it over, see?"

"I don't like the drift of this, Birch," said Wally.

Birch looked around. He was not anxious to be too explicit.

"So then the vote comes to Sally Brown—our dear friend Sally Brown."

"Dear, dear Sally! Angela's nemesis!"

"The papist!" said Birch.

"The angel!" said Wally.

"Sally Brown—she votes *for* him!" Birch exploded.

"Sally Brown voted for Devries?" Wally gasped. He put down his cigarette.

"I thought the fucking roof was going to fall in! I thought we had come to the end of the world," said Birch.

"Sally Brown voted for Devries? Birch, you're too much. You're making this up." Wally lit another cigarette and took a deep drag. "You're joking, right?"

"No."

"So are you telling me you lost the vote, in spite of the Hofsteder ploy?" Wally said in a voice suddenly small, without hilarity.

"Yes, that's right. But just hang on, Wally ... So after the vote, I says to Sally—'Sally, what are you *doing*? You just voted to renew Professor Devries. I thought you were going to vote the other way?' And everybody looks at me like I'm out of my mind, and of course the tape recorder is running and, get this, Dean Karla Marsh is sitting right there, eating it up. Dean Karla Marsh and her sidekick Olive Oyl!"

"You're doomed, Birch."

"I didn't get to that yet, Wally."

"So what were *they* doing there?"

"Looking around, you know."

"They'll kill you, Birch! Your life has ended."

"But see, just before the vote, I heard the tape-recorder click off. Angela had brought in a tape-recorder, but the tape had run out! Devries thought it was all on tape. But it wasn't. It's all just hearsay now, Wills. They can't prove a thing."

"You mean like 'I Dean Karla Marsh swear on oath,' " Wally mocked. "I don't even know you, Birch. You are a dead man."

"Sure, sure, so then Sally Brown says, 'Oh well Ray, in that case, uh, I guess ... I'll *change* my vote ... yes, I'll vote *No.*' "

Wally exploded, turning into cosmic fire.

"And then Angela Bellamy says, 'Well, the vote is over, Sally, and we *can't* change it now, so that's all there is to it, and what do you think you're *doing* anyhow? Frankly, I think this conversation is illegal.' "

"Leaders in their profession," said Harvey Vanderpool quietly.

"But then I says, 'Oh yes we *can* change the vote because we never adjourned the meeting.' All this time Devries is shitting in his pants. Karla Marsh is looking at me like I'm a slug, you know, over the tops of her glasses, but she doesn't make a peep, just sort of clenches her jaw. Get it? Olive Oyl ... she looked like somebody had just hit her on the back of the head with a two-by-four."

"So he *is* out, then, that prick," Wally said loudly with an odd tone of regret.

"*If* the vote stands. *C'est la grande question, mon ami.* Now it's up to the lawyers and … well, you know how that goes."

"*Mon ami!* Sally Brown," Wally hit the buzzer again, "and dear Karla Marsh was sitting right there … and Olive Oyl …!"

"Is Marsh the one who trashed your department, Wally?" someone asked.

"Doomed, Birch, you are doomed!" Wally said, ignoring the question.

The boy with the drinks just then came. He distributed them around the table. Birch threw in a ten dollar bill and others threw in money too—all except for Wally, that is. That was the rule—why if moneybags Wally Wills were to start buying drinks all around, where would it end?

"I can't believe you people really live like that," said Evelyn Cornel abruptly. Birch stared at her. Her face was translucent. She was beautiful in a way. She caught his eye and smiled. Birch wondered what kind of woman would take on a man like Eddy Cornel.

16. *The coldest summer on record*

"**V**oted for Devries and then changed her vote!" Wally repeated and threw back his head and bellowed until Birch thought that tears might burst from his eyes. "Well listen here, Birch, I've been suffering too—*children*, I've been all afternoon in the University Committee. I'm on it you know, and will probably be the next chair," Wally boasted without shame.

Wally meant the committee that made decisions on tenure

at the college level, passing on recommendations from the departments. Its members were elected through a university-wide competition, and of course Wally was well-known (if not always enjoyed!).

"What's that committee like," asked Harvey Vanderpool.

"Nooooh, you can't belieeeeve it," wailed Wally and lit another cigarette. "You say Karla Marsh dropped in—well these people live under Karla's house! They have come in from the star Sirius! Dr. Mengele and his ill designs!"

"Who's on it?" asked Eddy Cornel.

"Well of course there's Damasca Xingciaororili. She can't spell it either. She's as thin as a stick. Oh, but judicious. Her thing is central Asia."

"Do you think she's a virgin?" asked Eddy Cornel.

Wally curled his lip. "Actually she's OK. I know she has a weird name but she's really OK ... wouldn't like to get caught in a shower with her but ... Then there's Mohammed Mustafah something or other. Very multicultural. They make him leave his shoes at the door. He brings his prayer rug just in case. You can't understand a thing he says, but it doesn't matter because he's in favor of everything. But Mohammed is OK too, he's OK."

"Who else?" asked Harvey Vanderpool, the ceramicist.

"Jeremy Tatum—South Africa and very influential. An African-American. He pities the downtrodden."

"That leaves us out, hey Wills?" said Eddy Cornel.

"It's not really a review committee though, like it's supposed to be," Birch jumped in, feeling the beer and petulant about the Devries hearing. "I mean they pretend to be tough, but everyone gets through."

"Sure—law suits," someone said.

"Don't worry Birch, we do our work," Wally puffed.

"You do the work of Karla Marsh," Birch said.

"Unless you get there first, Birch!" Wally scowled.

"Birch is right," said Cornel heatedly. "Tenure is a fix."

"It sure fixed you," Wally scoffed.

"Really, is this conversation appropriate?" interrupted the mustachioed bureaucrat sitting in the corner. Birch realized with a start that he didn't really know who this man was.

"Well, I hear," Birch said, "that this is the coldest summer on record."

"I've heard that too," said Evelyn Cornel.

17. Last words

Wally sometimes stopped by Birch's house on Sunday mornings after returning from visiting Audrie Winter, a ninety-five year old matriarch with whom Wally had had Sunday breakfast for twenty-five years. Wally and Audrie were eerily devoted, but Birch was never sure why. Audrie was famous for her longevity and for all that she had seen. Even Birch knew her casually. She had lived upstairs in the apartment house across the street when he first came to town with his wife and family and five cats and tank of tropical fish. Wally was living downstairs with the well-endowed Jack Devries, who was then an undergraduate. The first time Birch was ever in Wally's apartment, Wally showed off to him an antique plush deep-upholstered captain's chair. Though the leather was shoddy and torn, Wally claimed it was a very fine piece.

"Audrie gave it to me … her father was a captain in the China trade and he loved this chair more than anything," Wally said, beaming with pride.

Then Jack DeVries had entered the room, emerging from the shadows of the living room and crossing to shake Birch's hand.

That was twenty years ago, when Birch first came to town, and since then Wally had lived in a dozen places before ending up in his cushy hip pad on the lake. Birch had moved up too, after recovering from his divorce, because the earnings from his books had been high enough to finance a cottage beside a wood in The Village, an exclusive separately incorporated neighborhood at the foot of campus, in fact one of the most desirable neighborhoods in the state for beauty, convenience, and elegant friendly living.

Birch's cottage was pre-Prairie style, designed in 1914 by Frank Lloyd Wright, a womb to protect him, to hole up in, keep his head down, and keep out of trouble. Birch thrilled every time he drove up the low hill of Harvard Drive and there was his little house, with its clean angled lines and immense overarching eaves and ceiling-to-floor swing-out windows that opened its dark-wooded interiors to the steamy woods bordering Birch's property. The house was even published in some book.

Yes, Birch had gone in deep, in spite of his book royalties. But if the going got rough, Birch thought secretly, he would touch Wally for a hundred big ones. That was the beauty of knowing a man of independent stature!

At first Wally feared that Birch had upstaged him by buying in The Village, but when he saw how really modest the cottage was compared with his own glorious location on the lake, he gave up all envy. Wally happily joined Birch on Sunday mornings, after Wallie headed home from Audrie Winter's.

They sat around a glass-topped table on the broad green lawn beneath the towering ancient oaks and drank coffee. They talked about Jack Devries and what had happened at the department meeting.

"So you think it will stick?" Wally said as he carefully, almost effeminately, placed down his cup of coffee on the table. The cup made a sharp tinkling sound. Birch hoped he didn't break the fucking glass! Wally was in an extra-fat phase, his enormous legs so tight inside his brown slacks that it seemed they would burst open like a squashed slug.

"If the vote holds," Birch cautioned.

"It will! But we mustn't gloat."

Wally clasped his thick hands across his enormous belly. The sun caught the ruby pinkie ring, whose obvious value contrasted with the tawdry and ridiculous silver French horn that held the ugly tie he always wore. Wally claimed once to have played

French horn in the Boston Pops, but Birch had never seen him near an instrument.

"Let's hire a woman this time—if she'll play our game," Birch suggested.

Wally lit a cigarette and exhaled the smoke in an elegant stream.

"My dear boy ... But yes, a woman—let them fight it out among themselves. You showed courage, you really did."

Wally's admiration was genuine but Birch understood him to refer to the attempted blackmail, of which he must have gotten wind.

"By the way Wills, I hate your tie. It's fantastically ugly. Do they make you wear things like that over in Art History?"

Wally smirked and shook his head with disappointment.

"Raymond Birch—I don't know what I'm going to do with you. You just don't understand ties."

Birch never wore them except on formal occasions and he wondered if in proper Bostonian circles ugly ties were a mark of taste, even.

After finishing his coffee, Wally got to his feet.

"You know it's my birthday—and Audrie's too. Our birthdays are on the same day. You want to see what I got to treat myself, just a little bit?"

"She got you a present?"

"She never leaves the house. You know she's blind—like you sometimes, old friend," Wally laughed.

Wally preened himself and puffed out as he strutted between the pines at the side of Birch's house. He crossed the quiet, shaded asphalt street. Parked beneath two overarching silver maples was a shining maroon Lexus V-8 LE with newly designed body, swung upward and backward—smart but too sassy for Birch's modest taste.

"I deserve something decent once in a while."

"How much?"

"$64,000—no, I mean $62,000."

"$62,000—yeah? That's cheap!"

Birch was not much for buying cars while Wally was always

driving up in something new. Of course he could afford it. When Wally was living across the street with Jack Devries in the apartment underneath Audrie Winter's, Wally owned a purple Jag which he kept in the garage all winter because of the road salt. In the summer he brought it out. Wally was so fat he could barely get in, so sometimes he loaned it to Jack Devries to drive around town and into the country. One day it was gone and up Wally drove up in a Mercedes-Benz.

"What happened to the Jag, Wally?"

"Oh, the Jag. Look, I pulled up to this parking light and this guy in the car next to me says, 'I *got* to have that car. $90,000, right now!' What could I do?"

"You sold the Jag?"

"Yes. And now I have the Benz. How do you like it?" he had said.

"I'm glad to see you've given up Benz's and are now firmly into Lexus," Birch said to Wally Wills as they stood in front of Birch's house on the warm Sunday morning. "But I wish you had told me you were going to sell your old Lexus because I'm in the market for a sedan myself. All I've got is my pickup and it's beat."

"Oh anybody would fuck you no matter what you're driving," Wally said. "But Gee, I wish I knew. I could have sold it to you. *C'est la vie, mon ami,*" he added with bonhomie and drove away.

Those were last words Wally Wills ever spoke to Raymond Birch.

18. rus in urbe

It was the land around Birch's house that cost so much, but of course that's what made his isolation possible. Birch's last set of neighbors, in his other house where he had lived as a married man and father, were oldsters on one side who liked to chat about who froze to death last winter wrestling garbage through the snow. On the other side lived a woman writer of miniaturist stories for *The New Yorker,* who stayed up till 4:00 in the morning and blasted her desk lamp straight across Birch's bed, keeping him awake for hours.

But now that he was semi-rich, not like the old days, he had moved up in the world. His enormous lot stretched from one street, where Wally parked his new car, up a low hill to the parallel street behind. Beyond the woods lived an eighty-five-year old woman in a big white house who came only two weeks a year to rake the leaves. Otherwise she lived in more genteel houses in Vermont and DC. On the other side lived a stand-offish childless middle-aged couple whom Birch had never met.

This was heaven, in a way.

The house had one appearance from the front, a one and a half story stucco with wide open porch and wicker furniture, and of course the overhanging eves and tall windows everywhere, but from the back it looked like a different place entirely—a little path wending through the woods, past a huge lawn, and against the street a big rose garden. Birch had planted it himself while kneeling in the hot pouring rain of the awful spring, wrapped in an L. L. Bean poncho, thrusting the bare-rooted plants into the hungry still-thawing soil.

In early summer he put a lawn chair next to the garden. He sat there as the setting sun drenched the roses. Their aroma filled the air. Though he was not on the lake, he was blocks from it, and anyway he didn't like the lake. It was much too cold, and from here he could walk to work or take his bike as he pleased along the lakeshore path. Sometimes the water of the lake was brown, sometimes crystal blue. Water birds of all kinds, including a pair of swans, lived in it or near it. Birch gradually became sensitive to which birds were there and which weren't, and he began to recognize individuals.

Certainly the birds were his friends.

19. *No man knows his hour*

In the afternoon, on the Tuesday after Wally stopped by, Birch answered the portable phone from its cradle on the post above the kitchen counter. There was only a buzzing, no one there. Now this could not be Jack Devries, because the calls had begun before that situation got dire. Maybe it was his ex phoning, or a malfunction in a transmitting station.

Birch went outside and stood at the corner of the house facing the wood and contemplated the redwood porch he would like to build there, if only the future were more certain. He would build it himself. Nothing like the satisfaction of a sturdy nail, snugly driven.

Birch stared at the big oak that overhung the back door where the porch would have to go. He was thinking about the big dead whitened limbs that would have to come down first, when the phone rang again inside the house.

Birch sighed but went up the cement steps to the sliding glass doors that any time now would lead to his redwood deck, once he built it. He circled around the mission-oak dining room table to pick up the phone. He would say nothing at first, setting a trap for the caller.

"Hello?" a voice said. It was a man.

What?

"Raymond—Professor Raymond Birch?"

"You're from the friends of the Sioux Nation, aren't you, asking for money."

"This is Vergil Rawlins. You remember me?"

"Vergil Rawlins?"

"Yeah—you know, Wally's neighbor."

"Oh. Sure."

"*Wally Wills is dead!*"

Birch, thinking about how much the removal of the tree limbs was going to cost him, if he ended up staying at all, was in no mood for bullshit.

"What's the joke?" he said

"Would I joke about something like that?"

The voice was hushed with anguish.

"What are you telling me, Vergil?"

"I'm telling you that Wally Wills is dead!"

"Are you serious?" Birch stalled.

"Look, this is it. Katy, my girlfriend—she heard the ambulance go down the street ... she said she knew there was something wrong at Wally's. I guess she's psychic or something. She went down there right away and, see ... the police were there ... she saw his body! Wally was at the bottom of the stairs—dead!"

Perhaps the man was crying. But Wally Wills was as permanent as the sun, as the wind, the rain, the seasons.

"Wally Wills—why, I saw him on Sunday. Are the cops there?"

"They've gone. They took the body."

"Where to?"

"The morgue, I guess."

"When did all this happen?"

"About three hours ago."

Outside in the graceful spread of green, beyond the high artistic windows and up the gentle slope to the back street, three enormous crows rummaged in the grass. Hundreds of these prophetic birds lived in The Village and Birch wondered if he should start feeding them. There was a movement among old-timers to have the raucous birds removed as a public nuisance. But how do you remove a flock of crows?

It was simply not possible that Wally was dead. Still, Birch was not surprised—Wally had beat himself up for years, drinking and smoking and taking dope and boasting how he would never live long but would go down like a bull to the slaughter, Whumph and Kapow, blood on the ground. He liked to say that. Birch guessed he got the image from ancient blood sacrifice where the priest moved in like a friend—sprinkling water so the dumb beast nodded its head, saying, 'Yes, please cut my throat,' then out with the knife from the basket of grain and Wham! the priest would cut his throat down to the gullet. Blurp! blood everywhere, drenching everything. The crowd went wild.

That's how he was going to die, Wally always said.

"OK, Vergil, I'll come out. You have a key to Wally's place?"

"Of course. Wally was like a brother to me!"

Rawlins was certainly crying.

"Lucky for us, hey Vergil Rawlins?"

"What do you mean?"

"I think you know what I mean."

20. Dead as a mackerel

Birch slammed the porto-phone back in its cradle. Obviously he was going to have to put the deck project aside. He couldn't believe it ...! Wally dead at the bottom of the stairs. What a pig ... Wally was too fat, apart from his other problems—a pig, his big feet ruined by gout. He was still a young man! Sometimes Wally had to wear specially enlarged shoes and he couldn't walk for days. Fell down the fucking stairs and killed himself!

"You pig Wills! And now you're dead," Birch said aloud. He wondered if he felt any regret. When you live in the pure white light of the spirit, you don't feel regret all that much. Of course none of this had sunk in.

Birch sat down at the round oak mission table. Outside it

was peaceful, the calming rays of the sun refracted through the pines and firs. He heard a spinning, whining sound in his head. What did he ever do to deserve living in this paradise? Maybe something was going to happen.

A jay swooped down in front of the window, screeching, complaining. But jays never told you anything about the world. The previous owner of this house, a little old lady, for forty years lived in this room where he was sitting. She was all alone and the carpet was green. The walls were cheaply paneled. Soon she went insane. That's why Birch was going insane. Her children finally did something with her and hastily sold the house. He had just walked into the deal. Her smell, her flesh, her cells, her hair had infected the hideous green carpet and Birch ripped it out and himself installed a prefinished hardwood floor over the particleboard subfloor, hammering in one sturdy nail every six inches with a mallet-driven machine. The work had been glorious. Then he built shelves along the tops of the walls for his Indian baskets. His wife had taken the car, but left him the baskets.

On top of the new hardwood floor Birch spread a huge blood-red oriental carpet whose deep colors picked up the earth tones of the baskets and contrasted with the yellow and blue feathers woven into the Pomos.

Unfortunately Birch had smoked the last cigarette from his emergency pack when Wally came over last Sunday.

"Rawlins must have got this wrong," Birch said to himself, got up, took down the phone directory from the shelf over the counter, and looked up the city coroner. He would phone the fucking coroner.

First he looked in the white pages, but he couldn't find anything and remembered he had to look in the business section, which had green pages for some reason. Then he found a blue section called CITY AND MUNICIPAL OFFICES and looked under the C's but there was nothing so he flipped to the table of contents.

"What if the house were burning down? Does anybody care? Who designed this fucking book!"

Birch dialed 411 and paced back and forth in the kitchen,

whose original badly decayed linoleum floor he had removed to expose the pine planking of the original subfloor. This he sanded silky smooth, then urethaned it to a golden lustrous finish. This call was going to cost him seventy-five cents and there was no reason for it, really.

"What city please?"

"Here—in town."

"Go ahead, please."

"The coroner. And why don't you have this number in your phone book? It's ridiculous," Birch said with irritation.

"I'm sorry, sir. You mean the city coroner?"

"Is there another?"

"There is only one city coroner."

He wasn't sure he liked the tone in her voice.

"That one."

"Here is your number."

Birch's subtle and sinewy mind, which had produced long books on arcane topics of lasting interest, did not extend to remembering phone numbers for even five seconds. Knowing his weakness, he repeated the recorded number over and over, then immediately flashed to the dial-tone on the porto-phone and punched it in. But already he was unsure whether the last number was 5 or 3. What if Wally Wills really were dead—?

As the phone buzzed, Birch paced around the oak table.

"Why should I?" he said into the phone, without thinking.

"I beg your pardon?"

"Oh—Hello, sorry, is this the coroner's office? I'm phoning about a man named Wallace Wills, former professor at the university, a friend, to see if he is dead."

"Wallace Wills—yes, he is dead. I am the assistant coroner. We have the body," said the voice.

"You do have the body. So he *is* dead, then?"

"Oh he's dead alright, sir."

"I see. Look, I'm Professor Raymond Birch. How did he die? Can you tell me?"

"I'm sorry sir, but we cannot be sure at this actual point in time. He was found at the bottom of the stairs in his home. There was bruising on his head, though not too serious. The autopsy is complete but we need to run toxicology tests."

They were going to find the dope! Birch realized that this was inevitable, now that death was in the act.

"I see, but what do you think he died of, I mean on first impression? Heart attack would you say?"

"Well, the Coroner found signs of mild heart disease but no infarction. Also, no signs of a stroke."

Sure, Wally just went over the edge. He had seemed OK on Sunday—of course he was pissed about the trashing Dean Karla Marsh had given his department ...

"So Wally really is dead. Well, when will you get your reports from the toxicology lab and all that?"

"That will take four to six weeks," the woman said apologetically.

"I'm sorry. I'm just a friend."

"I'm sorry too."

"Why, did you know him?"

"No, but I heard of him. Everybody had heard of Professor Wills," she said.

"Yes, he was a good man. A breath of fresh air, really."

Birch hung up. Obviously something was going to have to be done. The rats would be coming out of the woodwork, now.

21. We are brothers all

With a start Birch realized how logical it would be to speak to Angela Bellamy, of all people. In spite of the conspiracy against Devries, she and Wally had worked together for years as co-editors of a monograph series. Every time he saw them together at the Faculty Club they were touching heads and rubbing knees. Phonies, phonies—neither possessed one ounce of shame!

Birch fumbled with the book to find Angela Bellamy's number.

"Hello?" the female voice said.

Thank God it was Angela herself, speaking in a thick sluggish voice, and not her octogenarian Oxonian South African husband, who frightened Birch out of his mind with his small gray mustache, ruddy complexion, bright twinkling eyes, and his deferential manner.

He must have caught Angela sleeping. He was grateful he had a good excuse for phoning.

"Angela, it's Raymond Birch."

"Oh—"

She sounded remotely pleased, odd after what had happened with Devries, but Birch and Angela had always liked each other, and felt a nearly romantic affinity in their preference for the refinements of the heart over the abstractions of the intellect. Of course telephones always disguised one's true intent.

"Angela, terrible news. Wally is dead."

"Oh—I knew it, I had a dream."

"A dream?"

The jay returned, shrieking, carrying on. It settled in the pine outside the glass door, then became still. After awhile, Birch took up again.

"Yes, Angela, I know it is shocking. He was found dead in his house on the lake this afternoon. It's hard to believe and I don't know what happened because I haven't been out there but I knew that you would want to know about this right away."

"I still can't believe it ..." she said, scarcely audible.

"It's obviously a terrible thing and I don't know what exactly to do. But Angela—"

"Yes, Raymond?"

"Well, you know I wondered if maybe you might know who Wally's lawyer was or something like that? I mean he must have had a will and I suppose that the right thing would be to find it, to find who is the executor and then—well, you see what I mean?"

"Oh my goodness ... I cannot think straight. His lawyer—Oh no, he must have had several ... you know Wally was an art appraiser ... he had a business, and other things ... I mean for every occasion he must have had a separate lawyer ... but I really don't know ... This is terrible ..."

Her voice was broken, muted, distant, tired, sad. The burden of long years of conflict, and now this thing with Devries, and the general heaviness and malaise and feeling of exhaustion that hung over the department had broken her spirit.

Birch's heart went out to her.

"Yes, it is a terrible thing, Angela. But I think it's important to find the will as soon as possible, don't you? Then get in touch with relatives as soon as possible?"

He spoke gently, soothingly.

"Didn't he have a brother out West?"

Of course, Wally's brother! Why hadn't he thought of that? Wally was always going on about his Brahmin parents who had adopted him as an infant. Later, when Wally was twelve, they adopted a second child of his own age, after the boy's natural parents were killed in a terrible car accident. They were very close. Yes, Wally's brother!

"You're right," Birch said. "I'm glad I phoned, Angela. Yes of course, his brother by adoption. I don't know why I didn't think of that. What was his name?"

"Oh, I don't know ... I can't think ... he was supposed to be very wealthy since he had been an only child and the insurance policies were huge ... his parents died in an auto accident ... the double indemnity was huge. He and Wally were very close. The brother taught at Berkeley, maybe economics ... maybe he's famous or something ..."

Once Wally had described to Birch a visit to his brother's estate in the Berkeley hills, with its own tennis courts and swimming pool and life of refined sensuality. Wally said he had gone up to his brother's room on the upper floor of the sleek mansion when a naked boy came down the hall. Wally had no idea who he was. The boy nodded in a friendly way before going into one of the thirteen-year old daughter's rooms. Soon Wally heard them fucking. A thirteen year old girl ... And there was some incident in a hot tub ... big blubbery Wally invited in and everyone naked and his brother had provided a woman for Wally. That was pretty good!

"Oh yeah," Wally had said, "and my brother had this fantastic smoke. We were whirring like crickets. Wheeaaa!"

"Shame on you, fat boy," said Birch.

"Who, me?"

Wally spoke of visits to his brother with nostalgia and affection, and no doubt a little envy—not that Wally had anything to be ashamed of. A year or so before, the brother had quit Berkeley and taken a job down the coast, Wally told Birch, to be closer to the beach.

"Wow, if you could think of his name or the name of his lawyer—that would be great, Angela. Would you give me a call if you come up with something?"

"Oh yes, I certainly will."

"And Angela—"

"Yes?"

"I'm sorry about Jack Devries."

"Oh yes, I'm sure you are. Well that's not over yet, Raymond."

She hung up.

22. Feeling better

Birch didn't blame Angela, really. He was strangely excited. He crossed the kitchen, opened the hand-chamfered paneled birch and pine door and went into the living room and the hall. A walnut-paneled door concealed a narrow staircase leading to an upstairs library. He opened the door and mounted the stairs, passing his collection of beaded Indian artifacts from the northern plains—Cheyenne, Sioux, Arapaho, Blackfoot.

He spun around the landing. A Comanche war lance with fifty eagle feathers wrapped in trade cloth angled across it. If they caught him with that, that would be the end! Every time Birch passed the lance he relished the scent of its old and dusty feathers, as if he himself were mounted on a pony, his face painted black and yellow like the moon and the night sky, feathers knotted in his coarse black hair, his bone breastplate jouncing against his chest while his quiver decorated by bands of red quills and turquoise beads pulsed with his bursting heart as he eased the pony up a rise toward the enemy ... *It was a good day to die.*

If the Indians had worked with him, they would have done better against the white man, who of course would still have won in the end. The white man just didn't understand feathers, as Birch saw it.

Birch went into the bird room at the end of the hall that overlooked the quiet and restful street beneath a steep gable. The room was decorated with a dozen pairs of antique beaded moccasins suspended along the ceiling and a beaded saddle-blanket thrown over the day bed. The room was drenched in wealth, drenched in beauty.

When the umbrella cockatoo saw him, she whistled and pumped up and down on her perch in her large wire cage hung from the ceiling, while the blue-fronted Amazon, in the corner, fluffed her feathers and said 'I LOVE YOU.' She spread her wings to show her fancy inner feathers, stained red and blue. He had taught her to say that, and now he was sorry. He loved her too, but you can never unteach a parrot once it has learned something. That is a law of the wild.

The Amazon rubbed her beak vigorously on either side against the perch as Birch took a baggy out of a drawer that Wally gave him on Sunday. He sat down on the day bed and rolled a joint. The big birds leered, studying his every move.

"MARRY ME," said the Amazon.

"If you don't calm down, I will," Birch said, already feeling better.

He wanted to just lie there and think about Wally Wills being dead and what that might mean. Was he somewhere out there? or was he just gone? did he now live too in the pure white light of the spirit? or had Wally grown so tired of himself that he gave up everything just to get some peace of mind?

23. Always the last to know

Feeling slightly euphoric, Birch got up from the bed, blew kisses to the parrots, shut the door behind him, and threaded his way back through the library. He descended the stairs, through the kitchen, out the back door. Song birds twittered high in the fragrant trees. Birch was happy in a way. Wally was dead, but nothing could change that. The brilliant day was aflame with the sun.

Birch made his way up the path marked out with packed chips of wood, through the private forest to the one-car garage built on the back of his lot, facing the other street. The garage had the same cute little architectural flare on its eaves as the main house, but the building was useless for storing a car. It was too small and was, anyway, piled high with snow-blower, lawn-mower, seeder, pneumatic jack, spare lumber, and mountains of other stuff that Birch thought he might use some day. The fact is that he had paid a fortune for a house without a usable garage in a climate where winter dropped to twenty-five below!

Birch got in his Toyota 4-runner king-cab pickup parked in the drive and started the engine. It was 3:30 P.M. He pulled out onto Dartmouth, turned at Oxford, and made his way to Columbia, past the elegant houses set far back from the street on generous lots, or even acres. He wended his way up the hill and came down on the other side through the brick gate beside which stood The Village offices. The one and only police car was always parked there in this pacific community.

He pulled onto the main drag that led around the lake and switched on his Whistler radar-detector. He made his way through heavy traffic past pretentious high civic buildings at the edge of Blackhawk Golf Course, which belonged to The Village. According to legend Chief Blackhawk had once camped on this ground when fleeing from the US army, including a certain Abraham Lincoln, in 1832. The great chief had probably crossed Birch's own property. One of Birch's ancient oaks was bent in an L-shape against the sun, obviously an ancient trail marker from the nineteenth century. The Americans drove Blackhawk and his band to the Mississippi. When the Indians tried to cross, they shelled them from gunboats. Blackhawk was taken. They stripped the flesh from his bones which then were wired together and hung in a glass case that traveled the country in circus shows.

Where were the bones today, Birch wondered?

Birch drove through the haphazard commercial frontage as the road circled around the edge of the lake, passed through playing fields with clean, well-dressed handsome young men in red and white uniforms throwing balls. Then shopping malls on one side and lakeside housing on the other.

At the end of the lake he waited at the intersection with County F, which led along the lake's far side. After several miles on F, he turned off the main road onto Goldbug Street, which headed directly to the lake and Wally's pad.

Vergil Rawlins lived three blocks down Goldbug, two blocks from Wally's. Birch had been to Rawlins's house a couple of times with Wally. Evidently Birch was supposed to get along with this scumbag because he was Wally's pal, because he fixed Wally's windows when they leaked, and put in the dock, and sold him cocaine!

Vergil Rawlins's place was a four-bedroom ranch, its facade made of handsome local stone. A boat on a trailer was always parked in the drive and another boat on stands in a backyard surrounded by a waist-high cyclone fence.

Birch swung in the 4-runner behind Rawlins's vintage 1957 Chevrolet with high fins and high polish and a blue COLLECTOR license plate. He went up to the long covered porch to ring the bell. He turned his back to the door to look out at the street and wondered if maybe there was a cigarette somewhere in his glove compartment, lost in the muck of faded maps and gum wrappers and loose change. Birch stepped back off the porch to go look when Vergil Rawlins opened the door behind him.

Rawlins was a slight man of medium height, regular features, short hair, and wandering eyes, his mouth a little open. It seemed appropriate that he and Birch embrace in this moment of crisis, and Birch reached out to Rawlins. Rawlins missed the cue and bumped awkwardly against Birch's arm. Smoking a cigarette, Rawlins glanced away with a skittish look as Birch followed him into the living room.

The front room was large, its floor covered in a gray deep-pile rug. On the far wall was a stone fireplace. In the far corner was a dais with a low wall containing a dining set. Trophies of stuffed trout and antlered deer heads were mounted over flounced curtains. Birch wondered if Rawlins had killed these animals or if he bought them in a taxidermy shop. So bourgeois, Birch thought, for a dope dealer.

A plain blonde-haired woman of thirty-five was sitting on a couch that angled away from the hearth. Another woman, perhaps her sister, nearly her twin, sat beside her. Both were smoking. Birch didn't recognize them, though he must have met them—there were always so many people floating around Wally's house. One of the women got up and came over to him, glanced away, then hugged Birch tightly. Then she broke away, backed off, and wiped a tear.

"Oh, I'm so glad you came," she said.

Birch recognized Katy, Rawlins's girlfriend, the skinny one with the tiny breasts.

"Sure, the whole thing is terrible," Birch sympathized. "Tell me … what exactly happened?"

He put his arm around Katy and led her back to the couch,

then sat on another couch near the entrance hall. Rawlins plumped down beside him, tears streaming down his cheeks. They both started to speak at the same time.

"Go ahead," Birch said.

"OK. You want to know what happened? This is what happened. Katy's a nurse, see, that's how she saw that something was going on—when all these cars started going down the road."

A cokehead nurse, thought Birch.

Vergil Rawlins rubbed his brow.

"She went down to Wally's, see, to see what it was. The police were there and everything, and the coroner. Wally was lying at the bottom of the stairs, dead!"

In his mind's eye Birch saw him, flat out at the bottom of the tri-level deck that ran down to the lake from the glass-walled house. He wore a happy, cherubic grin. Home at last, home from the hill, eyes gently closed and pudgy black-bristled hand pulled to his once-warm, fuzzy cheek. His heart had given out, poor guy. Well, he was so fat. Wally never gave a fuck about his body. It was a miracle he had lived this long.

"See, on Sunday we were putting in the pier—" said Rawlins.

"You know he was at my place Sunday," interrupted Birch.

"I know, he told me. And on Friday we were together at the 666. That's why I can't believe it!"

"Wally mentioned on Sunday that he was coming back from Audrie Winter's," Birch said.

"Yeah, that old lady. He told me that too. Well look, earlier we were down at Wally's putting in the dock, like I say, and Wally comes out to help us."

"He never does that," added Katy, looking up. "*Never.*"

"He just watches," added the other woman.

"Wally seemed in such a good mood," said Vergil Rawlins mournfully. "And then these two guys showed up, one named Tom, and somebody else—someboy named Eric. I've seen this Tom guy around, but I never saw Eric before in my life."

"Nor have I," said the girl sitting next to Katy, lighting up another cigarette. Birch wondered if he should go over and just take one.

"So Wally goes back up the slope and starts to talk to these guys, you know, these Tom and Eric guys. They go inside and we go on working on the dock. After awhile, we come on back here. Wally was supposed to come up here for a cook-out, see, but instead later comes up by himself and wants to know, you know, if I can get him some stuff."

"Some cocaine?"

"Sure ... Well, I didn't have any. So they left and went back to his place. Then pretty soon I saw them drive by the house—they were going out somewhere."

"Wally and Tom and Eric?"

"Yeah. But pretty soon they came back. I saw them drive back."

"You're watching all the time?"

Vergil Rawlins looked at Birch in a funny way.

"That's why I live up the street, you know."

"OK. So anyway, they got some coke somewhere. Then what?"

"I don't know—I just know that I want Wally back!" Vergil Rawlins's face burst open like a summer rain. He dissolved into tears. The unabashed emotion surprised Birch because the human element in Vergil Rawlins always seemed rather dubious. Birch thought that dope-dealers were tougher than that.

The front door opened and a man wearing a sports coat and tie came into the room, stout, thick black mustache. The man greeted Birch as he passed. Birch couldn't place him, but maybe he was with the other girl on the couch, or maybe he was part of the 666 crowd. It was always that way in Wally's circle, people walking through you didn't really know. The man disappeared into a back room.

Birch too felt tears well in his eyes and pour down his face. He realized that everyone in the room was crying now, and everyone was smoking cigarettes—that is, everyone except Professor Raymond Birch.

24. Everybody's business

"**W**ell, let's go down and have a look," Birch said. "You've got a key,Vergil?"

"Sure. Wally's place was like a second home to me. And Wally said everything was to come to me if anything happened."

"Everything was to come to you, huh?" said Birch.

It was dusk as Birch, Vergil Rawlins, and thin Katy walked down the two blocks to the lake. The sun was a huge ball of red behind the black and orange clouds. In the distance sport fishermen plied the waters of the bay. Birch thought of Bruegel's painting THE FALL OF ICARUS, where the doomed son of Daedalus fell from the sky, a miniature man flailing in the background, while in the foreground was the picture of a peasant at his plow. W. H. Auden wrote a poem about this painting, and Birch thought now about the banality of sorrow that Bruegel represented. Everything just goes on as if it never happened. One day that would happen to you.

They turned into Iceman Walk, a private road just in from the lake that gave access to the back of Wally's house and to several other houses. Crunch, crunch they walked down the gravel path past the back of a neighbor's house. Birch had been in this neighbor's house once. It was a cold, gray, and rainy day. He couldn't remember who was this mustachioed ruddy guy who lived there, but he showed Birch a black powder muzzle loader that he'd made from a kit. It was huge. He explained how one day he'd tried it out, shooting through the low window to the ground. The noise was so loud that he hadn't heard a thing since.

Then that man moved away.

They came to the back of Wally's small frame rectangular structure with its simple peaked roof. The paint-job in deep cobalt blue was half-finished, just as handy-man fixer Eddy Cornel had left it when he moved out a year before. In the 1920s these were summer cottages for people who lived in town, but now the city had encompassed them and they were extremely valuable property. Wally liked to boast that his place, really just a big fancy room, was worth a fortune, twice what he'd paid for it. Obviously he lived as a modest bachelor and did not show off his wealth.

Still, he'd spared no expense in customizing the onetime summer home. He gutted the inside, tore out the knotty-pine walls (they actually had looked pretty good), and put up stark white walls on which he could show off his sensational art collection, mostly modern American. Wally knew many prominent artists, who drifted through town on temporary teaching positions. As the reigning art historian, who gave the best parties, Wally always got to know them pretty well. When they left, they'd would give him a painting. That's how he'd got the Jim Dine, for one.

Wally's redesign of the modest structure was brilliant with track lights in the ceiling to display the art to greatest advantage.

Wally also tore out the front portion of the upstairs floor so that what remained became an elegant loft, overseeing the lake through an enormous semi-circular window that he punched in the pediment of the lakeside wall. Now he could lie on his futon in the loft, edged by exotic plants, and watch the seasons change over the waters that began at the foot of his backyard. Wally called his house the Taj-Ma Cottage because of the exorbitantly high costs of reconstruction.

His new Toyota Lexus LE was parked on asphalt in the back. Hey, maybe Birch could get a good deal on the car ... Wally's birthday present to himself would then not go completely to waste!

The two men and a woman crowded onto the back screen porch. Plastic bags of garbage spilled over or leaned against the screen walls of the porch and bulged them outward. A gaping hole in the roof had let in recent heavy rains. The green carpet on the cement slab floor was badly stained. A drafting table, battered by rain, was pushed against the far corner. Birch couldn't imagine what function it served, unless perhaps it belonged to Eddy Cornel—Oh, Eddy was going to learn drafting along with his art hobby!

Birch laughed out loud at the thought of it.

"What's funny?" said Vergil Rawlins with a start.

"Nothing," said Birch.

Vergil fumbled with a key to the inner door when a vintage Volkswagen bug screeched up next to Wally's Lexus and without killing the engine out popped an elderly couple.

"Is it true? Is Wally dead?" the round and assertive no-doubt Jewish gray-haired woman asked, coming up onto the porch. The elderly man with her was tall, angular, and had soft intelligent eyes. Birch had never seen either of them before in his life.

"Who are you?" Birch asked.

"Why Professor Raymond Birch, you know me—I'm Marylou Stieglitz."

"And I'm Stan," said the man, taking Birch's hand.

Birch shook their hands as Vergil Rawlins and Katy watched like animals in the headlamps of a car. Maybe Wally had on several occasions referred to 'my close friendship with the Stieglitzes,' Birch remembered, or maybe 'I'm having dinner with the Stieglitzes.' That was possible. Maybe they lived in some swank mansion across the lake. Birch had met them at a garden party on Wally's lawn, when they pulled up in their sloop on the lake. Stan was some kind of famous doctor, Wally bragged, and she was a big philanthropist, both from New York.

"We came as soon as we heard," Marylou said.

"How did you hear?" Vergil Rawlins said, getting the door open. The Stieglitzes looked puzzled.

"And what did you hear?" said Katy.

"How? How did we hear, Stan ... ?"

"I think we should have a look inside," Stan said.

"Quick—we must go inside!" said Marylou.

Birch didn't know them, but he was glad they were there. It gave the invasion an air of legitimacy, considering their high standing in the community, and considering that Vergil Rawlins, though a friend of Wally's, was a low-life dirtbag dope dealer, and his girlfriend little better than a common whore.

25. Drugs?

In a bunch they crowded into an anteroom. There was an odd, unpleasant smell. From the double doors of a utility closet to the left spilled clothes in an avalanche from atop a washer and dryer. Dirty clothes fell in a river onto the floor, mingling with more clothes that burst from the closet.

Like a gaggle of tourists, they pushed through the anteroom, passed under an archway, and entered the large room that occupied the whole of the downstairs. The archway was flanked on one side by an extraordinary man-sized vase, an inverted blue ceramic cone with images of doves flying through an empyrean space, fixed in a squeegee base that sprang upward and outward like something alive. On the other side of the archway was an astounding six-foot high Chinese ceramic sort of mushroom shaped thing, glazed in bright Beijing orange and green with accents of purple. It was a humongous column made up of a half dozen ceramic drums fitted together that supported a mushroom-shaped cap.

"What the fuck is that?" Birch had asked when he dropped by one day to say Hello and, maybe, puff a joint.

"Hi guy. Hey, you like it? They gave it to me in an auction upstate ... I was the auctioneer, it was my fee."

"But what ... what is it?"

"What does it look like?"

"It doesn't look like anything. Like a mushroom."

"It's a Peking roof tile. Anyone can see that!"

Sometimes Birch and Wally would play around like this, just to put the other guy on the spot.

"That's no Peking roof tile! It's some kind of fucking garden ornament, I'd bet."

"But what would *you* know?"

At the far end of the big room, the sad summer gloaming seeped through the glass doors in the wall with the high semi-circular window. Just beyond the archway Wally had positioned two couches at right angles, sort of enclosing the hand-hewn stone fireplace set in the central wall—so he could flake out and watch a TV propped on a cardboard box, or read manuscripts. But now the near couch was shoved back against the wall beneath the open oak staircase that led to the loft.

Why?

"OK, here we are," said Birch breathlessly.

He moved ahead of the group across the debris scattered everywhere. He walked to the glass wall that faced the lake. A long white utility table was pushed in front of the windows, overarched by an antediluvian plant with elephant ears. The giant and luxurious plant was supported on a five-foot high one foot thick Victorian Corinthian column in wood and gesso. Zigzag rolling papers were scattered across the white table.

The kitchen, tucked at the far end in the corner beneath the windows, separated from the main room by a waist-high half-wall, was in complete chaos. A two-liter bottle of Vodka, two-thirds empty, perched on the edge of the counter. Beer cans and filthy dishes filled with cigarette butts lay everywhere. Another Vodka bottle lay empty on a pile of trash in the corner.

"Looks like some kind of party was going on here," said Stan Stieglitz sheepishly.

Birch turned around. Vergil Rawlins stood wide-eyed in the middle of the room. Maybe he was high. Rawlins moved his hands before him, as if swimming through a thick gelatinous sea.

"Let's look in the medicine cabinet to see if there are any dangerous drugs," said Stan Stieglitz cautiously, "or anything like that."

"Drugs?" said Vergil Rawlins and Birch at the same time.

26. I don't smoke

The open oak staircase that led to the loft went first to a landing fixed into the wall, then turned at right angles and led up to the loft. A Georgian wingchair stood at the bottom of the stairs, expensively upholstered in white silk with red stripes but disfigured by a patch of oil where Wally's bald head had come to rest—a million times.

"So they found him outside and at the bottom of the deck?" Birch wondered aloud. "Did he trip and fall down the steps of the deck then?"

"Oh no!" Katy protested in a hushed voice. "I didn't actually come in the house but he was right here—I stood by the door, and I did see him—There!" she pointed to the oak stairs. "His head was underneath the chair! He was bright red! He was dead!"

"Here? His head was down?" said Birch, pointing to the bottom of the stairs.

"Right!"

Birch felt disoriented. For some reason he had been positive that Wally died outside at the bottom of the deck. He must have got this somehow from Rawlins's description. Or where did he get that?

"He must have fallen down the stairs," said Stan.

Katy started to cry.

"He will have to be buried before sundown," said Marylou, taking her stand in front of the fireplace.

"Who was his lawyer?" Birch asked.

"What do you mean he has to be buried before sundown?" said Katy.

"Well, it's a Jewish custom," Marylou replied with some impatience.

Jewish custom now! Birch thought he must be losing his mind. Wally a Jew! True, Wally's adoptive mother had been a Sephardic Jew from an old French family, but she was irreligious and not his biological mother. Do you suppose that Wally's real parents were Jews? Birch wondered, thunderstruck.

"Look, Vergil, don't you know the name of Wally's lawyer or something?" Birch asked again, staring at a stupendous painting just beyond the end of the stairs, near the Georgian chair. It was an acrylic on the big white wall, the most hideous thing Birch had ever seen, a grotesquely fat piggish pink headless woman sitting on the edge of a gray iron bed. Her head had been ripped from her neck and her arms and legs were chopped away at the knees and shoulders. An ooze came out of the wounded thighs and shoulders and neck—it was eerie, horrifying, some sort of modern artistic crap.

"What is that piece of shit?" once he'd asked Wally. "Really, Wills you depress me."

Wally smiled enigmatically.

"That's a Jim Dine. Jim gave it to me. It's called ... *Venus*."

"I've never heard of Jim Dine," said Birch.

"But you will, you will," Wally bragged.

A couple of weeks after Wally moved in, Birch and Wally had gotten wildly drunk and hung up his whole art collection, including this thing, this *Venus*, which Wally insisted in placing so that it could greet all who entered.

"I suppose she reminds you of your mother," Birch had said.

"Yes, a monument to my mother, Birch," Wills said and laughed and laughed.

"I dunno, Wally—looks like university administration to me."

Wally laughed again, uproariously.

"You twit!" he said.

"Some guy named Fettman," Vergil Rawlins was stuttering and spluttering saliva "—yeah, Ron Fettman, that's the lawyer. That was

Wally's lawyer. I'll phone him right now. I don't know why I didn't think of him before."

"You knew the name of Wally's lawyer all this time?" Birch said, irritated.

"Yeah, like I said."

"Well, please phone him."

Vergil Rawlins rummaged in the trash on the floor and found a phone book that had slipped between the cardboard box that supported the TV and an antique spindled desk against the middle of the wall. Birch watched him dial, then walked close to the bottom of the stairs, where Wally's body must have lain. He stared at the wood.

Marylou Stieglitz prowled in and out of the lakeside room, up and down, looking for something. Katy, standing next to Birch, lit another cigarette.

"Hi Katy," said Birch. It crossed Birch's mind at some dim level that with Katy intercourse was always possible. Thank God he didn't do that anymore! "Think you could spare a cigarette, Katy?" Birch asked.

"Sure," she smiled and shook out a pack of Virginia Slim Menthols, the only cigarette in the world Birch absolutely hated. He lit the thing anyway.

27. The smell of death

"**H**ere, Fettman wants to talk to you," Vergil Rawlins said from the desk, extending the heavy black receiver.

Birch exhaled a long stale stream and took the phone.

"Hi, Ron Fettman here," said a boyish, well-spoken voice at the other end.

Birch had heard this voice before. Wally had recommended an attorney to him when Birch was thinking about buying The Village property. The man had told Birch that under no circumstances should he go in so deep, then billed him $200 for the call. That was Wally's style: high-class lawyers, and only the best, who rob you blind while giving bad advice. But what does it matter, when you're really loaded like Wally was?

"Sure, I know you Ron," Birch said. "When I was thinking about buying property over in The Village."

"I remember you, Professor Birch."

"Incidentally, I bought the property. My cockatoo is crazy about it."

"I'm glad everything worked out."

"Obviously we've other things to talk about."

"Wally Wills is really dead?" said the boyish voice. "I can't believe it."

"Do you have his will on file?" Birch asked.

"No. I just did his real estate. Like when Wally bought that house out in the country with that other fellow, and the house on the lake. Is that where you are now?"

"We're in the house on the lake. The place is a mess. We're trying to find his will. No one seems to know a thing. He had a brother out in California but I can't remember his name. Do you know him? We don't know who to get in touch with."

"No, I don't know the brother. Who was the fellow I was just talking to?"

"A neighbor." Birch turned from the phone. "Hey, anybody know the name of Wally's brother out in California?" Birch shouted to the people in the room. They stared, uncomprehending, and Birch returned to the phone.

"Anyway, do you have any idea where the will might be?" Birch said to Fettman.

"Wally never mentioned a will. I just did his real estate."

Attached to Fettman's voice Birch saw a hipster, young and ace-smart, a yuppie—probably he and Wally had done coke together.

"OK, Ron. Well—how 'bout if we keep in touch? Chances are, someone's going to need a lawyer."

Birch hung up.

"Wally said everything was to come to me, if anything happened," moaned Vergil Rawlins at Birch's side. He was crying again.

Stan Stieglitz stared, hunched over, hands in the back pockets of his brown gabardine slacks. Rolls of flesh descended on either side of his old face, giving him the appearance of some kind of dog.

"I was supposed to take care of everything and everything was to come to me," Rawlins repeated. "But really, I just want Wally back."

"Don't worry about it, Vergil. Wally told everybody the same fucking thing," Birch said bitterly.

"We want him back too," added Marylou Stieglitz.

"What's that awful smell?" said Katy. Katy lit another cigarette. "Probably the garbage," she said. "It's awful."

28. You do what you can

After inspecting the house, they all trailed outside. Vergil Rawlins locked the front door while the Stieglitzes got back in their Volkswagen bug, turned cautiously around, and drove away. Birch walked back up the street with Vergil and Katy. There was going to be a problem until somebody got hold of the will, or Wally's brother in California, because Rawlins had the only key to the house. He was a drug dealer! He could rip the place off and who could prove a thing, Birch realized.

Birch said Good-bye, got in his pickup, and drove back to his house. When he got to the back entrance of The Village, he turned in and took the more complicated and scenic route, which wound through gorgeous houses that overlooked the lake. He came up to his own property from the other direction, up a low rise, and parked on the drive in front of the unusable, but architecturally interesting, garage. He walked through the avenue of trees to his back door, unlocked it, and entered the broad square room. He sat down at the oak table to collect his thoughts.

Birch got up and went upstairs, through the library into the bird room, really a dormer through the steep roof, made up of complex intersecting angles. The short walls were lined with books. There was a day bed in the corner. The cockatoo and Amazon parrots were certainly glad to see him. That's what they did in life, waited for him to come home so they could squawk and carry on. "MARRY ME" said the Amazon. The cockatoo whistled a high sound and like a monkey swung down from her perch onto the side of the cage. The Amazon spread out her right wing and in a high pitched voice shrieked and shuffled her feathers with affection.

Birch opened the cockatoo cage and the big white bird raced down the wire draw bridge onto his shoulder. She rubbed her head obsessively against his cheek. She panted and bounced her soft head against him. Her feathers were dusky, covered with a powder that got all over everything when she shook her wings.

Birch held both hands around the bird's superheated body, her heart racing, and lay down on the day bed. He released her and she placed her black hooked beak against his lower lip. She tried to touch his tongue with her own dark bulbous protrusion, her breath not delicious like the Amazon's, but with an electric or acrid flavor.

"Leetle babee," Birch cooed in a special voice he had just for his birds.

They led lucky meaningless lives in big wire cages while Birch suffered the uncertainties of a moral life and its impossible uncertainties. If only birds were human! He was glad to have them, though, because otherwise Professor Birch would be all alone.

Yes, it was imperative to get hold of Wally's brother. And who were these Tom and Eric guys that Vergil was running on about?

The phone rang in the hall. Birch shook the cockatoo off his shoulder onto the bed and went to answer it. At the other end was a distant whine, a hum as on an international call, but nothing else.

29. The turning gyre

Birch awoke with a start from his nap. It was night. He'd been having a bad dream. In the dream he was trying to reattach some wires at the fuse box when he hit the main line. The dazzling shock ran through him. What were dreams anyway? Was somebody, or something, speaking to him, from the other side?

His head was still buzzing. The birds were quiet. He got up and went through the library and down the stairs to the kitchen. He sat down at the oak table in the dark. He had left the sliding door open. Beyond the screen the roar of crickets swelled and receded. He was badly shaken by the dream.

"*I need to talk to Sally Brown*," he said aloud and took up the porto-phone from the column above the counter. With his other hand he looked up her number. Sally had known Wally much longer than he. They were like brother and sister, after all. As far as he knew, Sally Brown didn't even know Wally was dead.

Sally's Swedish husband answered. His family spoke Swedish though they had been in America for generations. Birch couldn't remember his name, though he'd met him a thousand times—Siegfried or Sigmund or something.

"Oh—Hi, is Sally there? I hope it's not too late. Oh Sigmund—it's you? For a second I nearly forgot your name. No, just joking. But Sigmund, really. I have some terrible news. Wally Wills is dead."

"Wally Wills? Really?" said Sigmund in a cautious voice.

"I can't believe it either."

"Oh my goodness, here's Sally ..."

In the background he heard Sally ask, "Is this about Jack Devries?"

When Wally got his first big inheritance, around a cool but mere million dollars, he had taken Birch and his ex-wife and Sally and Sigmund to a fancy fish place at the edge of town. "The sky's the limit," he said, "order anything you want!"

"And fuck the world!" Birch said. Birch's wife was not so sure.

"I'm paying ..." Wally said.

Birch ordered plate after plate of raw oysters, lobster, crab and the wine came in buckets.

Then Wally leaned over and whispered, "Say Birch, in case this goes over the top—can I use your credit card? I mean I only brought so many bills, see what I mean?"

The words *credit card* made the tendons on Birch's fingers ache like hawsers in a hurricane. "No problem, Wally old buddy," he'd assured his friend, and slapped him on the shoulder, then canceled the last round of oysters.

Sally sounded tired.

"Raymond, can this be true?" she groaned.

"It's true, Sally. Now look, we need to find Wally's will, that's what I think. It might be at his house, or perhaps some lawyer has it. I went out there and I got inside but I couldn't find a thing. The place is a total mess."

"Oh dear, it's so hard to think straight. I still can't believe this. But no, didn't he have a brother out West?"

"Yes Sally, but what is his name?"

"Johnny—Johnny something. Oh, Johnny Carson. Like the man on television."

"Sally, that's right, Johnny Carson!" Birch agreed.

"Isn't he some kind of a sociologist or something?"

"I'm not sure. But great news, Sally Brown. You remembered his name. Much too obvious for me. Maybe I can run this guy down. But look, why don't you come to my house tomorrow, and we can go back out to Wally's and check out the place thoroughly? Like I say, I was just there, but we didn't want to touch anything very much. I've got a lead on Wally's real estate lawyer, a guy named Fettman. He knows nothing about the will, but just to keep things on the up and up … You know Vergil Rawlins, who lives up the street?"

"That sort of sleazy guy?"

"He's the only one with a key. But you and I probably knew Wally longer than anyone."

"Oh dear—"

"What?"

"I'll miss my Italian class. And for the second time in a row—"

"Your Italian class!"

"But no, this is more important," said Sally Brown.

"Are you crazy? Wally is dead."

"You're right, you're absolutely right. Wally *is* dead. The thing is, I had to miss the class yesterday too. Well, not to worry. I'll be there, not to worry …"

"I won't worry."

"And Raymond …"

"What?"

"I'm sorry about all that confusion with the vote over Devries."

"I can't believe you did that, Sally."

"But I *did* change my vote."

"Let's not think about that right now."

Birch clicked off. Her Italian class! Birch was going to have to get some cigarettes the next time he went out, for sure.

30. Secret things in secret places

Birch's phone rang.

"Hello, this is Eddy Cornel."

"Sure Eddy, sure."

"Is it true?"

"It's true all right. How did you find out?"

"Audrie Winter's daughter, Mimi Esperanto, talked to my wife Evelyn and told her."

Birch dimly remembered that the nonagenarian Audrie Winter, whom Wally visited every Sunday morning, did have an only daughter, but he wasn't sure he'd heard her name.

"Mimi Esperanto? Really? Audrie Winter's daughter? News travels fast."

"Have you tried to get in touch with Wally's relatives?" Cornel asked.

Birch could hear the eerie hoo-hoo of an owl in the woods next to his house. Crows in the day, owls in the night—like the island of Circe. He loved it!

"You mean his brother in California?"

"He had a brother?" said Eddie Cornel. "No—I was thinking of his daughter."

"His daughter ... !" Birch's breath caught in his throat. He was shouting, but that was to be expected.

"Wally has a daughter, you know," said Cornel patiently, at last. "At least that's what he always told me. Wally was married once and he had a daughter."

"You're out of your fucking *mind* Cornel! Wally was never married and he doesn't have any daughter!"

Birch put the porto-phone down on the counter and walked over to the far windows. Maybe he could see the owl—Nah, that was impossible. You could never see an owl in the day. But it could see you. Birch wished he were an owl, or maybe a weasel crawling through a hole in a hollow log.

He went back to the phone.

"Are you there? Look Eddy, sorry about the outburst, but all this is taking its toll. I've been having all this trouble at work and now—well, Wally's dead. Just between you and me, not everything Wally said was true. Wally Wills was never married, and there is no daughter. I can't believe that Wally told you that and I can't believe you believed it. Wally would say anything. But look, where are you now?"

"I'm in Paducah. But I can drive right over."

"Why would you come?"

"I can come over and help. Also, Wally had some of my things—but that doesn't matter. That doesn't matter at all. Who else knows about this? Any idea?"

Eddy sounded calm and was obviously sober for a change.

"Vergil Rawlins knows."

"We have to watch out for him," said Eddie.

"Uh-huh."

"That's where Wally got his stuff."

"He's also the only guy with a key," said Birch.

"No—I have a key."

"You have a key?"

Eddy didn't answer.

"OK, so you have a key. Look, Eddy, if you have a key, why don't you come over tomorrow morning. I was thinking I would go out there again anyway. Sally Brown—you remember her, Wally's friend? She's coming and we can all go out there together, the three of us, and check it out, if you've got a key. We'll bypass Rawlins. He won't last anyway."

"Another thing."

"What?"

"The safe—Wally had a secret safe."

Birch had been in Wally's house a hundred times and had never heard anything about a secret safe.

"Yes, there's a safe in the closet in the bathroom. Maybe he kept his will in the safe."

First a daughter and now a secret safe!

"Also, Wally had a big collection of antique paper money which he used to keep in the safe."

"Come at around ten o'clock," said Birch.

"Any idea who killed him?"

"They're calling it an accident. Some dudes were there, somebody named Tom, and an Eric. Know them?"

"No."

"Neither does anybody else.

"You know Wally was depressed," said Eddy Cornel. "Karla Marsh—she trashed him and she trashed his department. She was out to get Wally just like she got me."

Eddy didn't sound calm anymore.

"Also Jack Devries. There was something going on."

"We were trying to fire Devries," said Birch

"That's funny. Jack Devries was out at Wally's two weeks ago. As soon as I came, he left."

The call waiting beeped.

31. The ~~King's~~ Queen's English

"Hello—it's Dean Karla Marsh," said the gruff female voice on the phone.

"Speak of the fucking devil ..." he said under his breath.

"What do you mean by that Professor Birch?"

"Did I say anything?"

"I wasn't sure."

Birch had to be careful now. His troubles with Marsh began when she was just another professor on the University Committee, before she was appointed Dean. Birch had raised a question about a candidate, one of Karla's favorites, who had written a book comparing the facial gestures of castrated cross-dressing actors in Lesbian bars in New York, Chicago, and San Francisco with uncastrated performers in gay bars in Paducah, Illinois. In the meeting Birch had wondered if this was an appropriate topic.

"Oh you are all the same," Karla hissed, "foisting presentist standards down the throats of those more nurturant than you."

"Please, use the King's English, Professor Marsh," he'd replied.

"Shouldn't that be the *Queen's*?" Karla had said in glory.

Yes, it'd been downhill from there. And now this.

"What did you say?" Karla repeated over the phone in her deep voice.

"Really, Karla, nothing."

"I hear that Wally had no relatives."

"He has a brother in California. I need to get hold of him."

"I mean, I just can't believe that Wally Wills has died," Karla said. "I feel especially bad—I mean of course I am devastated anyway—but I'm also afraid that Wally died with anger in his heart, against me, if I may say so."

"Yes, Karla, he was upset, it's true. He said something to me about it. But he was calming down. I wouldn't worry. I mean, he is dead after all."

"That's just it. It's so terrible. I wanted to make it up to him. Was he ... on drugs?"

"Drink, I believe. The holy spirit of wine."

"Sure—he took a drink once in awhile, like the rest of us," she said humanely.

"Look, thanks for phoning, Karla. But I have to go. We'll chat, we'll chat."

"Oh," she said.

"What?"

"Wally always used to say that—when he didn't want to talk to you anymore."

32. Only the living suffer

No sooner had Birch hung up but the phone rang. The voice was sonorous, yet twangy—a woman's, like an empty wail down a dark hall.

"Hello Raymond. It's Mimi Esperanto, Audrie Winter's daughter."

Oh, it was *she* who had phoned Eddy Cornel and told him about Wally's death. But how did Mimi Esperanto find out?

Birch reached back in his memory twenty years, to the time when he first arrived in town in a U-Haul van with a VW bug in tow. Five caged cats on the seat beside him. And there was Wally sitting on the steps of the red-brick duplex across the street from the 1920s bungalow Birch had bought, his shirt off. Birch pulled the van to the curb. It was tremendously hot. Wally was a mountain of flesh humped on the cement, cascading downward and outward, his white firm meat bristling with black boarish hair. Rivers of sweat ran down his face and onto his breasts.

"Hey, aren't you Wally Wills?" Birch had shouted across the front seat and through the truck window, remembering Wally from his job interview, though Wally was more modestly dressed then.

"That's me, bro," he said. He came over and extended his thick arm through the window. His flesh had a strong, masculine smell.

The aged Audrie Winter just then came out of the building behind him. She crept down the stairs holding two glasses of lemonade, which she gave to the men. Then another woman came out behind her, yes—that was Mimi Esperanto, already old, huddling in the shadow of her ancient mother.

Wally was living in the downstairs apartment with Jack

Devries in those days. Then Jack and Wally split up, and Wally and Audrie became very close, depending on one another, loving one another. Audrie Winter surely was an anchor in the storm of Wally's life.

"It's terrible, Mimi," Birch said into the phone.

"You know I have to tell mother," Mimi said.

"Of course."

"It will kill her."

"Do you want me to tell her?" Birch offered.

"No—I'll tell her. Tomorrow. Now professor, don't phone, please! It's already too late in the day," Mimi Esperanto said. "She will need the entire day before her, to rest. If I tell her now, she won't sleep all night. You see?"

"I won't phone her," Birch promised.

"You know it is so amaaazing," Mimi whined, stretching out the word, "because Mother said that she had phoned Wally on Monday night and that all she could hear were these awful groans in the background. She thought something was terribly wrong so she hung up and phoned again and this time somebody *else* answered, who said that Wally wasn't there! But she could hear Wally in the background. He *was* there! Then Mama phoned again and this time nobody answered at all. Do you think there could be any connection between this and what happened?"

Uh-oh, a bleep on the line, call-waiting.

"I have to go now, Mimi," Birch apologized. "We'll chat tomorrow, OK?"

Birch opened the fridge to get out some orange juice while he hit the call-waiting. "Hello?" he said.

"It's Ron Fettman, the lawyer. I'm phoning because I've been nervous about the security of the house."

"I'm glad you phoned, Ron. Right now only Vergil Rawlins has a key, but there's another guy, name of Eddy Cornel—an old friend of Wally's who lives over by Lake Michigan—he has a key too. I've been thinking that it would be good if you could come out to the house with us tomorrow, Ron, since the legality of all this remains rather unclear. I mean you're a lawyer, aren't you?"

"Uh-huh."

"Somebody is going to have to keep us on the right side of the law. Want the job?"

"That's why they call me Fettman," he said.

Birch hung up and filled a glass with crushed ice. He then filled the glass half with OJ and half with water. The phone rang again.

"It's Marylou Stieglitz, Professor Birch. You have to get in touch with the east coast right away," said the philanthropist who had showed up at Wally's in the VW bug.

"Well, I know he had relatives out there, but Marylou, didn't he have a big fight with his mother before she died? Something about his father's inheritance? Wally spoke to me as if he were on bad terms with his eastern relatives."

"Yes, I heard that—that he had some fight with his mother," said Marylou. "You know that Wally's grandfather was big in the Burlington Mills out in Massachusetts. That's where all the family money came from," Marylou Stieglitz said. "When Wally's father died, Wally put his mother in MacClean's. They're the best hospital in Boston. MacClean's must have records of some kind. Maybe they will know the name of the attorney who has Wally's will?"

"MacClean's? Never heard of it, but what I'm worried about, Marylou, is that Wally was on such bad terms with his relatives back East … I mean there was some dispute about selling the mansion on the Cape—the place with twenty-six rooms. The relatives didn't get their proper share or something and sued Wally to get the money."

"Sued on what grounds?"

"Moral turpitude! Well, that's what Wally told me, I'm sorry to say. For this reason it doesn't seem like a good idea … to bring these people in until we actually find the will, see what I mean?"

"Yes, I do see," Marylou said.

Birch took a deep draft of the OJ. It was immensely refreshing. He didn't eat that much any more, but drank great quantities of OJ punch, to take off the gnawing edge of hunger.

33. A life of fun, pleasure

Birch sat down in the straight-backed chair in front of the mission table. He got up immediately, then sat down again. Wally had said his brother resigned his Berkeley job and took a new job ... sure, in Santa Barbara, Birch remembered. To be near the beach.

Easy just to phone. Get the area code and direct-dial. He phoned Santa Barbara info and *mirabile dictu* there was a listing for a John Carson. Probably the entertainer, Birch thought.

Birch rang the number. A woman's voice answered the phone—or it was a girl.

"Hello—is this the residence of John Carson, the brother of Wally Wills?"

"Well, sort of," the woman said with a high, merry laugh. Could this be Carson's wife? Or his daughter?

"Is John in?" Birch said.

"He's at work. Do you want to leave a message?"

Birch left his number and said Good-bye. He sat down, relieved that he'd found the brother so easily, a piece of cake. Then he got up and went upstairs to the bird room and lay down in the midst of the feathers, cedar chips, and the fine white dust that came from the cockatoo.

Birch was screaming something, and that's why the Amazon was making a throaty clucking cackling sound while the Cockatoo swung to the bottom of her cage on her massive gray antediluvian scaled black-nailed claws, and she burrowed with her massive beak in the cedar chips at the bottom of the cage, looking for something down there.

The phone rang downstairs. Birch put down the joint, rolled off the bed, which was a little wobbly, and made his way into the hall library. He took the call from the wall phone, which had the ringer turned off.

"Hello Mr. Birch, we've noticed that you have a cedar roof and this year we're offering—"

Birch cut him off. As if he didn't have enough problems. The phone rang again downstairs. Birch picked it up again and said "Hello."

"Hi, this is John Carson. You phoned earlier, about Wally? I just got home."

The man's voice was low, slithery.

"Thanks for phoning, John. I have terrible news. Wally is dead."

"You can't be serious."

"No, he's dead."

"How?" the man said, stunned.

"Maybe heart failure. I don't know. I'm sorry. As far I know you are his only living close relative."

"I'm not his relative."

"What do you mean you're not his relative? I mean you're his brother by adoption, aren't you?"

"Oh no, we are not related at all," the man half-laughed. "I just lived down the street from him in Worcester, Mass, where we grew up. But we're not related in any way. Did Wally tell you we were brothers?"

"He certainly did tell me you were brothers! And he told a lot of other people that too. You weren't brothers? The way I got the story is that your parents were killed in an automobile accident when you were ten years old and Wally's adoptive parents took you in."

Carson gave another little laugh.

"Yes, I guess Wally liked to call me his 'brother,' kind of as a joke, and really I did accept it, that he played that game—but that was Wally. In fact my parents are both alive. They still live in Worcester. Oddly, it was my father—a doctor—who arranged Wally's adoption."

"Your parents are alive?" Birch said.

"How well did you know Wally?"

"Well!" Birch emphasized, because he and Wally had spent thousands of hours together, and Wally had talked constantly, as a regular theme, of his complex relations with his family and especially all the trouble over selling the twenty-six room house on the Cape. "Wally always made a big deal out of you being his brother. He said that he had been adopted as an infant but his parents took you on later. Wally was bitter about his adoption—he said that his uncle used to introduce him on family occasions in front of ambassadors and other important people at their house on Cherry Hill in Boston as 'my adopted nephew'—this behavior chagrined and humiliated him, John, and Wally often talked about it."

"I wouldn't know. I've been to Boston probably five times in my life," the man laughed again. "Oh, maybe once in the airport. I don't think Wally had ever lived in Boston, if that's what you mean. But please don't get me wrong," Johnny Carson went on, "this is the most terrible news imaginable. As I say ... still, I would be more than happy to help out, I mean financially, if there's some way I can."

"Yes, of course. His body is in the morgue, I am told."

"Well let me know about developments. I mean Wally and I were quite close ... I—well, let it go for now ... but let's just say that I will do what I can. Wally was a very *very* good friend."

"How about his relatives then?"

"Well, his parents are dead, if that's what you mean."

"But I mean his cousins and so forth—his extended family?"

"Hmm, I don't know of any cousins. I don't think Wally had any relatives except for his mother and father, who of course had adopted him. Maybe there's somebody I don't know about."

Birch was stunned. His head was whirling. He was trying to make sense of it all.

"Do you have children?" he asked at last.

"Oh—well they're grown up. Another life and all that. I've been divorced for years. Why?"

"Did you have tennis courts in your place in Berkeley?"

"Berkeley? Tennis? I could never stand the game! And I've

never lived in Berkeley."

34. FLEISCHACKER, DORPFIELD, FETTMAN

The phone rang again.

"Hi, Birch, this is Ron Fettman. I'm phoning to say that I've gone ahead and drawn up documents that will make you personal representative. This will give you the legal right to enter Wally's house, inventory the contents, and search for the will. But you will need to come down to my office and sign the papers. That will give you the right to get his body out of the morgue and pick up his effects."

"Where are you?" Birch asked.

"You're going to have to look it up on a map. We're in one of the, uh, rapidly growing parts of town."

Fettman again sounded boyish, hip. Birch hung up and sat down in front of the round oak table and studied a map. He pulled on his short leather jacket that he had bought in Turkey and went outside to his four-runner king-cab pickup and drove over to the main thoroughfare. He followed the line he'd drawn on the map.

He came to a modern business complex in the west part of town where development was swiftly changing the character of the city. It felt good to be out of the house, where he spent too much time, even if on this dismal task. Birch wondered what it would be like to have a *real* job, to sit behind a desk every fucking day, drive to work, get up, go home. The thought seemed fantastic, insane!

It was nearly closing time when Birch entered the plushly carpeted hall and rode the elevator to the third floor. He walked down a silent glass corridor, to a blonde-paneled door in a glass wall inscribed FLEISCHACKER, DORPFIELD, & FETTMAN, the letters pecked out in the glass. Evidently some kind of legal partners.

But where was the name of Sam Spade?

Birch said Hello to the pert neatly-dressed receptionist. She slipped out of her nook and showed him across a waiting room decorated with potted palms, into a conference room filled by a large oblong table. The rays of the dimming sun played through the high glass panels, drowning the world in a lustrous hue of gold.

Immediately a man in a gray suit and tie, middle-aged with a plump face, came into the room. He sat down opposite to Birch.

"I'm Ron Fettman," he said.

Birch felt weak again. It was the same voice all right, but the body was entirely wrong. Where was the hipster, the yuppie, Wally's close advisor in real estate? This guy was a suit!

"Glad to meet you," Birch said, extending his hand.

35. Tragedy that breaks man's face

The Phone was ringing inside when Birch got back to the house. Birch rushed to get the door open. He picked up the receiver on the eighth ring.

"I already told Mama about Wally," said Mimi Esperanto in a plaintive voice without identifying herself. "She's crying about it right now. She's balling like a little baby. At ten o'clock the pastor is coming over from the church next door. You know that Mama lives in the house next to the church because she used to keep their daily accounts."

"She's taken the news pretty well?" Birch wondered.

"Oh no!"

There was a sharp voice in the background.

"Is that Professor Birch? I need to talk to him," the voice in the background demanded.

"No, Mama, you just relax—"

"Hello, Professor Birch?" a strong voice came in suddenly. "This is Audrie Winter. I'm on the other phone line. I just can't believe it! Can you?"

Her voice was clear, like a sharp breeze.

"That Wally's dead?"

"I simply can't believe it," her vigorous voice trailed off into soulful sobbing.

"Mamaaa!" cried Mimi.

"Oh hush, Mimi. Can't you see I'm trying to talk?" Then her voice trembled. "You know, Professor Birch, I just saw Wally on Sunday. He told me that funny story about Sally Brown—that when the renewal for that Jack Devries came up—that she had changed her vote. I couldn't believe it! But he seemed in such a good mood. What do you think happened?"

"Sure, and he came to my place after he visited you, Audrie. He seemed fine," said Birch.

"Of course he also complained about that dean who really did him dirt if you ask me. You know why? Because he was against the postmodernists! Can you believe that, Raymond Birch? I don't even know what a postmodernist is. He was a true scientist, Professor Birch."

"Uh-huh."

"You will have to notify his brother in California at once. His name is Johnny Carson, like the fellow that used to be on the TV."

"Audrie, but—this is incredible—I just talked to Johnny Carson and he's not his brother at all it turns out—only a childhood friend."

"Not his brother?" blurted Mimi onto the three-way line.

"Why I can't believe it," said Audrie. "Wally always said that John Carson was his brother ..."

"I spoke to John Carson and he says he isn't his brother.

And Carson's parents are still alive."

"My goodness," Audrie said, shaken.

"But you should get in touch with his relatives in Boston," said Mimi.

"Mimi, you know that Wally didn't get along with those relatives," Audrie snapped. "Oh no—he never got along with his mother at all, especially. Of course now she's dead. Wally told me that one of the most hurtful things in his entire life was when he came home from Oxford, England, where he had been a visiting professor, and his mother wouldn't even rise from her chair to greet him. This really wounded Wally deeply just like she had shot him in the heart. Those were his very words. I don't think he ever got over it. And she always spoke to him in French, never in English. That's why he hated to speak French!"

"But at least he learned it, Mama. We had to study French for years and never even learned it," Mimi Esperanto said in the background.

"Study is good for you, Mimi. We are talking about Wally. Oh I just can't believe I will never see him again ...."

Her voice trailed into a sob.

"Mama, I told you you shouldn't be talking."

"There there, I'm alright. Raymond, you know that both Wally's mother and his father are dead. He loved his father very much. He was a Unitarian and very wealthy. Their family earned their money from the Burlington carpet mills. They had a huge house on the Cape with twenty-six rooms. That's not far from my own home of Portsmouth, New Hampshire. It was a great sorrow to Wally when his father died. But Raymond—" her voice broke, "please, will you come see me on Sundays, now that Wally is dead?"

Birch had heard about Wally's parents' failing health and about their deaths. Wally had told him how it was when he had visited his father in a fancy rest home and he had to clean his bottom. That made a big impression on him. Then he had sold the house on the Cape. That's right, that's what started the dispute with his relatives over the proceeds and the charges of moral turpitude against him.

"Raymond," Mimi was saying, "just one thing."

"What?"

"Have you been out there to Wally's house? You know he has Mama's chair—"

"It was my Grandpa's. Grandpa just loved that chair," said Audrie.

"Do you think you could get that chair back for Mama?" Mimi asked.

"Professor Birch, could you, please? That would be so wonderful, if you only could."

"Well—I'm going out there today ... of course I will."

"Please phone soon then, Raymond. Tell me you've got the chair!"

36. Now he wants a match

Birch got out of bed, pulled on a robe, and went to the small cherry table in the living room. Maybe a cigarette had fallen out of an old pack. He used to keep a pack in that table for emergencies. His heart leaped when he spotted a broken Camel filter at the back of the drawer, underneath a stack of coasters. He found a paper of matches on the mantle and went into the backyard and along the path that led to the back lot.

The morning was gorgeous, scented, balmy. He sat down in the lawn chair beside the rose garden, tore away the broken portion of the cigarette, and fired it up. That was the thing about Wally— you could always go out to his place, sit on the deck around his Walmart wrought-iron table under the Cinzano awning and smoke a cigarette. He had been out to Wally's only two weeks before, just after the report came in from Karla Marsh. Wally's front door was open but Birch knocked anyway, lightly.

"Yeah?" said Wally from around the corner.

Wally was slumped over the long white utility table in front of the glass wall that faced the lake. He had bought the table after Eddy Cornel smashed his round oak work table for a second time. Wally was writing in his yellow note pad and Birch guessed he was working on his book on paleolithic art, for which he had signed a lucrative contract with a New York house. The kitchen was filthy. Empty glasses were scattered over the table among the papers.

"Hey Birch—hey man, wanna smoke?" Wally threw down his pen. "This stuff is dynamite … really knock you out … right out there … I got nothin to do anyhow …"

It had crossed Birch's mind that Wally might have some weed and that was probably one of the reasons he had come out in the first place.

"Hey … let's go out here …" Wally said.

The two men went outside onto the porch and sat down at the Walmart table.

"Hey … such a pleasure … to see you, guy … really beautiful out here … you are great, guy, I really love you … so class … so pizazzz … Karla Marsh! I'm going to chew her another asshole … you were right, Birch, you were right … Of course I'm not seething … but you know … I *am* seething …"

"Forget it, Wally, let it go," Birch advised. "It's not her fault. She and Olive Oyl are on the outs, I hear. Olive Oyl ran off, you know, with a man. I heard this."

"… she is? … I mean she did? … well, then … then that's OK … still, I want you to kill her, Birch … you used to be a karate guy, huh? … you kill her for me, would you …?"

"Sure, Wally."

"You can do it, Birch … for me … for old time's sake …"

"Great day, hey Wills?"

"… beautiful … I knew you would come, I knew it … you are so great … but that's alright … pizazzz … don't pay attention to me … I think I've had it, Birch … I wrote a book … I had a party and everybody came … and now nobody cares …"

Wally was referring to his highly successful symposium

volume on the principles of ancient art, to which luminaries from around the world contributed, an instant classic that established Wally's reputation. The book was brilliantly produced on fine paper with superb transparencies, heavily subsidized out of Wally's own deep pockets, and when the book came out Wally threw a tremendous black-tie party with a swing band that people *still* talked about.

Birch took one of Wally's cigarettes from the table, snapped alight Wally's Bic lighter, and lit Wally's cigarette, and then his own. Wally had not taken up cigarettes until he was thirty-five, when everybody else was quitting, but now he smoked often and with obvious enjoyment.

"Yeah, I know, Wally. Life is shit. But what else is there?"

"There's beer, for one thing … you wanna one? … wanna beer?"

"Oh, sure," Birch said to the offer.

Wally staggered to his feet and went inside and came out with three beers.

"Why three?" Birch asked.

"Ya gotta ask … one for you and two for me you twit … you fucking twit …"

"When you're out of beer you're out of gas, hey Wally?"

"Yessss."

Wally sat back down and they drank the beer and smoked.

"Wally, where's this weed you were carrying on about?"

"Funny you should ask … I just got some the other night … Just hang on—"

Wally got up again, knocking over the chair, then tripping on its leg so that he fell onto the deck with an enormous crash.

"Jesus Christ, are you OK?" Birch jumped up, actually alarmed.

"No, no … I meant to do that," Wally said, obviously toasted.

"You *meant* to fall down?"

Wally lay on the deck for a minute.

"Come on, man I'll help you up."

Birch took hold of Wally's massive shoulders but somehow

Wally regained his balance without him and rolled onto his feet.

"I meant to do that you know."

"Are you OK?"

Birch picked up the chair while Wally went back inside into the small kitchen and rummaged around on the highest shelf in the cupboard next to the sink. He brought down an antique gravy bowl. Inside was a baggy of grass and some cigarette papers that Wally carried outside and placed on the wrought-iron table.

"Hey, Birch, you do the honors ... you mind?"

Birch unrolled the baggy, took out a cigarette paper and made a new crease in it below the commercial center-line. He rolled a pinch of the light greenish-yellow marijuana between his fingers and dribbled it onto the paper.

"Light green is best, hey Wills?"

"... I hope a fuckin breeze ... doesn't fuckin come up ..."

"Don't worry about it."

Birch twisted the ends with a practiced air and inserted the whole joint in his mouth to wet it down so it would burn smoothly.

"... will you just light the fuckin thing?"

Birch tried the lighter, but it was out of gas and wouldn't catch.

"You got a match?"

"... now he wants a fuckin match ... ask Karla! ... I just want to be free of all that ... you know that ..."

"Freedom's hard to find, my man, in a land of slaves."

"... *land of slaves* my ass ... you fuckin twit ... !"

37. Friendship

Wally got to his feet and went inside the house, to the white utility table near the windows.

"How's the book coming?" Birch shouted through the open doors.

"Fuck you, Birch," he said, coming back and throwing a cigarette lighter on the table.

Birch lit the joint, took a drag, and passed it to Wally, who held it poised in his hand.

"Whaddya hear from your ex-wife?" Wally asked suddenly.

"Go to hell, Wills."

"... she was too good for you Birch ... that's the whole story ... you know it ..."

Psssah! Wally farted.

"... excuse me ... lucky we're outside ... anyway pal ... you are dead meat ..."

"You keep saying that, but I'm still alive," Birch replied with some irritation.

"... you know my mother was born in France ... she was very wealthy and always had everything ... my father wasn't exactly poor either ... but they never got along ..."

"Sure Wally, you've told me about it."

Birch offered the joint to Wally, but Wally at first refused, then took it anyway. The telephone rang inside. Wally got up and went inside. Birch could hear his muffled voice through the open door.

"Who was that?" Birch asked when Wally returned.

"... that was Audrie Winter ... such a dear *dear* friend ... such a dear old friend ... I was just at her house this morning ... she's ninety-five years old but as sharp as a tack ... she has a mind like a steel trap."

"Platonic?"

"What?"

"Your friendship."

Birch's eyes were red.

"... Raymond, Raymond—I don't know what I'm going to do with you ..."

Birch tore off the cover of a paper matchbook and rolled it into a cylinder around the end of the roach. He lit the roach and passed it to Wally.

"... no thanks, I'm fine ..."

Birch was glad to have the roach to himself. Then he stood up and went behind Wally's chair. He began to massage the muscles of Wally's huge neck. Wally relaxed under his hands. He let his heavy head slump forward like a dead man.

"... you're a wuss, Birch ..." he grunted and made animal sounds. "... but you're OK ..."

"You're OK too, Wally."

"... no, I mean it ... you're just saying that ... but you're really OK."

"... against the forces arrayed in mighty ranks, rapiers drawn ..."

"Ha, ha!"

"... relentless in purpose, devious, without heart or hesitation ..."

"... you're too much, Birch ... you're too much ... after all I did for them! ... I'm going to chew her another asshole ... I'm going to *kill* her Birch, I mean it."

"If she doesn't kill us first."

38. A voice from beyond

The dewy scents of morning were a wondrous drug as Birch lay in the chaise longue and let his eyes shut halfway in contemplation. Oh, now the phone was ringing inside the house. Birch flipped the cigarette stub into the rose garden and went back inside.

"This is Jean Fodamew," said the suave voice at the other end.

"Who did you say?" said Birch.

"I heard that Wally Wills died and that you are in charge."

"I don't know who is in charge, really."

"I can't believe it. You know I spoke to him on Monday."

"Who are you?"

"Well, Jean Fodamew, as I just told you. Ha, ha. I run an art gallery here in town. I was *such* a good friend of Wally's and I'm ... *very* good friends with Jack Devries you know. We're all just one big family. The thing is, Doctor Birch, that Wally was trying to arrange a, well, frankly, *very good deal* for me practically on the very day he died."

Birch held the phone out at a distance and looked through his windows, envisioning the glories of his redwood porch that would one day stand there. A shaft of light shined through the fronds of the big spruce and, bifurcating, struck Birch in the face. For a second he was blinded.

"... the sale of a painting, you see. That's why I phoned him on Monday. He was going to sell me a very valuable painting at a very good price. I mean, do you know just when he died by any chance?"

"I don't know *just when* he died, but his secretary found him on Tuesday around 1:20 P.M., when he didn't show up for work."

"But you see, that's just *it*," the voice cooed, "I spoke to Wally on Monday afternoon around 4:00 P.M. So near!"

"Did you notice anything unusual when you spoke to him?" asked Birch.

"Frankly, yes. That's just it. Wally was completely *out of his mind*! Yonko. Zatzville. Wally and I have tied one on a few times I can tell you, but I assure you—*this* was different. He was *completely incoherent*. He could barely speak—only grunts. I couldn't believe it."

"You didn't get much out of him, out of your conversation?"

"Hardly."

"I'm glad you phoned Mister, uh ... anything else?"

"There is a *little matter*, a *little matter* only ... Namely, *what's* to become of Wally's art collection?"

"Is it valuable?"

"Well, that Jim Dine, just for starters! ... let me tell you ...

some of it has a *lot* of value—the picture of the woman without her head, the Venus. And if that wing chair at the base of the stairs is really Georgian, which it may be, it could be worth $20,000—at least."

"The chair with the grease spot?"

"Oh me, oh my, that's nothing. Of course an expert would have to examine the *construction* of the chair to see if it really *is* Georgian. And of course he has those two Whistler drawings going up the stairs—"

The voice seemed to come from faraway, from a tunnel drilled into Birch's brain.

"Didn't you know? Yes, one is of a milkmaid and the other a fence across a field. They don't *look* like much, but they are *real* Whistlers."

"Real fucking Whistlers?"

"About $10,000 each, I would say. And then there is the Chinese primitive ... on the wall beside the lower course of the stairs, a village market scene, you know, sort of folksy acrylic, busy with detail kind of thing? It doesn't really look Asian but it is, and *quite* valuable."

"And the headless lady, you said?"

"You can bet *that's* worth a pretty good price. I'm very *interested* in the Jim Dine and even in all of the art when it comes up for sale, if you see what I mean."

There was a beep and Birch hit the FLASH button.

"Professor Birch—? It's Audrie Winter," said the voice of the old woman. "Where are you going to bury Wally?"

"Who makes that decision? His body is still in the morgue," Birch said.

"Please, Raymond, *please* ... you can do it ... Let him be buried in my family plot in Forest Hills Cemetery. He can lie next to Daddy and next to my brother Willie—and soon Mimi and I will be there too. Then we will all be together."

The call-waiting beeped still again.

"Audrie, that's a good idea. Let me try to get his body out of the morgue. I'll see what I can do."

"God bless you, Professor Birch! God bless you!"

Birch hit FLASH, but there was nobody there. An electronic sound like a long distance call, from a tunnel into the void.

39. You can always tell a fake—but you can't tell him much

Birch looked at his watch—8:15 A.M. The coroner's office would be open.

The sun was bright as he drove downtown into the maze of streets surrounding city hall. He got lucky and found a slot at the side of the building. He retrieved the leather school satchel that he brought to put Wally's things in. He must have had *some* things.

Birch swung up the broad granite steps of the courthouse, passed through high glass doors to the information desk. He asked where the Coroner's office was.

"Down the hall, turn left, then left. There is an elevator. Go to the basement," the small neatly dressed clerk said.

The echoing halls were empty. Polished floors reflected the overhead recessed fluorescent lighting.

Birch easily found the elevators with their massive, enormous doors—no doubt to accommodate corpses on gurneys! The elevator rumbled, descended, and opened into a basement, dimly lighted, but there was no sign, nothing that pointed the way to the Coroner's office.

Birch walked to the right down a passage that wended as in a maze beneath low ceilings, a mass of overhead pipes wrapped in gray tape. Something chugged behind the walls. A door was open. Was this the Coroner's office? Birch looked inside: It was a large closet for brooms and pails.

A heavily armed policeman swung around the corner and nearly ran Birch down. Fortunately, Birch had a lot of experience with police.

"Officer, could you help? I'm looking for the morgue?"

"It's down there, near the underground parking," said the policeman and pointed back in the direction he'd come.

Birch walked for a long time down the corridor. Then, where it opened out through large steel doors to somewhere, just before the doors, Birch found the sign CORONER on corrugated opaque glass. The door was old, of wood, and part of the sign was flaked away.

He went inside. The woman behind the counter shrieked and half-jumped from her chair, as if she'd seen a ghost.

"You frightened me," she said and clicked closed her cosmetic compact.

"I bet you were wishing it was five o'clock on Friday, huh?" Birch said.

She smiled prettily.

"Don't we wish!"

"We could have a drink—at some bar."

"Don't you wish!" she said coyly, somewhat flattered.

"I've come to release a corpse named Wally Wills."

"Oh, yes, Doctor Wally Wills. You must be Professor Birch? Your lawyer, Ron Fettman, gave us a call."

"No, that was me who phoned, or—"

"Was it? I thought he gave his name as Fettman."

A stout powerful man with strong white well-washed hands and a closely-cropped gray beard came into the room. He looked like the onetime surgeon general of the United States of America, the one that gave you confidence, but Birch couldn't remember his name.

"So you are Birch, the friend of Wally Wills?" the man interrupted the conversation in a commanding voice. "You know it's really amazing, but in thirty-five years on this job I've never received so many calls about anybody as I have about this Wills fellow."

The man was engaging, friendly.

"I hear he has a brother out in California," said the Coroner.

"Yes, but it turns out he didn't really."

"Really!"

"It's beginning to look as if he didn't have any relatives at all," said Birch. "There are rumors of relatives back East, but no leads," Birch said in a low voice.

"None! Really! Well that's an extremely unusual situation. Father and mother dead too, huh? Can't think of another case like it. Of course these street people, that's not unusual. But somebody like him, with a respected job, well known in the community—can't think of another case like that. No sirree. No close kin—just imagine."

The man was thick and clearly very strong.

"You're the Coroner?"

"Ralph Borgnine," he said and reached out his burly hand. Birch took it through the window over the counter.

"You did the autopsy? What did you find?"

"Not much. He had mild heart disease but nothing to kill him. No infarction. No stroke. His blood alcohol was .37. That's up there. That's really up there."

"Enough to kill him?"

"Oh no, I wouldn't say. Of course we sent in specimens for tests. We'll know in four to six weeks."

"I see. Specimens," Birch repeated.

"Yes, they'll do all the tests. He must have been quite a man. I've gotten so many inquiries. Imagine, no relatives. Well, if you can sign on this paper here, we can release him—I got a call from the Burning Light Funeral Home ..."

Birch signed the papers.

"Here's what we found," said the lady behind the desk, coming out with a manila envelope and emptying it onto the counter: an enormously fat wallet, a ring of keys, and a ruby pinkie ring.

"Also, these. They were in the open drawer of an antique wash stand."

From another envelope she brought out a handful of what seemed to be antique paper currencies. Birch had never seen anything like them. The bills were wrapped individually in plastic envelopes. They were beautiful, brilliant, mint-condition nineteenth century American greenbacks—images of locomotives chugging across fields of grain, Indians in full headdress, bare-breasted women lusting for Freedom, ones and fives and tens and fifties.

"The detective found them in the house and thought they might be valuable."

"Yes, well he collected things, I guess," Birch said and swept the objects into his satchel.

"Say, did you see this morning's paper?" the Coroner asked. He put down the *State Times*. In the lower right was a big picture of Wally, smiling like he'd just eaten a fistful of shit.

UNIVERSITY PROFESSOR FOUND DEAD IN HIS HOME

Wally Wills, a professor at the University, was found dead Tuesday at the foot of a stairway in his home. Wills, 45, died of unknown causes, said the County Coroner. "We're not suspecting foul play," the Coroner added.

The death came as a blow to Wills's colleagues. "He was totally devoted to his students," said Larry Brown, an art professor. "He had tremendous charisma and there are going to be lots of students who will be very upset." Students voted Wills one of the most popular professors on campus. In The Best Professors at the University, *a publication put out by the student Association, Wills is described as a man charmed, no tickled to death, by the magic of artistic creation.*

An anonymous student wrote about him:

"A truly amazing professor. He opened my eyes and challenged my views. Incredibly dynamic and challenging; above all, great fun."

"He was a super man, great to work for," said his secretary this

morning.

Wills was considered to be one of the world's foremost detectors of art forgeries. He appeared as expert witness in many art fraud cases and traveled the world advising museums on purchases and authenticating pieces. He once taught a class called, "Fakes, Forgeries, and Connoisseurship."

"I see," said Birch, pushing back the paper. "Except he was forty-seven."

"What do you mean?" said Ralph Borgnine, the city Coroner.

"Forty-seven years old, I think. Also, what if they find something in him?"

"Oh, you mean toxins? drugs? Things like that? Well, by then—you know, it will be weeks. You know how it is with these news people. Unless it's still bleeding, they haven't much interest."

"Gotcha," said Birch.

"I think it will be OK," said the coroner.

From his friendly manner Birch guessed that it would.

40. Some people get on my nerves

Birch returned home and threw the satchel on the oak table. It was nearly 10:00 A.M. He was washing his hands when the doorbell rang. Upstairs the cockatoo whistled, answered by the Amazon's shrieks. Through the inner and outer glass doors he saw Ron Fettman on the porch, looking the other away through the woods, toward the house on the hill.

Birch opened the outer door. He reached out his hand. The

clean-cut portly lawyer entered the living room and sat down on the couch that ran under the high dark-framed Frank Lloyd Wright windows, opposite the fireplace over which Birch had mounted his collection of nineteenth-century Indian pipes.

"Coffee—or tea?" he asked.

"I've had plenty, thanks," said Fettman. "I gather that others will be coming so I'll hold off on the spiel about your legal rights and all that."

"I'm going to fix some tea."

Birch went into the kitchen, but the doorbell rang again. He hastily filled the kettle and put it on the gas stove. He hurried to open the door for Sally Brown.

"It's beautiful out," she said idly, entering the room, "but I wish I could say it is a good morning."

"You're too gloomy. Wally has only joined the legions of the dead. Soon we'll be there too," said Birch.

"Oh—I don't think this is a good time for jokes Raymond," said the diminutive Sally Brown, suddenly self-possessed. She wore a hallowed quizzical smile. Her gaunt blonde-gray hair framed her face.

Just then a battered Ford van pulled up and Eddy Cornel got out on the driver's side. His wife Evelyn got out the other side and came around the car.

Cornel shouted a greeting as he came up the steps. Evelyn came behind. They came inside. Eddy sat on the couch next to Fettman. He leaned forward to support his elbows on his knees. Evelyn sat next to the fireplace on the old maid's rocker, casually dressed in shorts and a white shirt.

"Uh-huh," Birch smiled. "Well here we are. I guess we are going to go out to Wally's and see what we can find, eh? Thanks for coming. Our main purpose is to find the will, as I see it. I was there yesterday but the place is a total mess. We couldn't find anything. How does that sound, Ron? Look for the will?"

"That would be appropriate," he approved.

"Yes, Ron, we want you to come with us," said Sally Brown, who liked to repeat conclusions reached by others.

"Ron, I'm worried about this Vergil Rawlins character," said

Birch. "He's too shady to let in to this deal but he has his own key. Eddy has his key too so we can get in. Come to think of it, I also have a key—yes, I just got Wally's ring from the Coroner."

"You have his key ring?" asked Fettman. "If Vergil Rawlins shows, that will be no problem."

The tea kettle was whistling and Birch went into the kitchen. He dropped a bag of tea into a mug, filled it with water, and carried the steaming mug back to the living room.

"I made some tea for myself. Anybody interested?"

"You want to drink first?" asked Sally.

"Let's get going. I'll take it along."

They left through the glass door onto the covered porch, down the cement steps between the compact silver maples on either side of the walk to the street. Birch got in the front seat of Sally's ill-used Ford sedan. Eddy and Evelyn got into Fettman's new Nissan Pathfinder SUV.

"I got a call from Karla Marsh yesterday," said Birch quietly as Sally pulled away from the curb. "She claims to feel guilty for dissolving Wally's department. Karla Marsh thinks she killed Wally Wills."

"Oh dear." Sally was so small, she seemed engulfed by the steering wheel. "Did she say anything about ... the Jack Devries hearing?"

"Let's not talk about that now, Sally."

"I think the vote will stand, Raymond. But tell me, do you think there were any drugs involved in Wally's death?"

Birch looked at her askance.

"Why Sally, not as far as I know. Yesterday I didn't see anything. Of course the police had been there."

"But they didn't say anything?"

They drove in silence past the stately homes nestled in private groves.

"Anyway, drugs didn't kill Wally Wills, and neither did Karla Marsh."

"What do you mean?" She looked startled.

You always had to explain everything to Sally.

"I mean we are shocked and saddened by Wally's death,

naturally, but surprised? Wally was in too deep. He was supposed to be writing this book for Harcourt-Brace but he wasn't getting to first base. They paid him a lot of money so it wasn't like he could just sit on it. The thing with Karla Marsh—it was more of the same."

"You think he went over the edge? Oh dear. Have you heard from Jack Devries—about Wally's death?"

"Just because Wally's dead Jack Devries is suddenly phoning me up? Is that what you're asking?"

She was silent. Birch figured he better back off. There were probably limits even to the legendary patience of Sally Brown.

41. All is rank, all is foul

Birch led the way across the patch of grass at the back of the house and they entered the porch through the screen door. Eddy got out his keys on a long chain that he withdrew from a polished metal disk on his belt. He fiddled with the lock and got the door open. They pushed in behind, but Birch nearly gagged from the smell.

"What is that *smell*?" Sally asked.

"I don't know. It's awful. There's all those weeds rotting in the lake—swamp gas maybe," said Birch. "It gets into the house, doesn't it."

They all stood in silence for a moment in the antechamber strewn with clothes. Then Birch took charge, as if they were a team and he was giving orders.

"But look, Sally why don't you work in the bathroom? And Eddy—you said Wally has a safe? Check it out. Wally never said anything to me about a safe."

"Wally liked to keep things secret," said Eddy.

"While you guys are doing that, I'll inventory the property. Does that sound right, Fettman?"

Birch removed a clipboard with a yellow note pad from his satchel. Obviously what went down on paper in this inventory he was making right then—that existed, and what didn't go down, did not exist. That gave Birch a certain edge, in case he needed it.

But where was this going, really?

"I'll look through the desk," Fettman said and sat down in front of the antique low spindle-backed secretary stacked high with manuscripts and doo-dads against the long wall ten feet from the Georgian chair under which Wally had died.

"What about the stuff upstairs in the loft?" asked Evelyn Cornel.

"Check that out, yes," said Birch.

Sally Brown went dutifully into the bathroom that opened at the side of the stone fireplace. You'd never guess she had once been an associate dean!

"Does anyone have any toilet cleaner?" she called out immediately.

"I carry it with me," said Birch and laughed.

"Just for the record," Eddy spoke in a low voice—"that painting over there—the one leaning against the wall at the back of the white table—that's mine. I loaned Wally $350 on the security of it but he never paid me."

Eddy pointed to a small oil still life of a bowl with fruit, a nineteenth-century American with nice patina.

"You loaned Wally money?" Birch said with surprise. "Well, if the painting's yours, then take it. Why did you loan Wally money?"

"Yeah—all that crap on the mantle—those paintings, they are all mine too. I did those paintings. I know they're crap but I did them when I lived here."

"Didn't you teach golf in the athletics department?" asked Birch.

A half dozen amateur oils were scattered amidst the debris on the mantle.

"I teach English now."

"Well don't worry about it. Just take them," said Birch.

"I just wanted to straighten that out," said Eddy. "I'll go look in the safe now."

Eddy went into the bathroom where Sally Brown was rummaging around. He opened the closet behind the door.

"Looks like we got company," said Fettman. Birch looked up, expecting to see Vergil Rawlins, but into the room came the ceramicist Harvey Vanderpool, who had been at the 666 Club the Friday before. Harvey stood near the open door.

"Hello everybody, I came by to help."

Evelyn peeked down from the stairs where she was doing something and Sally stuck her head out of the bathroom door.

"How did you find out about this?" Birch asked.

"I bought a newspaper," said Harvey.

"Hi Harvey," said Eddy Cornel, coming out of the bathroom behind Sally.

"We're looking for the will," Birch announced.

"Best way to find it, is to clean everything up," Harvey said. "Everything."

He made his way to the small kitchen at the back of the house and began to work. Birch watched Harvey retrieve some black plastic garbage bags from beneath the sink. Swiftly he swept away the dozens of empty beer cans, bottles, and clogged ashtrays into a bag. Harvey knew how to get things done all right and Birch admired this quality in him. But Harvey saw the world as a right-wing conspiracy, which bored Birch and wore out Harvey's young wife, who divorced him after three years.

Still holding his clipboard, nothing on it, Birch looked over Fettman's shoulder onto the desk.

"Anything like a will Mister Fettman?"

"I found his passport," Fettman said, extending the green well-worn booklet toward Birch. He took it and flipped through it. Entry and exit stamps from Turkey, Egypt, Israel, Greece, Italy, Spain, Morocco, France, Germany, the UK.

"Wally got around all right," said Birch. "He had the time and he had the means and he had the know-how."

"He had a good life, eh?" Fettman said.

"O.K., so maybe the will is here somewhere, if the passport is. I mean maybe he kept his important stuff together."

"Here's a bunch of calling cards—look, his name is written in Greek on one side and in English on the other," said Fettman, holding up a large beige card.

"For the Dagos," said Birch.

"I didn't know they had Dagos any more," said Fettman.

"Not around here. But over there, they do."

42. Be careful of the sun

Birch began his inventory with the paintings. Just inside the front door, beneath the open oak staircase, was a four-foot high print of ICARUS above the couch pushed against the wall. Birch squinted to read the label. The figure's arms spread like gossamer, hovering in a tangle of lines, like a butterfly emerging from a pupa. The smell seemed worse here by the stairs, where Wally had died. In fact it smelled like death.

"You know this is weird—here is a painting of Icarus, like presaging how Wally died," Birch said aloud. "Fell down the fucking stairs."

"Who is Icarus?" asked Evelyn from up above on the stairs.

Birch looked up but only saw her calves at the edge of the stair.

"Ah—a guy who flew too close to the sun, and died."

"Hey you want me to go through this paper up here?" Evelyn called down. "All this stuff in the shelves by the stair?"

Birch walked up the stairs to inspect the built-in shelves on the inside wall, stuffed with books and stacks of papers. Half of one shelf was filled with reference works on antique paper currencies.

"Sure, check out the papers. Throw out anything worthless and keep it if it looks good. How's that?"

"Great advice," she beamed.

Standing close to Evelyn, Birch smelled her. She was delicious. He put down the clipboard on the stair and began to skim through the books—American pottery, the silk road to China, something by Charles Bukowski, a book on Roman cities, the red-figured pottery of Apulia. Birch wasn't trying to start anything with Eddy's wife, or with any other woman as far as that was concerned, so racking was the pain he had suffered from them. Still, it was nice to stand beside Evelyn and smell her, for just a moment.

"This must have been stuff he was fooling around with," Birch said aloud. He spotted a copy of his own first book. Wally had brow-beat him into surrendering one of the first five copies because Birch had given him a credit in the preface. Wally had, in fact, helped him on a certain small matter.

"Hey this book has my name on it!" Birch joked and removed it from the shelf. He went downstairs and put the book in his satchel. He could cut out the dedication and, well, give it to somebody else.

43. Haven't we met before?

A diminutive middle-aged man was standing at the front door and everyone noticed him at once.

"Hi, I came to see if I could help," the man said.

"Who are you?" Sally asked, peeking out from the

bathroom.

"Hey Paul West," said Harvey Vanderpool, coming from the kitchen nook. Now Birch remembered—he was the aging hippy who was always scrunched against the corner of the booth at the 666 Club.

"Hi Paul," said Evelyn from around the stairs without a railing.

"What can I do to help?" Paul asked timidly.

"Why don't you go upstairs and work on the closet off the loft?" Birch suggested. "I peeked in there the other day and there seems to be a lot of crap in there. We're trying to find the will but not having much luck. That's the main thing."

"Did he even have a will?" Paul West asked.

"Well just last month he told me he had established a trust fund for our son in his will for $200,000," Eddy Cornel shouted from the bathroom.

"He had a will all right," shouted Sally from the bathroom. "For one thing, didn't he leave a lot of money to the university press to continue the monograph series that he edited with Angela Bellamy?" Sally now came into the room. "He told me many times that he had a will. He was very generous to the University in it."

Fettman took all this in while he continued to sort through massive stacks of paper on the secretary.

"Yes," agreed Birch, "I remember that he was elected to the Lathrop Hill Society ... you have to drop a *lot* of money on the University to get into the Lathrop Hill Society, I think. Enough at least to endow a professorship, which costs 1.5 mill, as I recall."

"1.25 mill," agreed Sally, who had served on key committees.

"You only have to list them as beneficiary on your university insurance, though," said Harvey authoritatively, pausing briefly in his labors. "I admit that would be a big policy."

Sally Brown looked at Harvey's broad workman's face, lankish hair, gat-tooth, and intelligent eyes behind wire-rim glasses.

"But didn't he also serve on the governing board of the Credit Union?" Birch asked. "He told me after he got his last inheritance that he had put the whole shebang, two million bucks, in the Credit Union. Because he was such a large holder they made him a member of the board. So he *must* have had a will. Maybe it's in a safety-deposit box?"

Harvey gave Birch an odd look, then hoisted up a bag of garbage and tied its neck with a serrated plastic strip. "Don't count on it," he said.

"Look for a safe-deposit key," offered Fettman. "They have a certain shape."

"I guess you can phone the Credit Union," said Sally.

"Well it's not in the safe," said Eddy from the bathroom.

"You found the safe?" said Birch.

Birch went into the bathroom to see. Sally was gone—where was she? At the back of a lower shelf in the narrow closet—Eddy had cleared a channel through piles of poker chips and cards and backgammon boards—there was a secret safe, its door wide open.

"Man, I never knew this safe was here," said Birch.

"You said that already, Ray," said Eddy Cornel. "But Wally used to keep his shit in here. He had a big collection of old paper currencies, too. He used to keep them here too."

"The cops had a few of those currencies. I got them. They found them in the washstand. But no big collection or anything."

"Where *is* the collection of paper currencies?" said Eddy.

"I dunno. He's got a bunch of books on old money by the stairs," Birch said. "Well, keep on looking, Eddy. There's still a lot of stuff in this closet."

Birch went back into the living room.

"So I should work upstairs?" asked Paul West, still standing at the door.

"Yes, here, let's take a look—I'll go with you."

Birch put down the clipboard on the back of the couch and led the way up the four steps to the landing, taking his time past Evelyn, stepping over stacks of paper arranged on the steps. They reached the upstairs landing and entered into a small central walk-in closet to the right of the landing. Birch groped for a switch but couldn't find it.

"It's a little thingamajig just to the side of the bulb in the fixture overhead," said Paul West.

Paul West reached around and got the light on.

"You know this closet?" Birch said, surprised.

"Sure," Paul said.

There were a few ratty clothes on a rack, a shelf at the back stacked with papers and old LP records, dirty underwear, and trash on the floor in the corners.

"I've been here before," Paul said in a melancholy way.

"Well, there are garbage bags downstairs, Paul, so I guess we can toss out all this crap, unless you want some of these clothes."

"I don't think so."

Birch went downstairs.

"By the way, haven't we met before?" he said to Evelyn, standing on the stair beneath and looking up.

"You say that to every girl, I imagine," Evelyn said.

Birch laughed, then asked: "So how old is your baby?"

"Ten months."

"What's his name?"

"Actually we *have* met before," said Evelyn "I was out here one time with Eddy."

"We drank a beer on the porch?"

He did remember her now.

"And once I went on a double-date with your son."

"What?" Birch said, astounded.

"Well, not exactly—he was with another girl, or I should say a woman. She was a lot older than him."

"My son? You were with somebody else?"

She smiled, smart and sexy, obviously way out of Eddy's class. What was going on with her? What was in it for her?

Back downstairs, Birch picked up his clipboard. He spotted a small covered Pima basket on the mantle in the midst of the junk. He had himself given this basket to Wally as a house-warming gift, with a note MAY YOUR HOUSE BE AS WARM AS A BASKET. Birch went over to it and worked off the closely-fitting top. A ring of keys, tags, receipts, bits of paper. And there was the original note.

"Are these the keys to the safe-deposit box?" Birch said, tossing the ring of keys to Fettman across the room.

Fettman examined them.

"Not the right shape," Fettman said. "I don't know what these are."

Birch emptied the basket into the chaos on the mantle, replaced its top, and stuffed the basket in his satchel along with the book he had reclaimed from the stairs. He gave these things to Wally ... but now that Wally was dead, what would become of this stuff?

Just then Eddy Cornel dragged a black garbage bag stuffed with trash out of the bathroom. Eddy winked when he saw Birch put the basket in his bag.

"Too bad about that safe, hey Eddy?"

"Yeah, too bad."

44. Clothes make the man

At the turn of the stairs over the landing hung the Chinese primitive described by the art dealer who had phoned Birch. Then there was an eerie ceramic mask on the wall with a grotesque twisted nose, gaping nostrils, and dumbstruck death mask eyes. Surely a parody of Wally himself, a grim jest!

On the other side of the Chinese primitive, moving toward the front of the house, was an enormous semi-abstract print, a label scrawled in pencil HAMLET.

"Oh, he's holding the skull of Petronius," Birch realized.

"*Polonius*," corrected Sally from the bathroom.

"Yes—that's what I meant!" Birch said, somewhat chagrined.

Birch wrote down HAMLET on his yellow pad.

Next to Hamlet was a modest-sized acrylic painting of a bald-headed man seated on a couch, his heavy head drooped in despair, in a stark David Lynch room empty except for a portrait on the wall. The portrait was of a smiling middle-aged man in a green-check business suit, blonde-haired, bow-tied. He looked down and from behind at the man on the couch, scrutinized him, judged him, condemned him for his failure. Everything in the painting was reds and oranges and blues and the angle of view askew so that you could not see the features of the bald man on the couch, who had crossed his hands in despair, his white bare feet like dead things before him. Birch had never paid much attention to this picture, but he now saw that the baldheaded man was Wally too. But who was the man in the portrait?

"All these pictures are of Wally!" Birch shouted out loud.

"What?"

"Pictures in disguise. Yes—the mask, Hamlet who hated his mother, Icarus falling from the sky, and now this fat guy overwhelmed by superego—"

Birch wrote on his yellow pad, PICTURE OF MAN IN A ROOM.

"What about that Chinese thing? Is that Wally too?" Harvey asked.

"You mean the Chinese dick?" Birch said, indicating the immense orange and green ceramic thing just inside the door that Wills had called a Peking Roof Tile.

Evelyn's laughter came down from the stairs.

Hanging over the antique desk, where Fettman still plied through mounds of paper, was a Roualtish-water color showing two heads leaning together and touching at the crown. Wispy lines splayed here and there.

ROUALT IMITATION—TWO BROTHERS? Birch wrote.

Birch moved toward the front of the house, the lakeside. Here the light was beautiful, streaming through the glass. There was the ghastly Jim Dine, the HEADLESS PINK WOMAN.

"That's Venus, you know," said Sally, watching him.

"It looks like Venus," Birch said.

Because Birch had discovered the pure white light of the spirit, wherein he spent increasingly long periods of uninterrupted time, it didn't matter that he had learned little in life. But one thing he had learned was that from women flowed an ocean of pain, and the simplest tactic was simply to keep away from them. And above all, *never* sleep with them. Venus was the beginning and the end of all things, of that there could be no doubt. Sex and shit—that was life, and life only.

Thinking he would finish cataloguing the art before starting on the furniture, Birch went back across the room and up the stairs where Evelyn was still sorting through books on the shelves.

"Great job," he said for no reason.

"Thanks, prof. You already said that."

Birch came up on the landing. Paul West was carrying out clothes from the closet, placing them in a pile on the double futon mattress near the edge of the loft from which you could look down and through the wall of windows to the lake beyond. While Paul West sorted the clothes, Birch went into the closet to look around. He pulled back a poster leaning against the back wall that concealed a stack of magazines. He picked one up—a stud with a big dick fucking some guy in the ass while he sucked the dick of a teenager with a hairy chest.

Paul West came in.

"No need for anybody to see that," Paul said.

"No need at all," Birch agreed. He began to stuff the porno mags into a black plastic bag.

In the loft, a pillar supported the roof. Sky lights and abundant light. Dried-out dying potted ferns, one overturned, dry dirt splayed across the wood. Birch looked down into the kitchen just below the edge of the loft. An enormous rubber plant on top of the refrigerator spread its fronds up almost into the loft itself, quite glorious really.

The filthy coverlet of the futon was pulled down, a hand-knit comforter with zig-zag design, scrunched in a pile at the foot of the mattress. Next to the bed, Audrie Winter's black leather captain's chair, with its deep-inset buttons. On the opposite wall were two amateurish landscapes, a gilt-edged mirror, and a beat-up couch. A stereo receiver and turntable had fallen from an overturned milk crate. Small speakers were positioned at the very edge of the loft, between the dying unwatered palms.

"Quite a mess, eh Paul?" Birch said.

"Looks like there was a fight," said Paul West.

"Really? You think? But Wally was a big slob, do you think? Not much up here, actually."

Paul West was stuffing a black plastic garbage bag with old clothes.

"No, Wally didn't have much."

Birch wrote down, AMATEURISH LANDSCAPES, 2.

"Who do you think did these paintings?"

"Wally's friends. He was always collecting pictures done by his friends, even if they weren't any good."

"Think any of those clothes could be used by anybody? Give them to Saint Vinnies?"

"I doubt it!"

"It always amazes me because, you know," Birch said, "Wally was always going on a diet, losing fifty pounds, then gaining it back. He was like a balloon, puffing up and down. I used to think that he must have separate wardrobes, you know, for the different phases, complete sets of clothes into which he would slip and slide as he puffed up and down. Otherwise he'd have to get new clothes all the fucking time. Any sign of this system?"

Birch was nearly breathless.

"Nah, I don't think so," said Paul, tossing back his pony-tail. "Wally wasn't like that. He'd just wear stuff till it decayed and fell off. Then he would buy some more," Paul West said.

"How long did you know Wally?"

"Oh, I've known Wally for twenty-five years. Maybe more," Paul said. "We were great friends."

"Funny I never met you."

"You met me," Paul West corrected. "Several times."

Birch racked his brain but couldn't place him. Birch glanced in the closet. The poster and the porno mags were gone.

45. Sometimes it's hard to go on

Birch went back downstairs. A mound of plastic bags was now stacked in the middle of the room. Harvey Vanderpool added another. The front door was wide open and suddenly a man stood there in a uniform, hovering on the sill.

"Hi—Capital Lock," said the man in khaki.

"I took the liberty of phoning him," said Fettman from across the room. Fettman stood up and set aside the sheaf of papers he was sorting. "You remember we talked about this lock thing yesterday?"

"I'm glad you took the initiative, Ron," said Birch.

"Can you put new locks in both the front and back doors?" Fettman asked.

"That's what I do," said the small wizened middle-aged man.

After inspecting the locks, the man went out through the back screened porch to his van pulled up behind the other cars, its blinkers flashing. He returned to the house with a large green tool box.

Birch put down his clipboard on the back of the couch, crossed the long room, and went out through the glass wall onto the tiered deck that overlooked the lake. He pulled up one of the Walmart chairs to the table with the torn plastic Cinzano umbrella. A sail-boat glided a hundred yards from shore. The shoreline of the other side of the bay was clearly visible from here. Wally had got the best part of the lake alright, a bay protected from the powerful winds that in winter whipped across the wider lake, smashing floes of soul-chilling ice against the opposite shore, and the houses built there.

Of course Wally's pier had to be taken out of the water each fall before the ice came, then reassembled every spring. That was a headache. Now this summer's pier was mostly finished, except for the T platform at the end where you could sit on a lawn chair and watch the ducks and the carpet of slime that in hot months covered everything. Only the posts of the T platform had so far been driven into the lake mud—that was Vergil Rawlins's responsibility, in return for using the pier for his own boat.

A warm breeze blew, ruffling the blue water. A water scooter buzzed in the distance. Sure, Wally died in the bosom of what he loved.

Eddy Cornel came out onto the deck and stood near the table with an air of expectation.

"Nice day, hey Eddy?" Birch said.

"Yeah."

"This is a terrible thing about Wally. Why don't you sit down. Let's take a break," said Birch.

"Sure," said Eddy, pulling out a chair and speaking heatedly. "You know I think there's some blame to go around here and I'd like to see it go in the right place for a change. It wasn't just Karla Marsh."

"Well, sure, she's got a boss too."

"They've taken the money and they control the committees. You think you got Devries—forget it! Angela Bellamy will get to Marsh and they're going to get *you*, Birch."

Birch looked up at the top of the towering weeping willow that grew in the property next door. The tree hung mournfully over the dark lake.

"You know about that, huh?" Birch said at last. "Well I don't know, Eddy. I try to keep out of it as much as I can. I'm not political, my friend."

"That won't protect you." Eddy closed his jaw hard and flexed the muscles in his powerful hands. "This is supposed to be a university. But everything is agenda. There is no opposition. The

Germans won this war, Professor Birch."

"I know how you feel, Eddy."

"Admit it's true."

"OK. But what can I do about it?"

"Cover your ass, Birch. Wally thought he was cool—see what's happened."

"He got drunk and coked up and fell down the fucking stairs. That's what happened."

"The whole thing is sex, Birch. Everything is tagged—so much for this, so much for that. You were married, you know. You think a man would stay with a woman if it weren't for sex?"

Birch laughed.

"It's an interesting theory."

"That's it Birch, that's it."

"I'm not so sure. Look, I'm sorry about what happened, Eddy."

Birch had been watching the boats on the lake, talking to Eddy over his shoulder, but something made him turn around. He saw that Eddy Cornel's eyes were filled with tears.

The lock man just then came onto the deck and began to work on the glass door.

"I got to get back inside," Eddy whispered. "I just wanted to say that."

"Sure, we're all upset."

A rowboat was anchored a hundred yards off shore. A man fished from it, casting, casting, casting again.

46. Something to remember you by

"I guess that about does it," the lock man said after a few minutes.

"Already?" asked Birch.

Ron Fettman came out onto the porch.

"Hey Professor Birch, you got some of that green stuff? I think we better pay the man," Fettman said.

"You mean money, Fettman?"

"You want me to pay the lock man?" Fettman said.

"Why, you want me to pay? You're the lawyer. People pay you."

"Am I your first lawyer, Professor Birch?" asked Fettman with a smile.

Fettman was a good guy alright and knew his place. It was obvious that whoever paid the lock man was going to get every stitch and string of Wally's movable property, such as it was. Birch remembered that he had Wally's wallet from the coroner. The wallet, as he remembered, was fat, loaded with, he assumed, dollar bills.

"These are Wally's locks, so Wally can pay!" said Birch, got up, and went back inside the house. He retrieved his satchel from the couch, and went back onto the deck. He took out Wally's fat, black wallet, and flipped it open. From the front fold he counted a measly eighty-five dollars in small bills. In the back flap there was no money at all, but hundreds of small pieces of paper.

"How much do I owe you?" Birch asked.

"That'll be $67.50 for two locks," said the uniformed lock man, writing out a receipt.

Birch paid him and took the two keys on a ring.

"You take those keys," said Fettman.

"So only I have keys now, eh?" said Birch.

"What else is in Wally's wallet?" Fettman asked.

"We should have looked here first—how stupid of me."

Fettman sat down opposite Birch while Birch pulled out the masses of little pieces of paper stuffed in the back fold. They fluttered in a pile on the table. Birch began to describe each one, going through the papers one by one.

"—confirmation of a lunch date in 1976—cash receipt for the payment of $46 dollars to the clerk of the circuit court, 1986— telephone calling card, expired—United Airlines credit card, expired. Wow, looks like he had credit card problems," Birch said.

"Interesting."

"—Here's a receipt for a money order from the Rhode Island Hospital Trust, dated 1988—a temporary occupational operator's license allowing Wally to drive only to and from work— And to and from church!" Birch exclaimed.

"What?" Fettman asked, examining the pieces of paper as Birch passed them to him.

"His license must have been suspended—drunk again, I suppose," said Birch. "Here's a note from his secretary requesting office hours, dated 1982—the address of Gottfried the fraud Kroll in Wolcote Manner, the Bungalow, Stratford on Avon—Wow!— and now a warrant for Wally's arrest issued by The Village of Crestwood Hills—that's where I live!—for the non-payment of a parking fine."

"I hear they are sticklers for the law over there."

"Yikes! And here is a receipt in Greek from a restaurant in Heraklion, Crete, 1989—a receipt for $2.10 worth of bagels, 1989— a note on foolscap that rhapsodes have replaced singers—a bill for $520.68 from Gragender's Builders for, get this, 'trimming outhouse, build handrail, bookcase, ods'—spelled O D S— 'and ends, patsh'—spelled P A T S H—'dry wall ect, the coast of trim and suplies not included, September, 1990.' Wow, this guy can't spell for shit."

"Contractors," said Fettman.

"Here's an address at the Villa Corsi-Salviati in Florence, Italy, and one in Manhattan for a dealer in select Australian boulder opals."

"Uh-huh."

"A note from Cindy saying she was still working in Philadelphia as a jeweler and hopes to see him soon."

"Cindy."

"A notice of mail to be picked up at the main post office, 1990—*Le Bouddhisme et Les Grecs*, Revue de l'historie des religions, 1891, pp. 44 ff, S. Levi—one dollar reduction on a car wash, expired August 9, 1988—purple plastic membership from the Harvard Coop, dated 1973—receipt for $20.76 for the purchase of plums, asparagus, bananas, garlic melba, sunflower seeds, and Anacin—business card for Tents for Rent in Webster, Mass—receipt for a money order made out to American Eagle Fence—Scott Hudson, chairman of the Religion Division, director of Bachelor of Ministry at Brewton-Parker College, in Mount Vernon, Georgia."

"I know him well," jested Fettman.

"Well how about the Reverend Bill Vergil Wine, Assistant Professor at Mount Saint Mary's seminary in Emmitsburg, Maryland? Or Barbarosa Liquors, featuring a large variety of beers, wines, and liquors, imported and domestic, in Providence, RI?"

"Sure."

"Membership card for Nutri-System Weight loss center—Villas of the World, a Collection of World-Class Resorts, expired credit card—hand-drawn map leading to an address on the far east side of town—ticket stub to the Pink Floyd concert in the football stadium, Rain or Shine, 1986—business card of Christopher D. Bent, Managing Director of the Pacific Rim Press in Bangkok, Thailand—slip of paper offering TGIF FREE DRINK FACULTY CLUB—receipt for $57.50 from the Jean Fodamew Art Gallery, for picture framing—a business card in Turkish from the Anafartaler Oteliion, a telex number scribbled on the back—a yellow slip entitled ME and a phone number—Wally Wills, Auctioneer, Friends of UHC, Inc, Art & Antiques Auction ..."

"This goes on and on," Birch said with astonishment.

"Why did he keep all these things in his wallet?" Fettman wondered.

"*Lots* of phone numbers—Todd, Gerald, Phillip, Randy, Maggie, Pee, Brian, Peter, Jim, Jacques, Alan, Jeffery, Mike, Clayton, Jack, Richard ('Quick!'), Lonny, Don ('please call me on other matter ASAP'), Nick ('this is only scratched but scratchpaper happiness gives me solace'), Dale, David in Seattle, Boris, Tom, Christopher ('not for cocaine, but for friendship and love'), and wow—Jack Devries!"

"Who?" said Fettman, raising his eyebrows.

"They used to live together. Twenty years ago. He's a colleague—and an enemy of mine."

"Do you think he's carried that card in his wallet for twenty years?"

"Who knows? But apart from the weirdness of having all this junk in his wallet, Wally evidently didn't have a valid credit card. Of course he was totally irresponsible! What a guy! You know Wally told me he had somebody to handle his finances—somebody who gave him an allowance to live on, because he was so reckless. If we could find that guy we'd be in good shape, Fettman," Birch said.

"You know in all that stuff in the desk there were no canceled checks or even any bank statements," Fettman said.

"Maybe whoever it was who was giving him an allowance out of his estate ... Hey, look at this."

Birch held up a note scribbled on the back of a parking fine envelope. The note was in Wally's hand, but very hard to make out—

I only worry for several things. 1. His death by suicide. 2. His death by alcoholism or other drugs. He wants to die by the hand of his miserable life. He wishes it were different but it's not. Only time will tell. It's a difficult thing for me to hold. I must sell to survive. It's a cyclical—

"I can't make out the word after 'cyclical'—maybe 'bane'?"

bane thing for him to—

"It's dated December 4, 1990. It gets real sloppy toward the end. He must have been drunk," Birch said.

Fettman tried to follow the note.

"You do better than I, Professor, but this was a good while ago. Why would he keep something like this in his wallet? Do you think Wally's death was suicide?"

"Don't know. I couldn't say."

Fettman pushed back from the table and stood up and threw back his shoulders. He straightened his jacket and tie.

"Here's one more paper you can add to the bunch," he said and handed Birch a card that read RON FETTMAN, ATTORNEY

AT LAW, SPECIALIST IN DIVORCE, PROBATE, AND REAL ESTATE.

"You pass these out everywhere, Ron?"

"Can never be too careful," he smiled. "I have to be going."

"In that case, I think we should leave too. I wouldn't want to be caught here alone, Ron."

"I have to go too," said Sally Brown at the door, a strand of gray-blonde hair across her eyes. Through the glass wall Birch saw Harvey Vanderpool throw still another plastic bag on the pile, then take down some heavy plates from the kitchen cabinet and put them in a cardboard box.

47. Something always happens

It was late afternoon when Birch got back to his house and walked down the dappled walk through the private wood. When he got to the back door, he heard the phone ringing inside and he fumbled with his keys.

"Hello?" he was out of breath.

"Birch—it's Enrico Domingo. I heard about Wally."

Enrico Domingo was the professor of dramatic arts known for his publications on the Japanese Noh. He used to drink Friday afternoons at the 666 Club.

"Yeah, it's a pissing shame," said Birch.

"You know I have to say this about Wally ... he really was a breath of fresh air around this place. This is a pretty dull town and nobody gives a goddamn. But Wally had style. He made this town a better place to live in. I've got to go to England, so I won't be able to come to the funeral, if there's going to be one. But I wanted to phone now and say that."

"I'm glad you did, Enrico."

He hung up and the phone rang again. It was Harvey Vanderpool, phoning from a gas station.

"Do you want to go out and get some dinner?" Harvey asked.

"Oh, well, I'm beat. But come over, if you want to talk about things."

Birch thought that he would lie down for just a while until Vanderpool came, so he went upstairs into the bird room and lay down on the day bed. Almost immediately he heard a car door in the street. Vanderpool must have been around the corner! Birch got up and went downstairs. Through the glass doors he saw Vanderpool on the porch.

Harvey came in and sat down on the long couch in front of the fireplace while Birch stood against the mantel, resting his elbow on it.

"We didn't find much today, did we," Birch said. "How'd you get here?"

"In the old Rabbit. I still own it," said Harvey.

"Hey, maybe we should latch onto Wally's Lexus, huh?"

"Yeah, Wally always had nice cars. That's why Wally leased his cars. That way he could beat the hell out of them and there was nothing they could do. I guess you'll need to take the Lexus back to the dealer."

"What? Wait a minute … I don't get it—Wally got the Lexus for his birthday, he told me. It's the last thing he ever said to me, about the car. What a sweet ride it had."

"No way. Wally always leased his cars," Harvey said positively. He seemed exhausted.

"But he must have bought this one at least, Harvey, because he told me just last Sunday that he bought it for his birthday."

Harvey laughed.

"Nah—Wally always leased his cars."

"You mean that Wally fucking lied to me," Birch sighed. "Well Harvey, it's good to see you after so many years. I barely got a chance to say hello out at Wally's house. How's life treating you?"

"Things are good."

"Making money off your pots?" The last Birch had heard, Harvey was traveling around to art fares to sell his idiosyncratic ceramics.

"Three years ago I made $70,000. I admit that was a high. I meant to ask you—have you been in touch with Wally's brother in California?"

"Speaking of Wally's Lexus, and assorted lies, his brother turned out to be just some friend! There is no brother!" said Birch with an exasperated tone.

"I see," Harvey said and leaned his head back contemplatively into the couch. There were oriental carpets on the floor and artifacts on the walls and in an antique cupboard that stood against one wall. "And no will of course," Harvey said at last. "That was Wally."

They laughed aloud.

"You couldn't trust a fucking thing he said," Birch observed.

"Sure, Wally was a total liar," Harvey agreed.

"A lyin sonofabitch!"

"But look, now that we got rid of the crowd, you wanna go back and have a second look at Wally's place?" Harvey asked. "There were too many people there. And too much garbage and shit and chaos. I think we should take a second look out there."

"You think something happened?"

"Sure ... something happened," said Harvey.

48. Things are and things seem

The two men got up and went out on the porch and down the steps across the street to Vanderpool's beat-up VW Rabbit. An aged cocker spaniel lounged on the back seat.

"This dog your old sweetheart?" said Birch.

"Sure, that's Daisy—my sweetheart," Harvey said and got in the car. He reached around and kissed the dog on its wet black nose.

"I've taken up parrots," Birch said.

"How are they?"

"The beak keeps getting in the way."

They drove around the lake. Near Wally's, Harvey turned in past the mountain of green garbage bags piled high on the curb where Iceman's Walk met Goldbug Road. They drove down the narrow Iceman's Walk and parked in the apron next to the Lexus. The men got out of the Rabbit and crossed the grassy patch and walked up to the screen porch. Birch opened the door with his new key and Harvey went in first.

"What is that smell anyway? Like somethin' dead," said Harvey.

"I think it's the lake—all the weeds and stuff, rotting," said Birch. "I don't know. It's worse under the stairs."

"For some reason I'm not really that pissed at Wally," Harvey said, crossing to the glass door on the deck and opening it. There were still hours of daylight.

"Sure. He had a good life. Might as well die. Get it over with."

"Let's take another look in the desk," said Harvey.

"OK, but Fettman was plowing around in there."

Harvey pulled open the bottom drawer of the antique desk, its back a fence of spools. The drawer was crammed to overflow with letters and papers of all kinds. Harvey began to sort them while Birch pulled open a door in the other leg of the desk.

"Looks like Wally never paid his bills. I thought he had somebody handling his finances," Birch said, seeing the various threats from collection agencies.

Harvey laughed. "Yeah! Wally was a total deadbeat."

"Hey, here's his income tax return," said Birch. "Wow."

Birch opened the H. and R. Block slim paper folder on top

of the mountain of papers scattered around on the desk. Inside were three returns from previous years, simple without addenda, filled out by hand in pencil.

Vanderpool looked too. Birch knew a fair amount about Income Tax forms because he'd been audited twice and he saw in a glance that these were very primitive examples.

"Check it out, Vanderpool," Birch said. "Was Wally cheating the feds, huh? These are nothing!"

"Not really," said Harvey. "That's all he had, see—nothing. I know, you think Wally was rich. He told everybody he was rich and everybody thought he was rich. It was another lie. He had nothing. Believe me."

"What?"

"Wally even borrowed money from me." Harvey laughed. "That was the last straw between me and my ex—when I gave Wally 500 bucks she filed for divorce," Harvey laughed again. "Loaning money to Wally Wills was the last straw for her."

"You loaned *money* to Wally Wills?"

"He owed me three thousand bucks when he died."

Birch stood up.

"What—he blew it all, then? The stuff he inherited?"

"There was no inheritance. I found out all this when Wally went to Oxford. He had me pay his bills, see. Only I knew, and he swore me to secrecy."

"There was no money? I knew him for twenty years!"

"So did a lot of people."

Birch felt dizzy and sat down.

"He told me this story about some dinner party he went to in Oxford," Harvey continued—"this big fat English woman was sitting next to him, carrying on. I guess Wally wanted to brag so he started in about how his family made all their money making rugs. Of course it was total bullshit, but Wally thought it might do him some good. Then this Brit says, 'Oh, so you're family is in *trade*' and turned away with scorn. That was the end of Wally Wills at Oxford. After that he hated the Brits and wouldn't have anything to do with them."

"I'm trying to take this in Harvey. You're saying that Wally was a pauper?"

"Well, he had his university salary. That's about the same thing. As I'm sure you know."

49. Famous throughout the land

They heard a sound and looked up. A cop was standing in the doorway—a young woman, svelte in slacks and suit coat, standing at the front door that they had left open. On her hip was a gun in a Mexican-tooled leather holster. Birch wondered if it were a .38 caliber or if even here in this town they had switched to 9 millimeter Glocks. She was blonde, short-haired, mid-height, plain, and had hard eyes and one gold earring.

Birch instinctively raised his hands, like in the movies.

"What are you doing here?" the woman asked.

"Don't bother to shoot—we're respectable," Birch said, lowering his hands, but the words sounded absurd. "I mean, I'm Wally Wills's special administrator, and this is my assistant, Harvey Vanderpool. We even have a lawyer."

"I see. Well, could I please see some ID? I'm Lieutenant Karim Little of the Townsend Police."

She held up a badge and smiled in a suddenly friendly way. In fact, technically, Wally lived in Townsend, outside the city limits.

"Sorry about this. I'm sure you understand," she apologized.

"Sure, somebody could just rip this place off," Birch replied emphatically.

Birch and Vanderpool showed their IDs to the police officer.

"It does happen," she said. "But look, I'm glad I found you

fellas," she handed back the IDs, "because we've been making some inquiries about the death of Mr. Wills and a couple of things have turned up that we'd like to clarify. You see we've talked to people who said that they phoned here on Monday and it looks as if there might have been some people in the house when Mr. Wills died. Did you know friends of Mr. Wills named Eric or Tom?"

"No idea at all," said Birch. But maybe he recognized "Tom."

"We got these names from a Mr. Rawlins who lives up the street. We heard from another neighbor that there may have been others here, too, in addition to Tom and Eric. Do you know anything about any of this?"

"Not me," said Birch. "How about you, Harvey?"

"Can't say I do," Harvey said.

"We also understand that there was a Mercedes Benz with Illinois plates parked in the drive on Sunday night and Monday morning too."

"I see," said Birch.

"I have to be honest," the lieutenant said, coming further into the room and standing in front of the couch pushed against the wall berneath the stairs. "We found a plate with some white powder on it, on the mantle."

"White powder, you mean?" said Birch, trying to sound innocent.

"We have sent it to the lab for analysis."

"Uh-huh. You suspect foul play?" said Harvey.

"Not for the moment. I mean there are some suspicious circumstances and we are interested in knowing what actually happened on Monday night. But there were no wounds on the body or anything like that, and the bruise on his forehead may have come from the fall."

"Sure. He was lying on his back?" Birch asked.

"Yes, that's correct, but he may have turned over, see."

"You saw the body?" said Harvey.

"He was lying just behind you at the bottom of the stairs," the officer indicated with her hand.

Oh fuck! Birch thought, that was it. Wally came down to

take a pee, see. He was stoned out of his mind, of course. The lights were off. He missed a step, fell forward and down, hit his head, rolled around the landing and slid down the next three stairs and came to rest under the chair. It was obvious.

For the first time, though he must have stepped around it several times, Birch noticed a curious object poised at the edge of the landing, an orange papier-mâché jar two feet high. What was it—some kind of stage prop? had Wally stumbled on that when he came down the stairs? But it seemed made of paper.

"There is one little thing—"

"What?"

"At 8:00 on Monday morning Mr. Wills phoned in sick to his office. His secretary said he sounded terrible and that he could barely speak. At 10:00 a.m. Monday morning, he phoned HAVE 'MON' WILL TRAVEL AGENCY and booked a Wednesday flight to Burlington, Vermont, for one Eric Salton. Have you ever heard of Eric Salton?"

"Must be the Eric who was here," said Harvey.

"That's what we think too, Mr. Vanderpool. You see, Mr. Wills tried to put the ticket on a credit card, but the bank refused the charge." The lieutenant smiled. "And then he billed the flight to his department."

"No—that would be quite illegal!" Birch protested, astonished.

"Wally would never do that," Vanderpool objected.

In this Protestant town the misuse of public funds was more dangerous than Ebola, or fucking your grandmother in the street, but Birch realized immediately that Wally may in fact very well have done this.

"The travel agent said that Mr. Wills sounded very 'up' when he phoned at 10:00 A.M. Monday morning. Mr. Wills spoke of some sort of business deal, some opportunity."

"What kind of business deal?" Vanderpool asked.

"Eric Salton was a courier?" wondered Birch.

"But the plane ticket was never picked up," the lieutenant concluded. "We consider that to be very odd."

Vanderpool moved in close to Lieutenant Little and spoke

in a lowered voice.

"Look Officer Little, you should understand that Wally Wills was an important man. He was known throughout the world. He's dead and we don't see any reason to drag his name through the muck, if you see what I mean. Whatever happened on Monday night ... what does it matter, really? He's dead."

"Mr. Vanderpool, I take your point. But we are interested in the facts. After all, we are the police."

The lieutenant still seemed friendly.

"What facts?"

" 'There are no facts, only interpretations,' eh Professor Birch?" said Lieutenant Little and gave Birch an odd look from the corner of her eye. Birch was amazed, because he seemed to have heard this remark before. "You see I once had your course in Greek Myth," the lieutenant said. "Best course I ever had."

50. The sexual lives of human beings

"**D**id that woman really pull a gun on us?" Harvey asked after the lieutenant left.

"Nah, it never left her belt. Oh well, I'm used to that sort of thing—these days."

"You have any cigarettes?" Harvey asked.

"Sorry, Harvey. Gave 'em up long ago. So Wally had these guys over the night he died!"

"Sure, he wanted to suck their dicks," said Vanderpool.

"Uh-huh. Sure. Two guys—maybe more. Wally was always sucking the cocks of these young guys, I suppose," Birch complained. "I don't know, Harvey—maybe there's a cigarette lying around here in all this trash? We could share it. Or maybe we could find a butt in an ashtray."

"Yeah, cocks were the big thing in Wally's life," Harvey agreed.

"Do you suppose he sucked these guys off and then they killed him?"

Birch remembered the time when Wally had stopped by his house late one Saturday. They sat at Birch's antique oak dining room table. Wally pulled out the white dust and shook it onto a small glass plate. It seemed like speed and reminded Birch of shooting speed into his veins in the old days, for pleasure, something he'd forgotten about completely. Birch didn't like the feeling of the dust because everything went fast and then broke up so that he felt like he was living inside a shattered mirror. He had enough of that shit in life—he needed a little stability! Where was the fun in it?

Then Wally started in babbling about cocksucking. It was the only time he ever talked to Birch about it.

"... that's the whole thing ... that's what I do best, Ray ... like I like to get a big red one and just slobber away ..." Wally said. He wiped his mouth with the back of his hand and cut another line.

"... you know it's an art form really ... not anybody can do it right, you know ... I got some good old dogs down in Chicago ... Oh boy, I got some good dogs down in Big Chi Town, bro, I can tell you ... back in the good old days ..."

"I'll bet you did," Birch nodded, feeling as if he'd just been driven over by a semi-truck.

"Hey—has anybody found Wally's collection of old paper currencies?" Vanderpool asked. "You know he had this big collection he'd been working on since he was a kid. Wally was a pauper, but he bought the collection early and cheap, and prices have gone through the roof. He should have sold them and paid some of the people he owed money to, but he couldn't bring himself to it—I think he loved those old bills more than he loved his own life," Harvey said.

"Huh—he never mentioned them to me," Birch said. "The

cops found a few bills in plastic jackets in the drawer to the antique basin stand, when they took the body out. But they're no big collection or anything. I have them now. Eddy Cornel thought there was something in the safe in the bathroom, but the safe was empty. No dope either. Did you ever actually see these bills? Maybe that was a crock too."

"Where are the bills the cops gave you?"

"At my house."

"You know I was over here once," said Vanderpool, "and Wally was having this big fight with Eddy Cornel. Eddy was coming down on Wally, saying, 'All you ever do is suck my dick, Wally. Or watch me pound-off. I'm sick of it. This is getting to be pretty boring, Wally.' Stuff like that. And then Wally says, 'Why you little whore, you pathetic little whore!' He always called Eddy a whore when he was pissed off at him."

"I guess Wally could really suck dick all right," Birch agreed.

"He was the best cocksucker in the Midwest," Harvey laughed. "Course you always had to watch out when you were taking a piss. If you turned around—there was Wally, you know, sort of looking."

"Wow. Did he ever suck your dick?"

"He was dying to," said Harvey.

"He never tried any of that shit on me," said Birch after a long pause.

"That's because he respected you—you were a colleague."

"But what about Wally himself?"

"What do you mean?"

"I mean what was his angle exactly?"

"Zero," replied Vanderpool. "I don't think he ever had it up. He just liked to suck dick. That was his whole thing in life. That and art. He liked guys who had a fat roll and a big dick and he loved beautiful art."

"And now no money!" Birch snarled.

51. A good day to die

Birch looked across the open prairie. He could smell the smoke but not see it. There were Crow beyond the hills.

He hunched over and rubbed his pony's neck, an Appaloosa. He had painted a bright orange hand on the withers.

A wind blew up from the southwest, cold but fragrant with moisture. The smell of the smoke was gone. He wore a single feather in his long black hair.

His pony snorted and Birch eased him forward …

52. A touch of class

Birch sat down in front of Wally's desk and began to sort through papers. The fact was sinking in, that for twenty years Wally had completely deceived him. He had bamboozled him, taken him lock stock and barrel. It had simply never crossed his mind that everything Wally said was a lie. It was in any event incomprehensible.

Here were unopened envelopes from the phone company, a notice from Chemical Bank—account turned to collection agency in Atlanta without immediate payment of $2,903.92. A bill for $230.30 on automobile insurance.

"I have to admit these papers support your thesis," Birch groaned. "He owed the Faculty Club $840," Birch held up a bill.

"Sure," Vanderpool said from across the room, seated at the white utility table and sorting through other mounds of paper.

At the Faculty Club Wally always sat alone by himself in a far darkened corner, an imposing presence in the ornate wood-paneled Gothic room lit by lead-glass windows. Sometimes Birch went there just to find him, have a friendly chat or concoct some plot. Wally was always glad to see Birch and would point to the chair where he should sit. Then he would snap his black-haired fingers.

"Charlie, bring this gentleman a sandwich and a beer!"

"You picking this up?" Birch would ask.

"I think we can arrange it," Wally smiled and narrowed his eyes.

After lunch, Wally scribbled his name across the receipt. Birch liked that, very classy. Once Wally summoned the cook to compliment the beef, *vraiment superbe*. Wally knew everybody at the club by first name.

"Here's the bill from the party Wally threw in 1988 to celebrate his book on ancient art. It cost $1,120. He told me it cost $5,000 and that his mother footed the bill," said Birch.

"Yeah."

Wally's party was the only black-tie invitational anyone could remember. He hired a band. The downstairs of the Faculty Club was cleared and the lounge converted to a dance floor, with a long bar and free drinks in the foyer, elegant tables and low lamps for intimate talk in the dining room. The place was jammed with Wally's guests. Wally danced all night, amazing everyone with his brilliant muted understated style, so at odds with his bulk. He was a feather on toes.

"We should find Eric and Tom," said Vanderpool.

"Any ideas? Here's a bill for $52.90 from the Alumni Directory for Resurrection College in Worcester, Massachusetts. Ever hear of it?"

"Maybe his mother went there."

"Here's a paper granting him power of attorney over his mother, dated June 7, 1997. You know Wally told me he had some fight with his relatives over this power-of-attorney thing and his mother had disowned him. Here's a note from Le Ciel Funeral Home in Oxford, Mass, with a death certificate—his father's."

"Wasn't his mother a math professor at Boston College?" asked Vanderpool.

"I never heard *that* one. She was a French Jew and his father a Boston Unitarian, a constant source of conflict in the marriage," said Birch. "I mean that's what I heard."

"Wally always told me his mother was a math prof at Boston College."

"Here's a card from Johnny Carson, the fake brother. I talked to him on the phone—"

Birch handed Vanderpool a comic card, the picture of a wild-eyed leering man, fat cigar in sloppy lips, sitting behind an executive desk and speaking in the phone: CALL MY AGENT, WE'LL DO BUSINESS.

"Yeah, I guess Wally was a lonely man. Here's a bill from Centaur Enterprises for $21,223.36. Holy molah!"

Vanderpool stopped his sorting.

"I *told* Wally not to get into that. Those are the guys he hired to remodel this house. This used to be all knotty pine, but that wasn't good enough for Wally. He didn't even have a contract. He just said, 'Go ahead, do what's right.' Then he got the bill for twenty grand. That's why this place never got finished. These guys were coke heads. They'd come over at ten in the morning and bring half a gram. They'd sit around doing coke, then hammer one or two boards and go home. That's how Wally got mixed up with Vergil Rawlins. Rawlins was working with Centaur Enterprises."

"What?"

"Sure. Then when Centaur sent this big bill ... Wally didn't have a penny of course. *I* loaned him some of the fucking money, to save his ass. Can you dig it?"

Birch was silent.

"Sure—I had the money then, and I loaned it to him. Not the whole thing, but five grand—he gave them that, and then there was this big lawsuit over the rest. Virgil Rawlins took Wally's side. He broke up with the Centaur gang and went to work on his own. Really, he was tired of hammering boards and wanted to do dope all day long."

"How deep is Rawlins in?"

Harvey sighed.

"He's a big dealer. Wally had a big account. When I came over, Wally would take me up to Rawlins's house and get me to buy some coke. After awhile, before I'd come to the house, I'd take out all my money except for a ten dollar bill—then I could open my wallet and say, 'Look, Wally, I don't have a thing.' One time he wanted me to write Rawlins a check for the cocaine!"

"A check for dope! Wally had no shame. Did you do it?"

"Are you kidding? Sometimes he would phone and say, 'Harvey, I've *got* to have $600. I'm desperate. I absolutely *must* have $600.' You know, he wouldn't say why, but sometimes I'd lend it to him."

"I didn't know you were such a nice guy, Vanderpool. I was always going to borrow some money from Wally! Hit him up for ten thou!"

They were silent for awhile.

"Of course there's the motive," said Birch.

"What do you mean?"

"He owed Rawlins money. Vergil was with Wally Sunday night—he told me so—and Wally died Monday night or Tuesday morning," Birch said. "There was coke on the mantel. The cop said there were others here. Did she mean Sunday night?"

"Dunno," said Harvey.

"On the other hand, Rawlins was broken up over Wally, it seemed to me. Maybe I got that wrong—I get everything wrong these days."

"Murder makes you devious, yes."

"But what about this Eric and Tom? Goddamit Vanderpool, Wally was always going to take me out to this island he owned off Cape Cod. We were going to have a grand time. One time we planned a trip to his condo in Hawaii!"

Vanderpool laughed, but Birch persisted.

"Wally said his father always wanted this condo in Hawaii, and only after he retired had he been able to find one just to his taste."

Vanderpool laughed again. "What are we going to do with all these student papers? I've got two boxes and there are more."

"I'd say toss 'em. Throw them right out the window. They don't mean a fucking thing."

53. Eureka

"**O**K, here's a bill from Le Ciel Funeral Home, unpaid," said Birch. "Get this, they put a *Palmer Atlas* in his father's coffin, whatever that is."

"That's so he could find his way to the other world," Vanderpool said with a knowing grin.

Birch held up a greeting card all in gold. Inside was a brightly colored picture of a shrine to the Virgin, the Mother of God. The Virgin reached her arms upwards to heaven between baskets of lush red roses and golden lampstands. Above her was a magnificent cupola, the very image of heaven. Birch read aloud the inscription: THE CENTRAL ASSOCIATION OF THE MIRACULOUS MEDAL HAS THIS DAY PERPETUALLY ENROLLED GEORGE WILLS WHO WILL SHARE FOR ALL TIME IN THE TREASURE OF THE HOLY MASSES WE OFFER EACH YEAR ... O MARY, CONCEIVED WITHOUT SIN, PRAY FOR US WHO HAVE RECOURSE TO THEE.

"Yeah, Wally's family was bigtime Catholic," Harvey said.

"Yow! Wally always told me he was a Unitarian! I guess Unitarians are supposed to be better than Catholics, huh?"

"Sure. Catholics are scum. Rotten scum. Unitarians are much better."

"Especially in Boston, eh Harvey? Now here's a letter from a Father Louis, a.a. What does you suppose 'a.a.' means? This guy's a priest from Resurrection College—he's going to be in Detroit to preach on the Resurrection Mission in Zaire. He's driving to Dubuque and wants to visit Wally and have lunch. He praises him as 'one of their best students.' Wow—when Wally wanted to put somebody down big time, he always said they graduated from *Stigmata* U. That was the worse thing he could say about somebody. Looks like *Wally* went to Stigmata U. He told me he went to Tufts!"

"What is Tufts?"

"Some school back East. Hey, so you've known about this for years, eh Harvey? The deception, the lies?"

"I didn't know about Stigmata U."

"Find the will!" said Birch.

"There is no will. What is that horrible smell? It's driving me crazy. There's rotten meat somewhere."

"Here's a birthday card. 'The Fates were kind the day we met. Time makes the best friends of strangers, my Wally, my friend, and all we have is time—to repair the hurt of the past. Love in my heart and soul. J. D.' "

"Who's that?"

"Jack Devries do you suppose? *Jack Devries?* That would be good—!"

"Hey, did you check out the drawer in the antique washstand? That's a good place for a will."

"That's where they found some of the bills."

Abruptly Vanderpool went over to the washstand against the partition between the kitchen and the living room and pulled open the thin drawer. The drawer came all the way out and twisted over, spilling a melee of papers on the floor. On top was a video tape. FLAPJACK AND ANAL PERVERSION ON MUSCLE BEACH, CALIF.

"I don't think that's it," Birch said.

"That *is* it!" Vanderpool said.

54. I have given you the key to my heart

"**W**e didn't find much," Birch admitted to Vanderpool as they drove slowly past Virgil Rawlins's house. Rawlins was standing on the porch with his hands in his pocket. Birch waved, but Rawlins ran out to the truck so that Birch stopped.

"What the hell is going on here, Birch?" Rawlins shouted angrily through the driver's side.

"What now Vergil?"

"You've changed the locks in the house! I'd like to know what's going on. What are you doing with Wally's stuff?"

Birch glanced at Vanderpool.

"Wally said I was to get *everything* if anything happened to him," said Rawlins. "Also, he owed me money, Birch, big money. Did you find a will?"

"There is no will, Vergil, as far as we know," said Birch.

"Then everything is mine! He owed me money."

"He owed everybody money. Vergil, do you think this is a good place to talk, in the middle of the street?"

"Let's get a couple of things straight," Vergil Rawlins said and took a drag on his cigarette. He put his face close to Birch's window, and spoke in a whisper. "And that goes for you too, Vanderpool. Wally was into me for pretty big bucks, OK?"

"OK."

"These things count, OK?"

"Look Vergil, Harvey here has been telling me some surprising things about Wally. It looks as if he didn't have all the money he pretended to have, that he owed everybody money. He has completely taken us in, all of us."

"He owed me six grand," Harvey said, leaning across Birch to face off Vergil.

"So you have the new key to the house?" asked Rawlins. "There are things there. I want a key!"

"What things?"

"You know!" barked Rawlins. He brought down the flat of his hand on the hood of Birch's truck with a resounding smack. "Important things!"

55. A feverish dream

Birch slowed to make the turn into the Village, then hesitated.

"Look Harvey, I just remembered, I need to go over to Audrie Winter's place, the old lady—you know Wally's friend. She's been phoning me. It's still early enough and I think I'll go right now," Birch said.

"I know Audrie Winter."

"Want to come along?"

Birch had never been to Audrie's house but he knew that she lived directly next door to the Episcopal Church on the busy street near the campus stadium. Birch and Harvey drove past the church and parked down the block. They got out.

"This has got to be her house," Birch surmised, stopping in front of an old brick house beside the church. "She must live here."

They walked up the cement steps to a small porch. The inner door was open. A stale scent breathed from the inner darkness. Birch pushed the buzzer. A white-haired lady, small and frail, came slowly to the door.

"Oh Professor Birch—it is you! I'm so glad you have come," she said in a guttural voice and pushed back the door.

"Hello," said a taller, stout woman in a high whining voice standing behind her, smiling over broken yellowed buck teeth. That must be Mimi Esperanto, Audrie's Winter's daughter, Birch thought as he and Harvey squeezed into the dim forehall.

"I guess you know Harvey Vanderpool, is that right Audrey?"

"Oh yes, very well—let's see, is that you, Harvey? Let me see you—"

The old lady seemed to be mostly blind. She pulled Harvey's face down close to hers. She ran her eyes over his features.

"Yes, it is you, Harvey, it is you. Please forgive me! I can't see very well. And now let me see you too, Raymond."

She pulled Birch's face down and inspected it. She smelled of attar of rose, of must, of lavender, of something distant, something electronic. She too, Birch thought, lived in the pure white light of the spirit.

"Now let us go into the living room and sit down," Audrie said.

They followed her into the dim living room off the hall. Torn shades allowed in little light. The close air smelled like Audrie's own flesh. On the mantle at the far end of the room old china cups stood in wooden stands. There were dark pictures of landscapes on the walls over a broken old sofa.

"Here now, before I sit down, let me have a look at you again, Raymond—and you too Harvey. You know I'm nearly blind. Yes, it is wonderful to see you ... you haven't changed a bit since that day you drove up on Van Raven Avenue in that big truck, Raymond. You had five cats in the front seat and a bowl of tropical fish on the seat of the red Volkswagen you were towing. The day was fiercely hot. Wally was sitting on the steps with his shirt off and I gave you a nice tall glass of lemonade," Audrie reminisced.

"I can't believe you remember all that, Audrie," said Birch.

"Oh, I have a wonderful memory! I can remember anything. Now let me look at you again, Harvey." She pulled him down and rubbed his face with her eyes. Then she let him go.

"Yes, the light is better here ... I just can't believe it ... don't mind me ... I can't believe I'll never see Wally again ..."

Audrie began to weep, and her daughter, Mimi Esperanto, moved toward her.

"It's terrible," Birch said soothingly.

Audrie sat down in an easy chair near the window. In front

of the chair, two tin tables were covered with memorabilia. Propped against a small vase was a picture of Wally as a young man and a plastic envelope enclosing his obituary from the local newspaper.

"Raymond, Mama has something to say to you about Wally," said Mimi. "Tell him about the grave now, would you, Mama?" Mimi sat down on an upholstered chair in the far corner of the room. She was drowned in shadow.

"Oh Mimi hush up ... But since you mention it, yes ... Raymond, I already asked if you thought that Wally could be put to rest in my family plot over at Forest Hills ... Then he could lie next to me, beside and my own father, and my brother Willie."

"I'm sure we can arrange it, Audrie, to bury him there."

She breathed a sigh of relief.

"I'm so glad," said Mimi, getting up. She produced a slip of paper on which she had drawn a diagram of the gravesite. "You see, Mama will lie here, and Granddad is there, and Uncle Willie, and this is for me and Maspero and then Wally will be here ..."

Birch looked at her sketch.

"Isn't that a nice picture of Wally?" said Mimi, leaning forward and pointing to the picture in the paper. Tears sprang to her eyes.

"By the way, Mimi, thanks for spreading the word about what happened," Birch said. "Eddy Cornel came over with his wife to help out at Wally's house."

"Who's Eddy Cornel?" said Mimi.

"Don't be ridiculous!" snapped Audrie. "You know very well who Eddy Cornel is. He is that nice young professor who was fired for sexual harassment—whatever that is. I suppose every time a boy says to a girl that he likes her it is sexual harassment! How ridiculous!"

"You don't know Eddy Cornel?" Birch asked Mimi.

"Of course she knows Eddy," Audrie corrected and again fell to weeping. "I just can't believe I'll never see Wally again ... you know I came out here to the Midwest in 1906. We arrived on February 26. It was bitterly cold. I was born in New Hampshire. My father was a professor of mining engineering here at the university. I was the youngest of six. All the rest are gone. My oldest sister was in constant trouble with the men. She just couldn't keep her hands off them. She was married three times. My second oldest sister died at age 34 on June 4, 1928, of a fever. My oldest brother went to Alaska in the gold rush but never found a thing. He disappeared someplace in California, in Sacramento I think. My youngest brother Willie is buried here in town, next to Dad."

Then Audrie fell silent.

"I used to live in Oroville," Birch remarked, to keep the conversation going.

"*That* is a very terrible place! I know. I once was there. It is hotter than blazes in the summer. It is like death itself!" Audrie said.

"Mama, maybe Professor Birch doesn't like to hear that about his home town …"

"Oh hush up Mimi, he doesn't care," Audrie reproved her daughter. "And anyway he didn't say it was his home town. He just said he lived there. Well, then I got married, you see, and had Mimi, but my husband preferred another woman. He ran off with her and I never married again. That was on October 16, 1930, that he ran off. I was born on March 2, 1898, so I was 32 years old. Do you know something, Raymond Birch and Harvey Vanderpool?"

"What?" said Birch.

"Wally was born on the same day I was …" A spasm shook her small body. Tears poured from her eyes and danced into space.

She recovered. "Did you find out who killed him?" Audrie said.

"Mama—!"

"Well, I don't think he just fell down the stairs! Wally was a very strong man. I was an English teacher for thirty years. English and math, at Xavier College. But I was never a Catholic. I never had much use for religion, frankly. Wally and I were alike in that. You know Sally Brown—you know her? She once said that Wally just didn't care for 'organized religion.' Well, what other kind is there? She's a Roman Catholic, you know. Converted from the Anglican faith. Can you imagine? When Mimi went out to Texas to visit her father she came down with double pneumonia and nearly died. You see his new woman had the pneumonia but he never told us a thing about it. He was living in Texas then. He died long ago. Do you know this poem?

> *Remember thee! remember thee!*
> *Till Lethe quench life's burning stream,*
> *Remorse and shame shall cling to thee,*
> *And haunt thee like a feverish dream!*

That's Lord Byron."

"Mama can remember all kinds of poetry," Mimi interjected, hovering in the background, "but I've never been able to remember anything at all." Mimi brushed back a lock of hair from her wrinkled brow.

"Yes, that's right, Lord Byron. I always had my students memorize poetry, you know. It's a perfect thing. When trouble comes in life, then there's poetry to alleviate the pain."

Then she wept without shame, and Mimi cried too. Birch felt tears push from behind his eyes.

"Do you think I should go to the burial service? Is it scheduled yet?" Audrie suddenly asked.

"The coroner said he would send Wally's body over to the funeral home, so I guess it is there now, Audrie, but we haven't had time to arrange the burial. Still, I don't see any problem. He didn't have any family, so far as we know."

"And have you found the will?" Audrie brayed.

"No trace, I'm sorry to say."

Her eyes again filled with tears. Birch wanted to reach out and hold her, to calm her down.

"That's what Wally would have wanted, to be buried near me," she moaned. "And I want you to keep looking, Raymond, until you find out who did it. Not that it will bring him back. He is gone forever now."

"Mama, please!"

"Do you know this poem?

> *When we two parted*
> *in silence and tears,*
> *Half broken-hearted*

> *to sever for years,*
> *Pale grew thy cheek and cold,*
> *colder thy kiss;*
> *Truly that hour foretold*
> *sorrow to this."*

"Is that Lord Byron too, Mama?" asked Mimi.

Someone came in the front door and Birch and Vanderpool turned. A small portly man in a three-piece suit, wearing a gold watch chain, and behind him a tall thin man in a clerical collar. Mimi got up and straightened her skirt.

"Oh Father O'Dalley, and—Professor Birch and Harvey Vanderpool, do you know my husband Maspero?"

The men stood and greeted one another. The priest turned to Maspero and spoke in Spanish.

"Raymond and Harvey, before you go ..." said Audrie.

"What?"

"You know that Wally had my chair, the black leather chair with the deep buttons. That was my father's chair. Do you think I could have it back?" She fought back tears. "Wally loved that chair so much. And I loved him. And he loved me. I just can't believe that I'll never see that wonderful man again."

56. All flesh is grass

He was lost in the Grand Canyon, down near the river on a steep sundrenched slope covered in prickly pear. A helicopter droned overhead, but they could not see him.

> *Or was it a gigantic crow?*

The phone rang and he glanced at his watch. It was 7:00 A.M. Birch reached across a manuscript spread on the bed to answer it.

There was no one.

Birch hung up and went upstairs, showered in the small bathroom next to the bird room, dressed, then went back downstairs and poured a bowl of breakfast cereal and sat down at the round oak table. He turned on the TV with the remote control. *The Today Show* came on, special from Miami with Katy Couric and Matt Lauer in captain's chairs and sailor suits, sitting in front of a blue bay while Matt interviewed the local mayor about organized crime.

Birch shut off the TV and went outside and got in his pickup truck. He drove to the Burning Light Funeral Home to check on the body and make arrangements for the burial. The home was conveniently located across the street from Forest Hills cemetery where for years he had jogged through the pacific woods, through the cold and the sometimes impenetrable fog.

Birch parked in the asphalt lot. Even so early in the morning, blasts of the summer heat engulfed him as he walked to an overhang and through ponderous glass doors into a waiting room, like the lobby of a Holiday Inn.

There was a desk in the corner but no one there. Birch went into a hall and looked in a nearby office, but it too was empty. He went back to the lobby and sat on a couch covered in yellow Naugahyde. He thumbed through a portfolio of antique hearses on the parquet coffee table, a series of Polaroids recording the step-by-step restoration of a horse-drawn hearse, evidently the undertaker's hobby.

"May I be of assistance?" asked a small dark man suddenly standing over him, whom Birch had not heard approach.

"Yes, of course." He stood up. "Well, I've come for arrangements about a mister Wally Wills. The coroner said he would release the body to you."

"Yes, we have the body," the man said, holding his hands

together at navel height and bowing slightly. "Perhaps we should discuss this matter further, in another room?"

Birch followed across the lobby, back into the hall, then around a corner and down upholstered stairs to a lower level to a tunnel lined with puckered dull red wallpaper. The building was surprisingly large. From a back room on the lower level came a muffled rhythmical chanting. Vague shadowy forms moved on the pebbled glass door, illuminated by red.

"A Hmong funeral, you understand," hummed the dark man. He looked back over his shoulder. "They have their customs too."

"Of course."

"Please—after you." He invited Birch into a plushly carpeted room. Birch sat down in a deep chair behind a bare desk while the man sat behind the desk.

"We have the body, as I said."

"Good, well, things are somewhat confused, because Professor Wills died without kin and apparently there is no will. At least for the moment I am making the decisions. The point is, why don't you go ahead and cremate the body … and perhaps you can arrange for burial in the family plot of Audrie Winter in the cemetery across the street?"

"Oh yes, her daughter Mimi gave me a call this morning," the man said in somber tones. "You are, then, the personal representative of the deceased?"

"Like I said, I am making the decisions."

"You are the special administrator? May I see your papers?"

Birch reached into an inner pocket and produced the papers that Fettman had prepared. The man looked through them.

"Well, everything seems in order. I think, then, we can go ahead at your request."

The mortician opened a bottom file drawer and withdrew a folder of papers that he spread on the desk.

"You knew I was coming?" Birch asked.

"We knew *somebody* was coming," his thin lips smiled. "You will need to sign these papers. That is really all there is to it, Mr. Birch."

Birch signed.

"One thing—is it possible to see the body? I'd like to see the body."

The man stiffened. He was meant to act like this, with respectful sorrow. He did this for a living, ridding the world of human debris.

"Oh no! I'm afraid it would not be possible for you to see the body. The body is not suitable for viewing."

"What do you mean?"

"Well, you understand, Mr. Wills had been in an unusual position for a good while before he was found."

"Yes?"

"In an inverted position, you see. His face had turned a dark color."

"What color would that be?"

"Well, a crimson, a deep purple—like your shirt."

Birch glanced down at the purple flannel he was wearing beneath his black leather jerkin.

"In the position he was in, all the blood ran to his head, simply."

"I see."

"His tongue was protruded, sticking far out ... eyes opened. There was blood caked in the mouth and a bruise on the forehead."

Birch stared.

"Of course, well, somehow I had imagined it differently," Birch apologized. "But ... the coroner said that there was no evident cause of death, but between the two of us, I mean in the privacy of this room, what would you yourself say ... I mean how did he die, in your opinion?"

"I am not a doctor, but, yes, the condition of the body would be consistent with asphyxiation, yes."

"But not as if someone ... you mean you think the weight of his body, well, compressed his lungs and that's how he died?"

The man sighed.

"Yes, this is possible, from what I have seen, and from what I know. Still—he looks like, well—he might have swallowed something."

"*Swallowed* something?"

"Yes, or something caught in the throat. It's only that in cases of choking, when something is stuck in the throat, the symptoms are similar."

"But you said he hit his head? That he died of asphyxiation?"

"Well, we don't really know, do we?"

There was an acid smell in the air. The Hmong chanting grew louder now, joined by a drum, or hard sticks knocking.

"Would you mind, then—I hope it's all right—signing these documents?" the man said.

"You're sure about viewing the corpse?"

"Oh quite sure, Mr. Birch. Quite sure!"

57. The ashes of the dead

Birch wasn't sure why he wanted to see the body, but he did. But he wasn't going to see it. Maybe he should have insisted, but why? Wally was dead and that was that.

When he got home Birch went upstairs and out onto the second-story balcony of his house. He sat down in the filtered light coming through the leaves of the canopy of trees, casting complex shadows across the lawn. Beneath him squirrels chased in dizzying spirals around a high tree. Soon he dozed off in the chaise longue.

The phone was ringing downstairs.

He had been dreaming about a woman. Stiffly he got up from the chaise longue and went back inside to take the call on the upstairs phone. It was the funeral home.

"Mr. Birch, the ashes are ready."

"Wasn't I just there a few hours ago?"

"Oh, we mean to please at the Burning Light Funeral Home," the man said.

"You have your own crematorium?"

"Of course. We do all burning on the premises."

"I'll come by."

Birch hung up, but the phone rang again.

"Hi, Harvey here. How are the ashes coming?"

"That's good—they're ready," said Birch.

"I'm coming to town, so shall we pick them up? I've started working on the box to put them in. I've got a good pot too, for inside the box."

"Harvey, I've got to buy some groceries and run errands. Let's say two hours?"

When Birch got back, Harvey was waiting in front of the house in his Rabbit, listening to music on the radio and petting the head of the silky cocker spaniel, who sat in the passenger seat. He kissed the very old dog, got out, rolled up the window, and piled into Birch's truck. They drove to the funeral home and went into the lobby. The funeral director beckoned them from inside an office. Birch signed papers on a clipboard. The man left the room and returned with a heavy white paper box that he handed to Birch. The box was very warm.

"Those are the mortal remains of Mr. Wills."

"Any restrictions?"

"Oh no, they're just ashes. You can put them in your back yard, if you wish, or in a vase on the mantle. Some people like that. But didn't you say you were going to bury them in the family plot of Audrie Winter?"

"Right!"

Birch handed the ashes to Harvey. They went outside into the bright light.

"Heavy, wouldn't you say?" said Birch.

"Yeah," said Harvey. "And hot. Wally was a big motherfucker."

Birch opened the flap on the camper on the back of the

truck and Harvey placed the box inside next to the spare tire. They got in the cab and Birch started the truck. They pulled out of the lot into the stream of traffic on the broad street separating the funeral home from Forest Hills Cemetery.

"Yeah, that's right, Wally was a tub!" Birch laughed. "One time he came to my house and he sat on this big wing chair. It used to belong to my father. I was married then. It was my best chair. When he sat down, the frame broke! Crack! The thing went right to the ground! I had to throw the chair out in the street. Wally never admitted that he broke that chair."

"Wally was always doing things like that. You remember that VW bug I used to have?" said Harvey. "It had some bad rust. One time Wally got in on the passenger side—and the seat went right through to the ground and hit the pavement!"

They burst out laughing at the thought of Wally dragging on the pavement.

"Wally didn't apologize either," said Harvey. "He just got out, you know, and I sort of pried up the frame and wired it together and we took off. But the battery was cruising along about an inch above the ground. Every time I hit a bump, the battery crashed into the road. Finally I had to sell that car," Harvey said.

"You know we had Wally over to dinner once, when I was married, and he never ate a thing. He ate like a bird. He *always* refused desert," Birch said with amazement.

"That's because he always ate first, before he came! A big motherfucking meal, so that people wouldn't see what a disgusting pig he was," said Harvey.

"Wow ... I didn't know that."

"You know that first Benz he leased," said Harvey, "—he totally ruined it. On the driver's side there was a permanent list and all the tires were worn out on that side!"

"What a tub is right. Yeah, one time we were driving up north to some small town because he was going to be the auctioneer, see, in a big collection of weird shit. OK, we were driving up there to check out this collection, see," said Birch. "It was the only time I went on a trip with Wally. After about three hours, he starts to tremble really bad. He says he has to have some food, and quick we pull off in this small town and go into a bar and sit at the booth for a half hour. Wally was in a bad way—he couldn't talk. His hands were shaking. Finally they bring him three of those big mother cheeseburgers dripping with fat and tons of fries and ketchup and shit and Wally gobbled it all down like a madman. Then he felt better."

"Sure—what a slob," Harvey agreed.

"Hey, what do you say we go out to Wally's and get Audrie's chair?" Birch suggested. "You can help me carry it to the truck."

"I only hope that box don't break open back there," Harvey said.

"Hell, it's just ashes. We can sweep 'em out the back. The funeral guy said it was OK."

"Wally would like that!"

They turned onto the main boulevard that led around the lake.

"I guess we got to have a party now to celebrate," Harvey said. "We should put up an ad in the 666 Club. WALLY HITS THE ROPES, like that."

"In the 666? Maybe a little crass," objected Birch. "He had respectable friends too, Harvey."

"Yeah—like you."

"Yes, and Stan and Marylou Stieglitz. And of course Angela Bellamy. And Jack Devries. Let's pick some neutral ground, if we're going to have a party."

"The Faculty Club!" they both shouted at the same time.

58. Everything flows

They pulled up next to Wally's Lexus at the house.

"We've got to find what's causing this smell," Harvey said as they went in. "What are you going to do with all this art?"

"I'll put it in my garage, but not now. Let's just get the chair. Does this place have a basement?" Birch asked.

"I don't think so. It can't be Wally who smells—he's in the truck. I'll look in the john."

The place was more of a shambles than ever for some reason. It seemed to be falling down from every direction, returning to its constituent atoms, to the things it once was and might become again.

While Harvey was in the bathroom, Birch went upstairs, circling around the orange papier-mâché pot-like thing that stood on the landing.

"There's no railing on this fucking stair," he shouted down to Harvey as Harvey flushed the toilet. "Maybe if he had a fucking railing on these stairs, Wally would still be alive."

"No way," Harvey shouted from downstairs. "Wally designed this thing himself. He wanted everything to be his way. He didn't like the look of railings. Too bourgeois."

"He designed his own death you mean," Birch shouted.

Then Harvey came upstairs into the loft. Beside the futon stood Audrie's armchair. Birch had never noticed how great-looking this chair really was, with its deep-buttoned plush black-leather upholstery, which Wally had redone at exorbitant cost. Wally talked about this chair like it was his baby, his child.

"You take the front, and I'll get the back," said Harvey.

They wrestled the chair down to the landing.

"Watch out for that step on the landing, Harvey."

"What is this piece of orange shit here—this pot thing?"

"No idea."

They got the chair outside, loaded it in the truck, and drove back to Audrie's and parked in the street. They pulled open the back of the camper and hoisted the chair out, knocking over the cardboard box of Wally's ashes so that it fell into a wedge between the tire and the side of the truck. They carried the chair up the cement steps. Birch, bracing a leg against the door, rang the buzzer.

"Who is it?" came a sharp voice. "Oh yes, of course!"

Audrie emerged from the shadows behind the door, holding up her skirt with one hand. Birch pulled open the screen door. They stumbled inside and the door slammed behind them.

"Oh, did you bring something for me?" Audrie Winter asked from her blind eyes.

"We got the chair, Audrie, from Wally's, your father's black leather armchair, just like you asked."

"That's wonderful. There, put it in the corner. Now, let me have a look at you again. Here Harvey, come close and bend down. Yes, it is you, isn't it?"

She turned her back and sat down in a wingchair behind a metal tray beside a floor lamp with a yellowed torn shade. Through the window Birch could see the Episcopal Church.

"Now you boys sit down. There Raymond, you can sit on Daddy's chair. Is there going to be a funeral?"

"We thought we'd have a reception after the burial."

"When?"

"We thought next Wednesday," said Birch.

"That's right away. And you are going to bury him next to me and Daddy and my brother Willie?"

Audrie began to cry.

"Yes."

"That's so wonderful! I can't tell you how much difference this makes to me!"

"We thought we'd just have people close to Wally come to the graveside," Harvey said, "something intimate."

"*Quelquechose très intime*," said Audrie, "yes, of course. You know Wally and I always spoke French together. We should only have people who were really close to Wally."

"And then an open invitation to whoever wants to come to a public reception at the Faculty Club on the university campus that he loved so much," said Birch.

"Yes, but—I don't think I will come to the burial," said Audrie. "It's too much for me. Now that Wally's gone, I have to think about myself. You know Wally was upset about that report by that, what's her name—"

"Karla Marsh."

"Yes. They call her the Great Moogah but I don't know why. You know she's living in a house my mother owned?"

"The brown frame house on the heights?" said Birch.

"Yes, my mother bought that house in 1906. I have no idea why. We lived over on Patterson. She used to rent out that house. I guess that's why she bought it. William Ellery Leonard lived there with his parents. Do you know about William Ellery Leonard? He was a poet and a very dashing man. He was married four times, twice to the same woman. His first wife committed suicide and many in this community never forgave him for it. But she was unbalanced and *I* never blamed him."

Birch had heard stories about William Ellery Leonard, though he had been dead for fifty years. He was a minor American poet, a local legend. Late in life he became insane and lived in a rooming house that he never left except to go to the university campus, always by the same predetermined route.

"You knew William Ellery Leonard?" asked Harvey.

"He used to run after my sister!" Audrie exclaimed. "She was only eighteen and she just couldn't keep her hands off men. Well, we all have our problems and that was hers. Here he was in his mid-thirties, married several times—he always wore a big bow tie. When mother saw what was going on with Mr. William Ellery Leonard, she sent my sister to Seattle. Anything to keep them apart!"

"Did it work?" said Birch.

"Yes—sorry to say," Audrie smiled. "Of course I phoned up that Karla Marsh and told her all about it. She lives there with her partner, a tall thin woman, like a glass of water, Mimi said. Dean Karla Marsh was so excited that my mother had once owned the house that she said she was going to come down and talk to me about it, but she never did. I wish Mimi was here, she could make some coffee. Do you boys want to see my upstairs? Have you ever been there?"

The old lady got up, but her skirt slid down off her hips and she clung to it with one hand. Holding Birch's hand tightly, she preceded them up the stairs. They passed a bathroom with an old-fashioned toilet off the landing, with tank mounted near the ceiling, and down a short hall into a front bedroom with a four-poster bed.

"See that trunk there against the wall—that came from the China trade. It belonged to my great grandfather who was a sea captain out of Portsmouth."

The trunk was surely very old and studded with brass tacks. Once it had been painted a dull red, but most of the color was gone.

"Now come in here."

She went across the hall into another room, a parlor.

"See, there's my father—"

A yellowed daguerreotype hung over a sideboard pushed against the interior wall. Doilies and cheap Indian tourist baskets were on the sideboard, and the picture of a dashing young man wearing a close-cropped beard.

"And there's my mother ..."

There was another daguerreotype, of a beautiful woman lounging on a fainting couch.

"My mother was very beautiful. And there in the corner—see that bookshelf? I can't see it anymore, but I know it's there."

"Sure."

"See that picture over it?"

Birch and Harvey walked to the corner. In an oval frame over the shelf was a handsome young man wearing wire-rimmed glasses. He had a look of ferocious and angry intelligence.

"That's him—William Ellery Leonard!"

"The famous poet!"

"Yes, and you see the book *Two Lives* there? That's his sonnets. It's sort of a novel, but all in sonnets. It tells the story of his first marriage and his wife's suicide. My sister, you see, is the model for Clara, one of the characters in the book. Ellery was born in 1876, and he died in 1944. He was a wonderful man. Oh, how I loved him! I still do and I always will."

Beneath the picture, between book-ends, was a small collection of books. Birch picked up *The Locomotive God* by William Ellery Leonard. Inside, in an elegant Victorian hand, in brown ink on the title page, was written TO AUDRIE, WITH LOVE FOREVER. ELLERY.

A large truck passed on the busy street outside. The windows shook in the room. Birch turned to look but the picture of the street was askew through the ancient panes in their unvarnished frames, distorted by the flow of time.

59. Everything was going to be OK

It was the coldest summer since 1896, but on the morning they decided to bury Wally Wills the temperature took off and kept going. It was 90 degrees at 8:30 A.M when Birch got up, showered, and put on jeans and a white shirt and took the phone ringing downstairs on the fifth ring.

"It's me," said Mimi Esperanto. "I just wanted to be sure everything was alright for the service."

"It's OK, I think."

"It's at 2:00, right?"

"And afterwards there's a reception at the Faculty Club."

"Mama can't come to the grave side, you know," said Mimi. "She said it would be too much. I don't think she should come either. My husband Maspero and I will be there. You know Professor Birch—"

"What?"

"Thanks for everything you're doing."

"Sure, Mimi. As for the burial service, there should be only half a dozen people, I guess. I didn't tell anybody. Just those closest to Wally, I figure, will be coming."

"Mama said that his colleague Sally Brown will say something."

"She and Wally were good friends," said Birch.

"And her little girl is going to sing?" said Mimi Esperanto.

"I heard that."

"But Professor Birch—Mama has a special poem that she would like you to read. Can you stop by and pick it up?"

"Sure. I will."

After he hung up, the phone rang again.

"It's me, Vergil Rawlins. So the funeral's today?"

"I'm glad you phoned Vergil, because I wanted to ask you about all that stuff in Wally's garage?"

"Most of it's mine. So you're in charge, huh?"

"Please get it out, Vergil. I'm going to have to sell the house, which should be enough to pay off the bank, which was about to foreclose. Did you know that?"

"Foreclose?"

"As far as I can tell Wally had nothing of value. I'm telling you this because, you know, of our conversation the other day, about the money he owed you."

"What about the will?"

"Zero."

"No will? And the art?"

"The art seems to be local stuff, of little commercial value."

"I can't believe that. Wally said I would get everything!"

"I don't see what I can do, Vergil. He told me that too."

"He owed me money. Did you get in touch with his wife?"

"Oh for Chrissake—"

"Wally was married for ten years before he came to town and—"

"Married! Just think about it, Rawlins. That sounds like one of his stories. I gotta go. You'll get your stuff out of the garage?"

"I can't believe any of this is happening."

Call-waiting beeped.

"Is this Professor Birch? My name is Alice Taylor. I heard about Wally Wills. He was going to do some appraisal work for me, a painting I inherited from my grandmother. I paid him $600 but he hadn't gotten to it yet. Do you think I could get back my $600?"

"Write me a letter, please, and enclose a copy of the canceled check."

The call-waiting beeped again.

"Hi—my name is Ralph Anderson. You met me once but you may have forgot. You know I've got a lot of stuff at Wally's, and I wondered if I could maybe get it."

Ralph Anderson had been at the 666 on the Friday before Wally died, Birch remembered.

"Like what?"

"There's a CD player upstairs, and a crate it's sitting on. And they're two paintings on the wall upstairs too. And a fan at the foot of the bed. And a brown armchair in the garage."

"What do you want me to do about it?"

"I thought that maybe after the funeral we could go out and get my stuff."

"Look, I'll put that stuff in the garage and you can get it anytime."

The call-waiting beeped. It was Harvey.

"You got the box?" Birch asked.

"A really nice one. I put the ashes in a real nice jar and I put the jar inside the box."

"A great find for archaeologists, eh. What's next?"

"I'll meet you at the cemetery," said Harvey, "at the entrance. There's a little house there, an office."

"Have you checked the grave? Do you know where it is?"

"I went over there yesterday and checked it out."

Harvey hung up. The phone rang immediately.

"You know I'm not coming," Audrie said.

"This is the right decision, Audrie."

"Did you find any pictures out at Wally's—there's one of Mimi standing with my father in front of a big white house."

Birch thought that he had seen something like this on the mantle.

"Oh, and you can read the poem I've picked out at the funeral? Please come by to get it, Raymond. And God bless you for letting him be buried next to me!"

"I'll be by before the service."

Birch hung up and put on some water for coffee when the phone rang.

"Hi—it's Marylou Stieglitz."

It seemed like years since she and her husband Stan had driven up in front of Wally's.

"You know I want to help with the arrangements in any way I can." Her voice was low and brusque.

"Thanks for the offer."

"I thought it would be nice if there could be some live music at the reception, you know. I'm quite shocked to learn that Wally wasn't Jewish. Many a time he's sat at Seder with us. Anyway, I've found the reggae band that Wally liked so much, that he had at his last party at the end of the semester, you know after that play they put on?"

Wally always had a big blast at his house at the end of the semester, after the performance of a comedy by Plautus put on by his large lecture class in ancient art. The lead role was always rewritten to resemble Wally himself, with a fat pillow for girth and an argyle sweater. 'Not *skism* but *shism*,' the actor kept saying, mimicking Wally's tone. 'Not *skism* but *schism*,' mocking Wally's pedantry. The audience went mad as Wally then rose from his seat in the center of the hall, a glutton for attention, cynosure of the world, surrounded by adoring students.

"Yeah, I know the band," Birch said to Marylou Stieglitz.

"They say they'll play at the memorial for $175 as a favor. I can give them the money if the estate will pay me back."

"Well, why not. I can find $175."

"I wanted to check."

The water in the tea pot was boiling, but the phone rang again.

"Hi, it's Sally Brown."

"Yeah."

"I hear there's going to be live music at Wally's reception," she said in a chirping voice.

"I just heard that myself, Sally. I was speaking to Marylou Stieglitz—do you know her, the philanthropist? She said she was going to get some band that played at Wally's last party."

"Well, you know I heard about that too, Raymond, but do you really think that would be appropriate? I also heard that somebody was going to put up a sign in the 666 Club. I mean Wally had his noble side too, Ray."

"In addition to the sleaze, you mean."

"I don't think that's fair, Ray. I spoke to Georgia Nugent who runs the Faculty Club and she said that Harvey Vanderpool had spoken to her about having an open bar at the reception, but I don't think that would be right at all. Just think of how he died."

"How did he die?"

"You know Ray, there are lurid stories going around."

"Like what?"

"I really think that an open bar would be inappropriate and so I arranged for Georgia to have a *cash* bar. Is that OK with you Raymond?"

"No free wine?"

"I don't see how you can have it both ways. You know I've worked with Georgia Nugent over the years, and she agreed that she'd put out a spread and that she would wait to be paid."

"Nice."

"It wasn't easy persuading her, I have to admit."

"I'm glad you've shown some initiative, Sally, because I just haven't had time to think about details like this. Let's get together some time and chat, OK Sally? We'll chat, we'll chat."

The call-waiting beeped.

"Hi, this is Eddy Cornel. I'm in town. Evelyn is with me. We're at the Pancake House. I wanted to find out about the burial."

"It's at 2:00. Why don't you come over and we can go to the cemetery?"

As soon as he hung up, the phone rang.

"Hi, this is Marylou Stieglitz again. You know I totally forgot when I spoke to you a minute ago. Wally had some plates that were made by the famous potter Don Wright. You know he gave us three of those but three is really not enough for a service. If I could get just one more plate from Wally's house, then we'd have a complete set. Do you think that would be possible?"

In his mind's eye Birch saw Harvey Vanderpool lifting out some heavy hand-thrown plates from the shelves in the kitchen and loading them into a cardboard box.

"Ouch! You know Marylou, I think that Harvey Vanderpool must have latched onto those plates."

"Who's he?"

"Oh, an artist type, an old friend of Wally."

"I never heard of him. And what is his right to the plates if I might ask?"

"Look, Marylou, I'll do my best."

"That's all I want—one plate. You've been wonderful about everything."

"Well, Wally was a friend."

"He was a friend to all of us."

60. Division of the spoils

The phone rang. It was Vergil Rawlins again.

"We need to talk," he said.

"What about?"

"Money! Wally owed me ten big ones, let's say in round figures. I have to have the money!"

"Calm down."

"I'm calm."

"How'd Wally get to owe you so much?"

"I'm not sure it's your business, but let's just say I trusted him. He told me just before he died that he was going to make a certain transaction, which would realize him a big profit—so that he could return the whole sum—this is what I'm thinking about here."

"What are you thinking about?"

"I'm telling you that Wally was about to conclude a deal! I don't know what. Maybe a painting. Wally had a lot of stuff."

"You know in fact Wally told a guy at a travel agency when he bought a ticket for this Eric, whoever he is, that he was cooking up some business deal—that's what the police said anyway. But the plane ticket was never picked up. Is this what you're talking about Vergil?"

"I never saw this Eric before—before that Sunday I mean."

"What has all this got to do with me?"

"Don't fuck with me, Birch! I know what's going on. I need to get this money one way or the other—Wally *owed* me. Now do you see?" Vergil Rawlins said breathlessly and hung up.

The doorbell rang. Birch went to the door and admitted Eddy and Evelyn Cornel. Evelyn was lovely in a pink dress of a flimsy fabric that showed her body beneath, and Eddy was wearing a light blue blazer and dark blue tie. Birch shook his hand and kissed Evelyn on the cheek. She smelled of rosewater.

"Ah, rosewater—I used to know a woman who wore rosewater," Birch said.

"What, your wife?" she said and smiled.

Evelyn wore a blue flower in her hair, too, and Birch wondered if blue flowers were really the right thing for the funeral.

"You guys look great," Birch said.

"We feel good," said Eddy.

They were all standing in Birch's living room.

"I know you just came inside, but what do you say we go outside again and sit around under the trees? It's a helluva hot day," Birch suggested.

"It's supposed to be blasting later on," said Evelyn.

They followed Birch through the kitchen and out the back. They sat in lawn chairs on the lawn around a glass-topped table.

"Too bad we don't smoke cigarettes any more, hey guys?" Birch plumped.

"We could go get some," suggested Evelyn.

Even in the shade it was hot. Cicadas screamed in the bushes in the woods next to Birch's house. Beads of sweat swelled on their faces. There was something about the way Evelyn held her head.

"So what's on the schedule?" asked Eddy.

"Why don't we relax for now," insisted Birch. "We're sitting here now, aren't we, and that doesn't seem bad. In a little while we can go over to the cemetery. I have to pick up a book at Audrie Winter's, that's all."

"Fine," said Eddy.

"I guess there is some minor business though, so why don't we do that first."

"What's that?" said Eveyln.

A neighbor's orange marmalade cat walked across the lawn, right up to Evelyn. The cat rubbed its head against her leg. This cat had taken control of this section of the Village and daily prowled its rounds, demanding food and some respect. Birch wasn't sure what house it lived in. The cat had been a favorite of Wally's, but he was certainly treacherous. Birch feared he would jump on Evelyn's skirt and give her a good scratching.

"What, for example, am I going to do with all of Wally's crap? Vergil Rawlins thinks Wally's stuff is worth a lot of money and claims that Wally owed him ten grand, but as far as I can see the art is mostly local stuff. Some local art dealer named Fodamew, or something like that, phoned me, but frankly I'd just as soon see it went to his friends, other things being equal," Birch said.

"But how do you know who Wally's friends are?" Evelyn asked.

"You know them by their fruits." Birch smiled and Cornel laughed. "What I'm saying is that I think you were his friends, so why don't you give me a little something for this, a little something for that ... you take what you want, I take what I want, something to Vanderpool, some stuff to Audrie Winter, and so forth. . that's how it will go, what do you think? Legally speaking, I'm in charge."

"We're all his heirs," said Eddy.

Evelyn smiled. She no doubt married Eddy because he ran around with hotshots like Wally Wills. Birch had seen this before—a woman marries a broken man because he shares a vice with a great one. For such indiscretions they pay a terrible price, and Evelyn was paying it now.

"The point is, what do you want from Wally's stuff?"

Evelyn's eyes widened.

"Think of something."

"How about the Jim Dine? The pink lady with her head and limbs chopped off?" said Eddy. "I think that was Wally's favorite."

Birch was happy to hear the suggestion, because he feared that this ghastly painting was going to live against the wall of his basement behind a stack of lumber until it became covered with mold and ended in the trash. Either that, or sell it to the art dealer Fodamew.

"Fine," agreed Evelyn.

"You really want the headless lady? So make me an offer."

"$100."

"How about $20. I'll take cash or checks."

Eddy smiled broadly, showing his well-ordered bright teeth. He opened his wallet and put a twenty dollar bill on the table. The crows made a loud racket and suddenly one swooped down over their heads and with a horrific scream, making a pass at the cat beside Evelyn's chair. The cat lay back its ears and crouched. The crow perched in a tree and kept up the racket.

"Wow, are you often attacked by crows?" Evelyn asked.

"When there's money on the table," said Birch.

Evelyn hoisted the cat on her lap, and the cat drooped over her thighs and purred.

"Here, little sweetie, I'll protect you," she said.

"There's another thing," said former Assistant Professor Eddy Cornel. "Wally had a gold ring, a ruby pinkie-ring he always used to wear. It was supposed to be worth a lot of bucks."

"Yeah, well."

"I'd sure like to have that ring."

"You know, I thought something like this might happen," said Birch. He pulled the very ring from his coat pocket and rolled it across the table. Eddy picked it up and stared in a melancholy way.

"You know I brought along a turquoise ring to trade you for this, if you want it," Eddy said and fumbled in his pocket.

"Are you crazy? Now let's go over to the cemetery and get this over with. You take your car, I'll take my truck. After the reception, come by and get the headless lady. It's in my garage."

"Where are we going to put it?" Evelyn asked Eddy.

"I guess over the couch," said Eddy. "That's where I always wanted it anyway."

61. The isles of Greece

Audrie handed Birch the slender black volume through the screen door. When he got to the cemetery he was surprised to see long rows of cars along the drive on either side of the entrance and several dozen people milling on the sidewalk in front of the cemetery office. Birch used to live in this neighborhood before moving to the Village and he had jogged through this cemetery a thousand times. In summer it was a fine park with imperial oaks and rainbow flowers blooming on the graves. In winter the footing was good because the crews kept the roads clean for the mourners and the gravediggers who set up metal canopies over the fresh gravesites and fired jets of propane thundering beneath them through day and night to thaw the frozen ground.

The crowds astounded Birch as he drove through the gates to the head of the row of cars. He had told no one, really, about the funeral. He parked his truck and walked slowly back to the crowd around the office. The engulfing heat rolled in waves across the highway beyond the office and boiled on the asphalt like the sea at tide. Sweat poured down Birch's face in streams.

Near the edge of the crowd he saw a man he had met years ago when Wally lived in the country, in the stone house with his true love Sean Stand. Nervously Birch went up to him and shook his hand, though he couldn't remember his name.

"Hi—George Peach," the man reminded him, thinner and

mustachioed now. Maybe he had been a pettifogger who lost his earnings by investing in solar technology. Sure, Wally had rented an apartment from him in town, a close oppressive attic that Wally called the Crypt. Harvey Vanderpool and Wally used to snort coke up there and play backgammon all night long.

"Hi," Birch said to George Peach's wife, who had already lost the bloom of youth.

Wally's secretary, who found him dead at the bottom of the stairs, came up to Birch and over her shoulder he espied Marylou and Stan Stieglitz in a group of elderly men and women.

"I'm glad you're here," the secretary said softly.

"Oh, thanks, but who are all these people?"

"They're people who loved Wally, I think."

"Fine, only I thought this was supposed to a burial *intime*. How did all these people find out about this?" Birch whispered.

The woman, who was very fat, seemed offended.

"Oh no, you don't understand. These were friends of Wally."

"OK fine. It's just that I'm surprised. There must be a hundred people here."

"Please Professor Birch, don't be that way."

Marylou Stieglitz worked her way over and greeted Birch in low tones. Birch noticed that everyone was speaking softly, afraid to wake the dead he supposed. Birch himself wanted to shout but he shook Marylou's hand. Then he spotted Sean Stand in the crowd, Wally's old flame, looking worn and tired and wearing a three-piece suit and dark tie in the ferocious heat. Sean Stand caught Birch's eye and nodded.

"Are we going to drive to the graveside?" Marylou asked. "Or shall we walk? Do you know where it is?"

"I guess we should drive," said Birch. "I think it's a good ways, though I haven't actually been there. It's fantastically hot, isn't it? Some of these people seem ridiculously dressed."

Harvey Vanderpool drove through the gate in his beat VW Rabbit and parked down the line. He joined Birch as the lawyer Ron Fettman turned in at the gate.

"When shall we head up?" Harvey asked in a low voice,

coming up.

Vergil Rawlins and his girlfriend Katy huddled like mice in the grass. Birch spotted Eddy and Evelyn Cornel near them, under some trees. Ron Fettman came down the road covered in sweat.

"We've been holding up the whole thing for you, Ron."

"You haven't!"

"No. But I guess we can get started now, eh?"

Birch collected himself.

"HELLO, everybody, HELLO," Birch boomed and hushed the crowd with outspread hands as he had done so many times in large lectures at the university. "I'm afraid we now have to get back in our cars to head out to the graveside. It's too far and too hot to walk. So please follow Harvey Vanderpool here—he knows the way."

Harvey nodded and headed back toward his car at the head of the parked cars. Like sheep the crowd followed. By the time Birch got back to his truck other cars were moving out, creeping past him. He followed the mélange of cars.

The procession passed on the left a special portion of the cemetery reserved for the Confederate dead, surrounded by a low cement wall. There had been a prisoner-of-war camp here in the Civil War, where the Yanks shipped the southern boys to die like animals in the savage cold. A local southern woman cared for them in their agony. She was buried here too, in front of the plot just inside the low wall. A hundred times Birch had stopped beside the southern graves while jogging, to read their tombstones. Stones across the road marked the graves of pioneers, written in German or Norwegian, the writing so faint you could barely make out the lettering. Some of the stones had fallen down or were broken in half, impressed into the earth. In the dim twilight of a March morning, as mists of the breaking ice rolled around and engulfed the letters, Birch had made out the story of an eighteen year old Midwestern Yankee shot through the heart by a southern sniper as he guarded a bridge ten days after Appomattox, not having heard of the war's end. But the boy's name had crumbled away.

The procession entered the forest of oaks and turned on a subsidiary road up a hill toward the Jewish section, past the tombs of once-great supreme court judges and brazen developers, their mortal remains surmounted by obelisks of granite, glowing in the dull sun. Cackling crows leaped from tree to tree and followed the cars.

At the top of the hill the procession stopped. Well back in the line, Birch pulled his truck over and got out. He walked across the neatly-tended plots to a knot of people gathered around a mound of fresh earth piled in an open area. A shovel was thrust into the mound. People drifted and formed a circle around the mounded earth but no one spoke. Even the crows had fallen silent, though they whooshed with their wings as they took up position around the grave.

Birch went up to Harvey beside the mound.

"We set?" he whispered. "Where is Sally Brown? Isn't she supposed to do something?"

"When has Sally Brown ever been on time?" Harvey asked, knowing her reputation.

Then Birch glimpsed Jack Devries, hanging out in the background among the trees. He wondered if Karla Marsh had made it, but the petite and exhausted Sally Brown just then worked her way through the crowd. She was dressed all in black crepe. She came into the open space behind the grave, next to Birch and Harvey. Behind her stood her jet-headed ten-year old daughter, skin so white it seemed translucent or diseased. The blistering sun pored through a gap in the trees. An aura of expectancy gripped the crowd. An energy or vibration hovered above them like a mirage.

Birch removed from his satchel the book that Audrie had given him. He stepped forward to the earthen mound and the open grave and flipped to the marked page. A dragon of feeling dropped on the crowd and struck with its sharp spines the hearts of the mourners, and against his own will a great emotion overcame Birch, as from a deep animal well, and tears flooded Birch's eyes as broken sobs and gasps came from the crowd.

He read the passage marked by Audrie Winters:

"The isles of Greece, the isles of Greece,
Where burning Sappho loved and sung,

Where grew the arts of war and peace,
         Where Delos rose and Phoebus sprung!
Eternal summer gilds them yet
But all except their sun is set.

The mountains look on Marathon
         And Marathon looks on the sea,
And musing there an hour alone
         I dreamed that Greece might still be free.
And standing on the Persians' grave
I could not deem myself a slave.

A king sat on the rocky brow
         Which looks o'er sea-born Salamis.
And ships by thousands lay below
         And men in nations—all were his!
He counted them at break of day—
And when the sun set where were they?

And where are they? and where art thou,
         My country? On thy voiceless shore
The heroic lay is tuneless now—
         The heroic bosom beats no more.
And must thy lyre so long divine
Degenerate into hands like mine?"

The words of Lord Byron broke the mourners' spirit. Without shame the moans of the people filled the air. Birch crossed his arms and stepped back as the jet-headed girl stepped forward and in a sweet falsetto sang Walter Savage Landor's *Fate! I have asked few things of thee*. Then Sally Brown spoke of how the Roman poet Catullus journeyed through many countries and over many seas to see his brother's grave in Asia. There he left a token of his esteem—*atque in perpetuum, frater, ave atque vale*.

Sally Brown stepped back. Birch and Harvey went up to the grave. Harvey had placed his handsome box containing Wally's ashes on a square ply board over the hole. WALLY WILLS was chiseled handsomely into the polished wood. A system of ropes permitted Harvey and Birch to slip the board out from beneath the box and lower it into the ground. When the box was down, Birch picked up the shovel. The dirt made a clumping sound on the box. He handed the shovel to Harvey and the two men stepped back. One by one the crowd came forward, took up the shovel, and cast dirt into the grave.

All were complicit now.

62. Make that three, would you

By the time Birch got to the Faculty Club in the late afternoon the place was packed. He pushed through the mobs in the foyer off which opened a capacious reception area usually set up like a living room, but the couches were now pushed against the wall. At the far end was a high stone fireplace. A long table in the middle of the room supported a punch bowl and plates of hors d'oeuvres.

Birch wended through the crowd, making for the bar in the hall behind the foyer. He was surprised to see Angela Bellamy just inside the door and wondered if she had been hidden in the crowds at the burying ground. There at her side stood little Jack Devries, the poet, huddling for comfort in a tan sport coat with red tie and dark slacks and high-piled blonde curly hair stacked foppishly on his head.

Birch stopped in mid-stride and stared. Certainly Angela was putting on weight. Just behind her was Charlotte something or other, the graduate student who had sterilized herself so she could get on with the work. Birch shuddered when he saw them.

And now Angela came towards Birch, Devries just behind

her.

"Hello Raymond," Angela said.

"You look well, Angela. And you too, Jack."

Jack avoided Birch's eyes. Birch wondered if he should kiss Angela on the cheek, in spite of everything, or if maybe he should even shake Jack's hand, in light of the occasion.

"Well, I'm glad you could make it," Birch finally said, deciding to survive. "I hope you'll forgive me, but I have to get a drink now."

"No, you go ahead," Angela smiled wanly. "You need one."

Birch turned and pushed through the crowd. There was Harvey Vanderpool. He went up to him and touched Harvey on the shoulder.

"So what are we drinking today, buddy?"

"Gin and tonic," Harvey grinned like death.

"You took the words from my mouth."

"I'm having two."

"I'll have two too," Birch agreed and muscled his way in closer against the counter. The bartender was the same slim dark-haired youth who always served Wally at lunch, taciturn, with a slight sneer, as if he were in a state of perpetual anger. In fact he seemed to recognize Birch and he poured out two plastic cups especially for him, and two for Harvey.

The heat was smothering and Birch's shirt was drenched in sweat as he downed one cup in a single swallow. He felt a little better. Then he downed the second.

"You had the right idea, old bean," Birch said to Harvey. "By the way, nice fucking box. Wally will like it."

"When should the band start playing?" asked Marylou Stieglitz suddenly at their side.

"I didn't see you, Marylou. They're set up, are they? Those South American guys?"

"They're here and everything, in the other room," said Marylou.

"Who did that?" Harvey asked.

"I did! I set it up myself," Marylou said proudly.

"I'm glad somebody's taking charge," said Birch.

Harvey wandered off and Birch held up two fingers to the dark-haired bartender. He'd got a buzz off the first two G & Ts but he was going to need more than that.

"I thought Wally would like it," said Marylou. "Shall I tell them to go ahead then?"

"Yes, yes, let's have some music."

Somebody tugged at Birch's jacket from the other side.

"Very nice service at the grave site," said the fat man with a beard. Birch remembered him from the distant past—an artist, maybe from California. Birch met him a couple of times at the 666 and had played poker with him at Wally's.

"How'd you like the poem I read?" Birch asked.

"Did you write that?" asked the fat man.

"Ha! Pretty good! I can also swim the Hellespont with both hands tied behind my back!"

Birch craned his neck to see how the bartender was coming with the G & Ts. The boy looked up from beneath his brows. Oh my God—Wally had been at him too.

"What—are you crazy?" Birch repeated and reached out for the second round. He drank one of the cups and began to feel much better while trilling high flutes came from the other room and the syncopated drumming of marimbas. The music and the heat and the press of bodies went to Birch's head. The bearded fat man disappeared. Clutching the remaining gin and tonic, Birch forced his way into the other room to have a look at the band.

Through heads and arms he made out in the corner two white men, one playing a flute and the other a marimba, and a small handsome black man, who worked the percussion. Birch slid along the windows and came in behind the black man and cupped his hand in front of his mouth. Birch shouted into his ear, "Not quite so loud ... it's great, but not quite so loud ..."

"Too loud, mahn? Eez it too loud? We donna play too loud no moah, if you donna wan."

"Like, you know," Birch shouted, "it's a fucking funeral. It's a party too, but people want to talk and shit like that."

"Gotcha, mahn," the Jamaican said, winked, and made an O with his thumb and index finger. "Gotcha—it's a fuckin funeral!"

"Hi, I'm Michael Mitanni," said a medium-sized muscular man near the band.

"Who is that?"

"Are you Professor Birch? I was Wally's childhood friend."

The man's voice sounded familiar. The man was forty years old, dressed in a gray check suit, and in good physical shape. Sweat ran down his hardened face.

"What do you mean?"

"I'm from Oxford, Massachusetts. I came out for the funeral."

"For the funeral? How did you find out about it?"

"Oh, I think everybody knows about it."

"You were his friend?"

"I loved him like a brother. Of course he had his faults."

"Lucky we're spared any of those, hey Michael?"

"I'm sorry—I shouldn't have said that."

"Don't worry about it. Hey Harvey," Birch shouted, seeing Vanderpool through the crowd, "this is some guy from Massachusetts—he knew Wally when he was a kid and came out here for the funeral!"

Harvey worked his way over to them, but they were standing so close to the band that it was hard to speak. Taking Harvey with one hand and Wally's childhood friend with the other Birch guided them away from the band toward the bay windows at the other end of the room that overlooked the plaza and the broad lake.

"Wally always had the biggest collection of forty-five hit singles in the neighborhood," reminisced Michael Mitanni. "He was fantastically proud of them," the man was saying as Birch eased away and headed back toward the bar.

He turned. It was Paul West, the aging pony-tailed hippy who had cleaned out Wally's upstairs closet.

"Sorry about all this, Paul."

"No, everything is wonderful," Paul said, crocodile tears running down his cheeks and mingling with the sweat. Birch wanted to embrace him but he immediately ran into Mimi Esperanto.

"Oh that was lovely," she said in a grisly way from behind

her protruding twisted teeth. She was certainly old, very old. "I just love that poem, Professor Birch, about Marathon and the sea. That's Mama's favorite poem. 'The mountains look on Marathon, And Marathon looks on the sea.' I just love that." Tears welled behind her old yellow eyes. "And the way you read it—it was beautiful. Every word was magic. Every word brought me a chill. I wish Mother could have heard it."

"Thanks, Mimi."

Another fat man, one of Birch's colleagues, a professor of Chinese art, came up.

"Are there going to be speeches or what?"

"Excuse me, Mimi, let me talk to this man."

"That's no problem," she moved away.

"Are you going to give a speech?" asked the professor.

"Oh, no. I wrote a poem for Wally," Birch said. "I'll read that and that's all. That's it."

"Boy, it's hot in here. When will we get to it then?"

"Don't you dig the music? Have another drink," said Birch.

"Hello Professor Birch—I was at the funeral," said a woman with pimples and gray hair at the temples and distended nostrils. "I just loved the poem. I'm Alice Packwood. I knew Wally Wills in high school, in Oxford, Massachusetts."

"Oh? You came out her from Massachusetts?"

"Yes, because you know I really loved Wally. You know he took me to the high school prom. We had seats together in homeroom for four years. Probably you remember him as a *dignified professor* but I'll never forget how at the prom he signed an autograph hound directly under its tail! It was so funny! And he was such a good dancer!"

Big tears were running down her cheeks.

"Please excuse me," Birch said.

"Oh Raymond," said Sally Brown from the other side, "there's something I need to ask you about."

"What?"

"You know Ralph Anderson don't you?"

"No."

"Yes you do. He said he just phoned you—about his CD

player that he left at Wally's and some other things."

"So what?"

Birch needed to get back to the bar.

"You know, he told me that he had left an ashtray at Wally's, a big one with a kind of loop over the top and German writing on it. He wonders if he could get it back," Sally laughed cheerfully.

Birch had snuffed out thousands of cigarettes in this ashtray over the years. At Wally's poker parties it was always crammed with hundreds of butts flowing over the table and mixed with dribbles of wine and beer and every kind of filth, a silly thing whose WEIN AUF BIER, DAS RAT ICH DIR on one side and BIER AUF WEIN, DAS IST NICHT FEIN on the other echoed the Kraut clichés in the University Rathskeller. Wally had that fucking ashtray from the day he was born.

"Sally, I know the ashtray, but it doesn't belong to Ralph Anderson, whoever he is. Anyway, if this guy wants this ashtray why doesn't he ask me for it?"

"Oh yes, he's here somewhere but he was afraid to ask you for it and that's why he asked me."

"Well, might as well ask somebody!"

63. He was there all right

"**A**re you Professor Birch?" asked a thin man, pushing himself past Sally Brown.

"Everybody says I am so maybe I am."

The man was twenty years old, a flush of dishwater blonde hair over one eye. He was large and had probably sensual lips and wide ears, big eyes, and wore a sports coat and tie.

"I'm Tom Allen."

"So what?"

"I was at Wally's the day he died."

Birch stared.

"You're *Tom*?"

"Sure, I'm Tom. Why do you say it that way?"

His voice was thin, excited, nervous.

"So you're the man who killed Wally Wills?"

The boy blanched.

"I don't think that's very funny."

"We've been looking for you buddy, and so have the police."

"The *police*?"

"Was that your Benz parked outside with the Illinois plates on Sunday night then?"

"My father's Benz. That was my *father's* car."

"So tell me what happened, Tom, I'd like to hear it from you."

Birch wished Tom would make his explanation fast so he could get back to the bar, though obviously this was a big deal, if Tom had something to do with Wally's death, and if Birch could bring himself to care.

"OK, well, you know," said Tom, "I was in town with my old college roommate, this guy named Eric Salton. He'd never met Wally, see, but Wally and I were old friends. I—"

"This is the *Eric* we've been hearing about?"

"I don't know what you mean. I'm from Chicago."

"We knew you were there, that's all, at Wally's house."

"Yeah, like I said."

"How old are you?"

"Twenty-two."

"You were a student of Wally's?"

"Yeah, sure."

"OK, I'm listening."

"So we drove out to Wally's on Sunday. Wally was down at the pier. Me and Eric."

"Vergil Rawlins was there?"

"I dunno—some neighbor was working on the pier. There

were a couple of other people with them."

"You didn't know these people?"

"Sort of—like I say, Wally and I were old friends."

"Then what?"

"Wally came up from the pier. We had a couple of beers. Wally was supposed to go up to the neighbor's for dinner, the guy putting in the dock, but we decided to go out for pizza."

"This is Sunday night?"

"Yeah, Sunday night. Then we went back to Wally's. We had, you know, a sort of party. We drank beer and played cards. We sacked out late, around one o'clock."

"And the next morning Wally phoned in sick to work?"

"That's right. He was hung-over, see."

"But around ten o'clock he phoned a travel agency and booked a flight for your friend Eric. Did you know that?"

"Sure—how do you know all this? That's right. Because you see Eric needed to get back to the East Coast. He had an Amtrak ticket but the trains were on strike and Wally did it as a favor. I mean the plane ticket."

"He billed the ticket to his department?"

"Yeah, because I guess his credit card was overdrawn or something. I dunno, but anyway he said he'd front the money to Eric because, see, Eric really needed to get back to the East Coast for an interview. Also, Wally wanted him to take something back there or something."

The music was loud again and Birch could barely make out Tom's words through the torrent of sound, sweat, and fear, though now he hung onto every word.

"What?" said Birch.

"What *what*?"

"You said this Eric Salton guy was going to take something back to the east coast?"

"I dunno, some old money or something. He was going to take some old money to a dealer—in New York."

"Look Tom, the man at the travel agency said that Wally sounded 'up' when he phoned, in a good mood, but then his secretary said that when he phoned at eight A.M. he sounded 'down,' depressed."

"Yeah, well that's because he started drinking Bloody Marys just after he phoned his office."

"Yeah? Bloody Marys?"

"Yeah, he said the tomato juice made it a kind of a breakfast. Wally was a great guy but sometimes he liked to get real fucked up. He could be pretty hard to take when he was totally fucked up."

"So what then?"

"So he went on drinking Bloody Marys and got so fucked up he could barely talk. When we left he was lying on the couch— he was barely conscious. He was wearing a T-shirt and filthy shorts—God they were dirty. I couldn't believe he could wear clothes like that. Eric even poured some water on his head and he sort of came around and sat up but I don't think he knew who we were. He sort of grunted and got up and went into the kitchen and made himself another Bloody Mary. That's when we left."

"You and Eric? All of this is Monday morning?"

"Yeah. Then we just drove around town and went to see some other friends."

"But you went back to the house?"

"Nah, we never went back. Nope. I still can't believe that Wally is dead. How do you think it happened?"

"I thought you were going to tell me."

"No way, Professor Birch, when Eric and I left he was lying on the couch so fucked up he couldn't talk. I really couldn't stand Wally when he got like that."

"Look here Tom, several people phoned Wally on Monday afternoon, from around three to five P.M. and they all said that somebody *else* answered the phone—that it wasn't Wally. Are you saying that wasn't you on the phone? That somebody came by *after* you guys left?"

"Me? No, like I say, we didn't go back. We left around two o'clock."

"What about Eric?"

"Well, that's weird, you know, because I thought that he was going to fly back east, you know, the next day, but when I tried to get hold of him at his house in Burlington the phone was disconnected. I haven't heard from him since."

Tom Allen fidgeted and looked across the crowd. He put his hands in his pockets, then pulled them out again.

"But this old money that Eric was supposed to take to New York—I mean did Wally give the money to him or what?"

"No. Wally was way too fucked up to do anything. I figured he'd just forgotten about it."

"But that was the idea. That's why Wally bought Eric the ticket. So he could take this old money to a dealer in New York?"

"Yes." Birch eyed him coldly. "I just don't understand your attitude, that's all," Tom Allen said.

"And you haven't heard from this Eric Salton since that night?"

"Well, it's not so unusual—I mean we were sort of friends in college, but nothing special."

"The plane ticket was never picked up."

"Huh? I dunno."

"At the travel agency—the ticket was never picked up."

"I dunno. I mean I had to go back to Chicago. Like I say, I haven't heard from Eric. But why are the police looking for me—you said?"

"Cocaine, I guess."

Allen backed off.

"Oh no you don't! I don't know anything about that, if there was any cocaine or anything."

He was lying but Birch pretended to believe him.

"Nice to meet you, Tom. Let me know when you hear from Eric, would you?"

"Sure, why sure—OK," Tom said as Birch broke away and headed for the bar.

64. The eye of the sun

As he was pressing in against the back of the crowd that surrounded the bar Birch saw Jack Devries bearing down on him. Devries had a drink in his hand.

"Say, you know, there is something I want to ask you, Raymond," he said in a husky voice.

"Really, Jack? I wasn't sure we were speaking. What did you want to ask me?"

"Well, you know, there's some of Wally's property that, you know, I'd be interested in. You know we used to be roommates."

"Sure, I remember that. When you lived across from us on that shady tree-lined street. I guess that slipped my mind. What are you interested in?"

"Well, there is that black chair with the leather upholstery ... upstairs next to the bed—"

"You know, Devries, for the record, you're a weird sonofabitch. The chair belongs to Audrie Winter. Didn't Audrie live upstairs when you and Wally were roommates?"

"Yeah, but she gave the chair to Wally. It's his now."

"How did you know the chair was next to the bed?"

Devries flashed a brilliant red.

"Come to think of it Birch," he said angrily, "what gives you the right to make these decisions? I mean, how did you get to be in charge? I heard there was no will and that you were taking all his stuff."

"Let's just say I got there first," Birch said.

"Professor Birch—" pleaded Marylou Stieglitz from his other side, "don't you think we should get the presentations over with? It's so hot people are going to start fainting."

Birch turned his back on Devries.

"OK, but where shall we do them?" he said to Marylou Stieglitz.

"Can't you just stand between the two rooms and—"

"Hi—I'm Jean Fodamew," said a man in his mid-thirties in dapper dress, a three-piece suit, short hair and trim mustache with a good upper body and biceps clear through the clothes.

Marylou looked at him.

"You know, I phoned about Wally's art. Puhleeze don't forget me when the time comes!" He put his hand on Birch's sleeve.

"Ray, we really need to get going," Marylou insisted.

"Nobody will hear a thing if I just stand between the rooms—but look, I'll get a chair or something and set it against the wall over there in the foyer, to get some altitude."

"Sure, fine, Professor, and then you can signal to me when you want the band to stop," said Marylou.

"Fodamew—about the art—we'll chat ..." Birch said and held up two fingers to the bar boy. Birch looked around, scoured the corners and walls for a chair, and at last spotted one against the wall inside the main door, grabbed the drinks from the bar, dropped a five-dollar bill on the counter, and jostled his way toward the door. He tossed off one of the G & Ts and nested the empty cup in the full one. He picked up the straight back chair by one leg, raised it high, and carried it over the heads of the crowd to the closed mullioned doors that led into the formal dining area where Wally used to eat lunch.

"You might need this," said Harvey, appearing at his side and handing him another gin and tonic.

"Thanks Harvey."

Tossing off the doubled cup he already held, he handed the empties to Harvey, took the new drink and got up on the chair. The heat boomed around him like a presence, a spirit. He caught Marylou Stieglitz's eye from across the room and signaled. She disappeared toward the back. The music stopped.

"HELLO, HELLO, HELLO ..." Birch called over the heads of the crowd but at first no one could hear him.

"HELLO, HELLO," he repeated "QUIET, PLEASE ... QUIET PLEASE ... I HAVE JUST A FEW WORDS ... Thank you ..."

A silence fell over the crowd.

"… We are gathered in honor of WALLY WILLS … a FRIEND to all of us … this great crowd is a wonderful testimony to him … don't doubt it … Wally was our friend and we are SHOCKED and SADDENED by his death …"

Someone coughed.

"Sure, Wally was many things to many people," Birch said and took a gulp from the G & T.

" … he had the USUAL ACCOMPLISHMENTS … fine scholar, exemplary teacher, beloved colleague, all that … COMMON qualities … We expect them … take them for granted and there they are at every turn … but Wally was GREATER than that …"

Birch paused as mourners crowded from the far room into the foyer to hear better.

"… Wally was a BIG man." Birch extended his hands before him, as if touching an unseen belly " … and we are so SMALL … little things … like FROGS huddled around the pond of his greatness … Wally died young, sure, but he had a good life … he got WHAT he wanted … WHEN he wanted and HOW he wanted … he DIED AS HE LIVED with style and panache … a life full and a death sudden and tasteful … We're going to miss him and—his gift for FRIENDSHIP … Wally Wills valued friendship … loyal to the end … you could always count on Wally Wills …"

The crowd liked this talk and many murmured approval. Far in the background Birch spotted Dean Karla Marsh. He paused and craned his neck.

"Speaking of FRIENDSHIP, I have brought with me a poem that I wrote just for Wally … cause you know there are scholars and there are poets … this poem is called THE GARDEN PARTY OF DEATH and I wrote it for fat Wally Wills …"

Birch stopped, tossed off what remained of the gin, then cast the cup in the air. Somebody must have caught it because he didn't hear it drop. Then he read the poem.

"The milky mist came on so fast,
across the muddy windswept street
from the night—

he had no time to think
for its blinding light,
the quick air,
left him breathless.
It's God, he told his friends,
but the mist was gone,
trailing a putrid air.

They never believed what he said.
They listened only to themselves.
'Then explain this morning light,'
he challenged, 'when before it was night.
Then explain this mountain peak,
when before it was heated plain.
Then explain this snowy canyon, there!'
It was true.
Everything was changed, changed utterly.
It was the work he'd never do,
the work he sorrowed for.

This was not the bombing at the bunker,
beneath the mountain of sand
where the water dripped-dripped
into black pools,
where they sought him out with guns and fire
until invisibility proved to me
we were no more there to see.
And we will join him too,
in the dimmèd sun,
and shall all be gathered,
as we are now,
all hate gone,
gathered as one
in the Garden Party of Death!"

Birch stopped but no one spoke or breathed. There was a
screaming in Birch's head as the ceiling lifted from its pillars and

crashed into the sun.

65. At last, sorrow

Birch walked along the lake until the dark sun fell beneath the horizon and the air cooled. He made his way back to his truck and drove to his house in the Village. It was late and he was surprised to see a light on upstairs in the library because he rarely left lights on. Everything seemed normal when he went inside the house until he got upstairs to check on his little babies and he saw the cockatoo on her back, her legs absurdly protruding upward, her black claws curled, her deep black eyes open. Behind the door in her own cage the Amazon's little head was half-tucked inside her wing. Her own gray lifeless lids were half-closed, dreaming of time. Birch cocked his head and sniffed—there was a scent of burned almonds.

Birch fell to his knees, as if someone had kicked him from behind, and his breath left him in a puff. He remembered all the terrible things he had done to so many people, starting with his wife, and then their children, who saw him as a monster, a freak, a curse on their own lives. A feeling he'd not felt for a long time, since he was a child, came from somewhere, an animal feeling, of deep sorrow. Just behind his eyes the feeling hung and pushed outward as tears, and he realized that his chest was heaving and that he was sobbing as the river of that feeling, whose existence he had forgotten, swept over him, rolling his mind like pebbles in a flood

"Oh God, I'm so sorry," he said aloud. "So very very sorry!"

66. The real thing

The phone rang downstairs. He took the call in the library, but there was no one there—only a hum, or a whine.

Birch went back into the bird room and carefully removed the corpses of his little babies from their cages. He wrapped them in paper towels and carried them downstairs to the basement and put them in the freezer. Then he went back upstairs and plowed around in one of the low closets built under the eaves until he found his silver-plated Smith and Wesson .38 and a box of ammunition. He went down into his basement and set up a firing range with a paper target and a bag of premixed cement for a backup. He sprayed the action of the gun with WD-40 and worked it back and forth several times until it felt silky smooth. Then he loaded the gun, put noise mufflers on his ears, and fired to see if the ammunition was still good. The gun worked well and the pistol felt familiar in his grip. Birch had grown up with guns in the foothills of the Sierra Nevada Mountains.

He placed the pistol in the glove compartment of the Toyota truck and headed out around the lake. He pulled over a block from Vergil Rawlins's house but left the engine running. The house was dark and the twin tone '57 Chevy gone. Of course it wasn't likely that Rawlins was going to hang around town to see how the threat went down!

Birch drove down the block and pulled into Goldbug Walk. He parked his car on the apron, thinking maybe he would go into Wally's and wait around there. Maybe he could find a cigarette in the trash on the mantle (though he had looked before), or in the cushions of the couch.

Birch went into the screened porch. Beyond the screen, as

in a reflection across the lawn, he thought he saw a sliver of light. He unlocked the door and pushed it open with his foot. The evil smell engulfed him. There was something else—a cigarette.

"Helloooo," he said in a low voice, but there could be nobody in the house because he had the only key and no way anyone could get in through the big glass doors in the front. He stayed in the dark and edged into the front room. He remembered that he had left the pistol in the truck. He turned to go back when he saw the shadow to his right and a powerful arm grasped him from behind and pulled against his esophagus with an intense pain.

Birch tried to speak but he couldn't and the man pulled still tighter. Birch saw a horizon of dancing stars above the line of his sight when he came to himself and smashed down and back with his right heel and caught the man in the shin. At the same time he twisted his head into the man's armpit, smelling the rank stench of nicotine. When the man loosened from the pain Birch slipped his head out of his arm and spun and caught the man in the side of the head with the point of his elbow while shrieking something from a time long ago. He saw a flash of light and heard a voice in his head, from behind his nose. Something crashed backward into something under the stairs.

Birch was catching his breath when the form came at him again and caught him this time in the groin and imprisoned one testicle against his crotch so he would never stand again as something made of wood actually broke where his neck joined the shoulder. Birch was somehow on the other side of the room near the glass doors. The faint light of a beclouded moon lit the mounds of chaos. A hulk in the middle was breathing and making some kind of sound.

Birch felt himself in the air. He was screaming like a god when he caught the man in the side of the face with the heel of his foot. There was no pain in his groin any more, nor had there ever been. He had torn the leg from his pants while he brought the back of his fist against the man's temple with a whumph and dug razorback knuckles into the soft pathetic flesh.

Somehow the light was on. The man was slumped against the washstand against the divider to the kitchen. He was small, dark, and muscular. He wore a dark suit and white shirt with no tie. It was Wally's friend, Michael something or other, from the funeral. The man needed a haircut. A packet of Pall Mall straights peered from his suit pocket. As Birch leaned over to remove one he got a whiff of nicotine again from the man's flesh.

He had found a real smoker at last!

67. Potato salad for everyone

Birch sat down in front of the white utility table and pulled up the fancy ashtray with the WEIN AUF BIER slogan on it. Though his hand was shaking, he lit the cigarette and took a deep drag.

"I'm sorry—I didn't mean to hurt you," Birch said when the man opened his eyes, but he didn't attempt to stand up. Birch rubbed the back of his hand. "Someone killed my parrots and I'm in a stinking foul mood." (Where was the pure white light of the spirit?) "You were at the funeral—you're Wally's friend, Michael something."

"OK pal, you got the edge, I admit. I'll put you out of your misery. I said I was Michael Mitanni at the funeral, sure, but really I'm Johnny Carson."

"Wally's fake brother, you mean?" Birch stiffened.

"I'm sorry about jumping on you like that," Carson said. I thought you were that guy Vergil Rawlins. My guess is that he has his eye on this place. Where'd you learn to fight like that?"

"Really."

"Look let's try it from the top, Birch, and cut the bullshit. Do you mind if I stand up? I'm no college professor—that's what Wally liked to say, I know, but I'm a lawyer."

"I get it. Whatever Wally said, it was just the opposite."

"Yeah sure. He was a pathological liar. I don't think he was psychologically well, frankly."

Birch watched the man slowly unwind and then move across the room. Gently he let himself down in the allegedly Georgian chair with the oil spot from Wally's bald head.

"Look, Birch, I'm in something of a jam. The fact is that Wally owed me a pretty fat sum of money and I'm really not in a position to let the matter go. What is that sickening smell? But the thing is that Wally was going to pay me. You know Wally and I were very tight. Now I've got interests to protect."

"How much?"

"Big bucks."

"Ouch. Wally was broke, Carson."

"I know that. But he was going to recoup. He was going to sell this big collection he had—he'd been working on it since he was a kid. It was fantastically valuable. Antique currencies. He had some of them when we were kids even. They were the center of his life, really. Wally was desperate. He was going to sell and pay. He swore it. I've got to have that money, Birch."

"Funny thing about this famous collection—it's disappeared."

"Really? Well maybe you just haven't looked hard enough. I spoke to Wally on the Wednesday before he died. He had arranged some connection in New York."

"The collection has not been found and nobody has any idea where it might be. Only a few bills were in the washstand. There were a couple of young men here that night and one was at the funeral, Tom Allen by name. I don't think he knows anything. There was another guy, named Eric Salton, who was here too, but nobody knows where he is. I gather that he was supposed to be the courier for the sale you're talking about. Wally bought him a plane ticket, but Salton never used it. I don't think any of Wally's other stuff—this so-called art—is worth very much, Carson. It's sentimental stuff that his friends did to satisfy Wally's sense of himself."

"Yeah, well where is all the art anyway?" Carson said and

gestured to the empty walls. "And how about that big Chinese dick-like thing over there—that must be worth something."

"The art's put away, mostly. I don't think the Chinese dick is worth anything either. How'd you get in the house?"

"Over the balcony in the front. The door was unlocked."

Birch had forgotten about the door that opened just off the head of the upstairs onto a tiny and dilapidated platform above the covered porch at the front of the house.

"Do you mind if I smoke one of my own cigarettes?" Johnny Carson asked.

"Always a pleasure," Birch conceded and shook out a cigarette from the red and white pack on the white utility table and threw it across the room. He crushed out the butt of his own cigarette and lit another.

"How did you even know about the funeral?"

"Some guy named Jack Devries told me. I guess he and Wally were good friends. Somehow he had my phone number."

"*Devries* phoned you?"

Of course, Angela knew Carson's name so that made sense, Birch thought to himself, and she must have given it to Devries.

"How'd you get to town?"

"I flew. How do you think?"

"Who was the girl on the phone, when I phoned your place?"

"My old lady. She doesn't know anything about this. She doesn't even know I have a brother."

"A fake brother, you mean."

"Yeah, sure," the man flicked his cigarette, "and that's the most amazing thing. Wally and I always played this game about our being brothers but the fucking fact is that we really *were* brothers. Wally never knew it. I didn't know this myself until a couple of months ago. My father was dying. He told me. I was going to tell Wally, see, after he paid me the wad he owed—as a kind of surprise."

"I really don't get this."

"It's an old-fashioned tale. My old man knocked up some chick back in Massachusetts and that's how it happened. He was fucking this sixteen year old. My mother knew all about it. They were Catholics for Christ's sake. The priest fixed it up on the hush-hush and they farmed out the brat to a local parishioner. That child was Wally Wills. We had the same father!"

Birch slammed down his foot on the floor and the man jumped.

"Why did you do that?" Carson asked.

"And your father never told you?"

"Are you crazy? I guess he wanted to clear his conscience, see, before he died. I'll bet you been trying to find out about Wally's past, right?"

"Sure."

"Bet you haven't found much, have you?"

"That's right."

"Because he covered his fat ass. Wally threw up a smokescreen around his background ten miles thick. He was my half-brother and I did love him but frankly Wally Wills was a phony. When we were little and almost never saw each other he told me that he lived in a big white house, you know, with pillars like a southern mansion. Then one day I went to his house. It turned out to be a tract house piece of shit. I guess he forgot what he'd said because he took me home to meet his parents. That was when we lived in Worcester, Mass."

"Wally always said he was from Boston."

Carson laughed, then coughed. He took another drag on his cigarette.

"I don't think Wally ever set foot in Boston. Maybe the airport."

"This stuff about his father being some kind of entrepreneur—in carpets or something?"

Carson laughed again.

"His father was in charge of the storeroom at the Worcester knitting mills, if that's what you mean. Maybe he was a foreman. He worked there all his life. He was a Kanuck nobody. They were all big Roman Catholics—fucking Canadian immigrant Catholic fucks. That's why it was such a big deal when my old man knocked up the teenager."

"Where is Worcester, Mass?"

"It's a factory town is southern Massachusetts. A real asshole town, let me tell you. Then Wally's father—I mean his adopted father—got some sort of transfer to Oxford, Mass, when Wally and I were around twelve. That's when they moved. After that I didn't see him until we went to college."

"You went to Resurrection College too?"

"That's right. So you know that about Wally?"

"I did find that out. Wally always said he went to Tufts. I found some papers. I don't guess that Wally's mother was really a math professor at Boston College either?"

The man started to cough again and he coughed until a froth of bubbly blood appeared at the corner of his mouth, which he wiped off with the back of his hand.

"Take it easy on the upholstery, would you," Birch said.

"Yeah sure, sorry. Anyway I'm not sure that his so-called mother ever worked. Did Wally tell you she was a math professor? That's good! Wally had no fucking shame. Not one ounce. She may have been a waitress at some time but I couldn't be sure even about that. She was a housewife. Speaking of which, Birch, if you're interested, I found this when I was rummaging around in all this shit before you arrived—in a suitcase in the closet over there by the door—"

Carson fumbled in his jacket pocket and pulled out a piece of paper. Birch crossed the room and took it from him. It was a faded news clipping, the picture of a woman peeling potatoes. She held a paring knife in one hand and was crouched behind piles of potatoes on a table. She had a dumpy face and short hair curled around piggish ears and was wearing a checked sleeveless dress. She glowered at the camera. The clipping read:

MRS. GEORGE F. WILLS IS KNOWN FOR HER SPECIALTY, POTATO SALAD. MRS. WILLS AND A HELPER WILL PREPARE 150 POUNDS OF POTATOES FOR A SALAD TO BE SERVED AT A CHICKEN BARBECUE. OXFORD CHURCH 10TH ANNUAL FAIR.

A teen-age dance will launch the festivities at 8 P.M. Sept. 15 in the church hall. Music will be provided by THE INSPIRATIONS, an all-girl rock group from Webster. On Sept. 16 and 17 booths on the church grounds will be offering homemade handicrafts and barbecued chicken as well as games for all ages and hay rides for the children. A special booth will contain many new items obtained with trading stamps donated by parish members.

"That's Wally's Mom. Pathetic, really. Both of them—his parents—they were extremely small. Wally towered over them and weighed five times as much of course. You know he loved his father like crazy. I mean his adopted father. They always kissed when they saw each other. His mother loved him too but honestly she was a world-class bitch. World-class!"

"Wally said she always spoke in French."

Carson guffawed and threw the broken cigarette across the room toward the fireplace where it struck the screen and showered sparks.

"You suppose Wally left anything to drink around here?" he asked.

"Forget it."

"I don't think his mother knew a word of French, though who knows—being a fucking Kanuck and all that maybe she knew *commentallezvous*. In fact she could barely speak English. I suppose she ruined Wally's life, why not, but we all have our problems. Wally was fantastically ashamed of his parents, no doubt of that. You know we were altar boys together in Worcester. Not that either of us were religious. He came back from Oxford to attend Resurrection College in Worcester. Like I say, I saw him there occasionally. Really, from what I saw his parents were pretty affectionate toward him. The truth is that he was their pride and joy."

"Damn—we had grown fond of Wally as the Boston Brahmin."

"Sorry to disappoint you. You know a strange thing is that Wally phoned me on the Monday before he died, after we'd talked about his selling the collection and all that. I wasn't home but he left this very weird message on my answering machine, like his voice was wrought-up, excited."

"What did he say?"

"That he loved me very much. But there was something really off in his tone."

"Did he ever do that before?"

"Never."

"After somebody dies, looking back, everything is different."

"Frankly, I can't believe he's dead."

"He's dead all right."

Or what he stood for was dead. Wally himself seemed very much to be in the room, to be near them, watching them, knowing their thoughts. Birch understood the importance of ghosts and how people came to make sacrifice in their name.

68. We are lonely all

"So what else?"

"What do want to know?"

"More about his past, shit like that."

"I don't know—Wally never had a penny, but when he was in college somehow he used to get hold of nice cars to drive around. Once he had a big fucking black Cadillac. He worked in a bakery after classes, see. In order to make it seem like he had lots of money he always asked to be paid in one dollar bills. That way his wallet made a big bulge in his hip pocket and when he took it out it looked real fat and flashed a lot of green."

"Yeah, when he died he had a big wallet too."

"Sure. I must say he wasn't much of a student—the worst in fact. The priests didn't give a shit about him and he returned the compliment. They misspelled his name in the graduation brochure. Can you imagine? They were all faggots anyway. Only afterward did Wally become a good student, when he went to Chicago. Wally used to say that anyone could get a Ph.D. All you had to do was to jump through enough hoops and suck enough dick. He was good at that!"

"I guess he was."

"You know he was the most entertaining man I ever knew. That's why I kept up with him all these years, played that game about being his brother. Every once in a while he'd pull some of his bullshit on me and I'd just say, 'For Christ sake, Wally, get the fuck off—I was *there*,' and he *would* get off. I guess he was a big success out here—chairman of the department for so many years?"

Birch laughed. "Yeah, since last year and then from default. Wally was a bit too clean-cut for the locals, I'm afraid."

"Sure, he lied to me too, big surprise. Hey come on Birch, there must be a little something in a bottle around here somewhere? I need a drink. You hit me hard."

Carson rubbed the side of his face.

"I don't think so. Anyway, I'm in a really really foul mood. What was this big fight that Wally got into with his parents and relatives he was always carrying on about? I know he was always flying to the coast to *take care* of business."

"Oh yes, well after his father died, Wally got power of attorney over the bitch his mother, see. Then he sold everything she owned, including her house, and put all the money in his own account. Then he put her in a state-run nursing home. Once she was legally impecunious, he made her a ward of the state. Get it? In comes Medicaid to pick up the bills. Very sweet, really, and also standard operating procedure. That's what I'm trying to do with my own old man, I don't mind telling you. Anyway by then she had gone flippo. This sort of thing is usually done by agreement—but I think that in some way Wally went too far. I mean he has no close relatives—except me!—but some or other distant cousins were extremely pissed off by the way he had treated his mother, you know shoveling her into the death house and all that like she was so much stinking meat. Of course it wasn't REALLY his mother, see? I think they're all dead now. Come to think of it, I am probably Wally's last living relative. There was no will, huh?"

"We haven't found one."

"I was out of my fucking mind for getting in so deep with Wally. Frankly, Birch, I'd watch my ass if I were you."

"What do you mean?"

"I mean when it comes out that you've been stealing all his shit—including the collection of old money, huh? It was here the weekend before he died, bro."

"Maybe Wally was lying about that too. Maybe he sold the collection a long time ago."

"Maybe. You were the first one in this place?"

Birch silently regarded the tight rumpled man.

"Anyway Carson, you were saying—about Wally's distant cousins."

"Actually his mother's cousins, I think—"

"They didn't think he had acted properly in taking his mother's property?"

"Not that there could have been much. Just the sale of the tract house, really. But you know how things are these days."

"That's how he got the money to get into this place?"

"I don't know. I had heard it was splendiferous—with many halls and high ceilings—sorry to complain."

Birch felt a shudder of loneliness. He felt desolate, like weeping, and there was an emptiness in his heart.

69. Why not?

Carson was gone. He dropped his business card on the utility table before he straightened his jacket and brushed back his hair and left by the front door. There was a family resemblance all right— receding hairline, bouncy jowls and thighs. Not far gone like Wally, but drifting in the same direction. Johnny Carson said they'd be in touch, whether Birch liked it or not.

Maybe Wally had in fact stashed some booze somewhere. Birch had never really looked through the kitchen cabinets that Harvey had worked on. Best to get the hell out of there, but annoyed and sickened by the foul odor Birch went to the end of the room under the stairs. He swung back the couch from the wall. He got a puff so strong he thought he was going to vomit. He pulled up his shirt over his nose. For the first time he noticed beneath the open-work stairs in the shadows a small brass ring embedded in the oak floor. There was an outline in the floorboards—a trap door in the fucking floor!

Wally never said anything about a trapdoor. Birch kicked aside the debris. Still holding his shirt over his nose, he pulled up the ring. The door easily swung back against the angle of the stairs, assisted by an invisible counterweight. The smell hit him like a freight train and Birch reeled back and doubled over, useless to resist a rush of bile that filled the back of his throat. He spit into a heap of clothes on the floor and pushed outside into the night air.

After a few minutes he felt better. He went to his truck and opened the glove compartment, picked up the revolver and slipped it into his coat pocket, then took out a red bandanna and tied it around his face. He went around to the back of the truck and opened the camper flap. He crawled up into the truck bed over the layer of dirt and threw open the long black tool box where he kept his emergency supplies. He took out a five-battery magnum light and went back into the house.

Even from the door where Birch directed the powerful beam down into the black hole along a steep white wooden stair he saw it at the bottom. Pinching the bandanna around his nose, he edged down the steps. It looked like a dummy, but he couldn't see its face because the chin was deep into the chest and pitched into the angle between the bottom of the stairs and the floor of the cellar. Long blond hair draped across the face. Birch crouched at the bare blackened feet where some animal had worked away the flesh, exposing white bone. Grimacing behind the bandanna and directing the light with one hand, Birch seized the cold hard ankles and twisted the corpse so that it tipped to the side. The head angled into the rubbish overflowing between the stairs and the wall of the cellar. The man was wearing jeans and a loose shirt. Birch worked gingerly at the bulge against his buttocks and removed a wallet. He crept quickly back up the stairs and hurried to the big glass doors and out onto the deck. A quarter moon hung like bull's horns pinned to the purple sky.

After he caught his breath Birch shone the magnum light on the wallet and flipped it open. It was made of snakeskin and very handsome. Behind a plastic window he read *ERIC SALTON, Burlington Vermont.*

Birch guessed that he wouldn't have to kill Vergil Leach after all.

70. Life is the shadow of a dream

Birch was in a race, just for the fun of it. His pony was doing well against the others. The grass was high and acrid, the sun stark, cicadas buzzing. A stream up ahead, the horse shied at the deep mud and Birch swung down. He had his new leggins on and they needed to soften. They were very handsome, and he was very proud of them. This was a race he was going to win.

What day was it? He had to get up. Birch needed to tend his little babies, then get to campus. The house felt empty. But his little babies were dead. He saw the dark open eyes of the cockatoo as she lay on her back in the horror house of his mind. Vergil Rawlins, in all probability, had murdered them and now they were in his freezer downstairs.

Birch was fully awake. Wally's death and all that had happened afterward had disoriented him, but it was time to get back on track. The discovery of Eric Salton in Wally's basement had created an enormous sensation in town. *CORPSE FOUND IN DEAD PROFESSOR'S BASEMENT.* Hysterical speculation—this exhausted him. Salton died of a broken neck and everyone had a theory but after the hoopla the police found nothing. Wally's death was "accidental" and the death of Eric Salton, a rootless drifter, "unsolved, probably accidental."

Birch answered the phone. It was an old, an ancient voice.

"Do you think that this Eric Salton person was the one who killed Wally?" Audrie Winter asked.

"Mama!" Birch heard in the background. "Leave him alone!"

"Oh Audrie, it's you. I just got up and I'm a little groggy. I'd stopped thinking about it. I only wonder how he got down in that hole?"

"Well, he just fell down and died. That's what I think!"

"Audrie, he was in a cellar—underneath a trap door."

"Yes, well don't you give up Raymond. I want you to find out who killed Wally."

"Uh-huh."

"I loved him so much. That darling man."

"I know. But Audrie, I have to get on with my life and you should get on with yours."

"What life? What life do I have now?"

"Mamaaa," wailed the voice in the background.

Birch hung up and lay back in the bed. The phone rang again and when Birch picked it up from its cradle the line went dead, crackling in the wind.

71. The intellect can unravel all

In an unprecedented shift of season at the end of summer and the beginning of the fall term cold winds drove down from the Arctic across the Canadian plains, dispelling the breathless heat. In the earliest recorded frost the cold shadowed the leaves of Birch's regal oaks with reds, golds, and ambers.

Walking outside to his truck Birch said to himself that he would never again rake these leaves across the broad back yard but let them lie where they fell so that the land might return to what once it was, in the days of Blackhawk, who had once crossed his property, when a riot of oaks and saplings and willows and a woodland carpet of crisp mottled browns and yellows and scarlets covered the land.

Birch was late to the last day of the international oral poetry conference. In his confusion he went into the wrong end of the auditorium and suddenly the whole audience was staring at him as he entered in full view, just below the podium. The speaker hesitated and glanced down with annoyance as he stalked across the carpeted orchestra and dropped into a seat in the empty front row. A hundred people were behind him, gathered to hear this last speech of the conference by some famous speaker, some clown named Rosenmeyer. To Birch these people seemed pretty much the same—the conference was on "contextualizing the historical body," but Birch had no idea what that meant, or what any of it meant.

"An impassionate person's passionate need to rebuild the text from within, freed from authorial intention and reveling in the oceanic feminine that underlies the stiff (and stiffening) clarity of male cannibalistic gendered greed," the speaker, an elderly male, was saying.

Birch really wasn't feeling very well. He leaned his head forward on his knees and stared at the carpet. He thought of the spirit world that like an ocean of light surrounded the material realm, a kind of refraction of the spirit, but always it was the pure white light of the spirit itself. This room was that spirit and he was that spirit. One day the lines of his sight would join at an apex, and he would diverge outwardly into that ocean of light, he thought, as he straightened up to gaze along the row of gilt chairs. In fact he was the only one sitting in the first ten rows. Nobody wanted to be too close to a speaker of this greatness and magnitude!

"While the modern scholar needs to make concessions," Rosenmeyer was saying, "she or he has still to hang onto the hog, or the hog is going to get lickety-split away down the path!"

"What is this shit anyway?" Birch said under his breath, but louder than he had intended. Oh no, what if somebody had heard!

The conference reception was in the university art museum in a modern building just behind the faculty club and Birch was the first one to get there. He went straight to the cash bar and ordered a double scotch. Long tables of sliced pastrami, salami, cheddar, strips of celery, Swiss cheese, and other substances were set out on paper plates. As the crowds drifted in, a student in a stained waist-length white frock coat circulated with a tray of plastic cups of Chablis and Burgundy. Birch, nursing the scotch, waved him on— Oh no, it was the dark-haired boy that used to serve Wally.

Birch turned his back because he didn't want to smile and he didn't want to talk to these people, but he did need to be there because he was in a rather tight spot now that Bellamy was preparing to move against him. The proceedings against Jack Devries and the disputed vote still dragged on in committee hearings, but more and more it appeared that the initial vote would stand. That meant that Devries was still in and Birch couldn't afford just now to be seen as a curmudgeon who had no interest in current developments in the field of oral theory!

On top of everything Jack Devries had retained a personal

lawyer who was threatening Birch with a civil suit for having voted against Devries in the first place, alleging defamation of character on the basis of sexual orientation, although Birch wasn't sure how that was to be argued. Nonetheless he'd been on the phone to Ron Fettman about the matter and had sent Fettman a small retainer.

Birch stood away from the crowd beneath a close-cropped oriental plane tree whose health was maintained artificially through the long winter by specially fashioned gro-lights. Four of these truncated trees grew in the court, each surrounded by wooden benches. The artificial light from the distant ceiling suffused the court and warmed it as Birch finished his scotch and went back to the bar for another. He went back again behind the trees.

"Whatcha doin over here in the shadows?" somebody asked, coming up from behind. It was Ralph Anderson, the sad sack who had wanted Wally's ashtray. "Trying to get out of the light?" Anderson asked and flashed a golden first incisor which Birch had not noticed before.

"Too much light for one life," Birch said.

The man smiled faintly.

"Last summer was terrible, with everything that happened," said Ralph Anderson.

"Yeah, what happened?"

Ralph Anderson gave a forced laugh at Birch's joke.

"Say—whatever happened to that ashtray that Wally had, the one with the German inscription on it?"

"What?"

Birch espied Sally Brown in the crowd, looking more bedraggled than ever. Three weeks earlier she had been diagnosed with ovarian cancer and now it looked like she would be dead in six months.

"*Che cosa faci?*" Birch waved to her, lipping the words waggishly in Italian and hoping to get away from Anderson even at the expense of having to talk to Sally Brown. He wondered if Sally had caught up in her Italian studies after the interruption caused by Wally's death.

"*Io faci* any *cosa* I can," she said coming over, smiling, showing off her yellowed teeth. Birch bit into a piece of bread and cheese. Sally Brown had lost a lot of weight, probably because of the cancer, and Birch wondered if they were shooting her up with chemo and all the other stuff they did to sick people until they died. Sally was wearing a purple shirt with a black tie and she sprayed saliva in an arc as she spoke.

"I'll bet you do, *professore*," he said. "And that's why everyone admires us so much."

Sally looked puzzled.

"So what're you working on these days, Ray?" she asked.

"Working on?"

Anderson continued to stand near them, hands in his pockets that pulled down his loose pants. Probably best just to make excuses and get the fuck out of here, make a run for the door, thought Birch.

"Speak of the devil—!" Sally said.

"Huh?"

"There's Jack Devries," Sally said.

Birch saw him too, locked in conversation with Angela Bellamy on the other side of the room.

"Right, Sally. Look, I gotta go pretty quick. Would you excuse us for a moment, Anderson?"

Birch took Sally Brown by the upper arm and moved her to the side. He waited until Anderson wandered away.

"So, heard anything recently about the hearings on the Devries case?" Birch asked.

"No," she sighed.

Without Wally's skillful diplomacy, differences were swiftly emerging between Birch and Sally Brown.

"Except that now he's living with Angela," she said.

"Devries is living with Bellamy?"

"You know her husband is not well ..."

"You know that Devries is trying to sue me because I voted against him—on some or other hyped up grounds—because he's a woofer I guess. Is that right? Is Devries a woofer, Sally?"

"Well, you know he used to live with Wally."

"That was twenty years ago! It takes more than that. Anyway, is he suing you too Sally?"

"Not yet."

"Yeah. Because you voted both ways. Look I do have to go—you take care."

72. The death of Milman Parry

By now the hall was filled with conferees and luminaries, some from the former Soviet Union, and Birch put down his plastic cup on a trestle table and left Sally Brown. He went toward the main door but he sidled past the bar set-up on a glass-topped table just inside the patio doors and, what the hell, he signaled to the bartender for one more Scotch. The man in front of him—medium build, clean shaven, fiftyish, wearing a gray suit and a red bow tie—turned suddenly and saw Birch's name tag.

"Oh, how fortunate—Professor Raymond Birch."

"Oh Hi—you are ... Professor Hajji," said Birch, reading the man's tag and knowing him by reputation, though they had never met. To Birch's irritation the man began to ask him about his background and mutual acquaintances and about current projects and about the presentations. The man let slip that he had been curator of the Milman Parry collection at Harvard, a mass of undigested data gathered from illiterate poets, mostly Muslim, in the Serbian hill country in the 1930s. Milman Parry proved that the *Iliad* and the *Odyssey* were composed without the aid of writing. He was the greatest Homeric scholar of the twentieth century and had single-handedly revolutionized understanding of the origins of Western culture.

"Really?" Birch said and emptied his new drink. At last he

felt a good buzz coming on. He only hoped that Sally Brown across the room didn't see him lingering here.

"Yes!" Professor Hajji nodded eagerly and raised his eyebrows.

"You know—it's hard to believe now," Birch said, "but it was Parry's work that first got me interested in oral poetry. A teacher of mine, a classicist named Bundy—Bundy was an undergraduate in the 1950s and he told me this story how once he found one of Parry's original books, the very one with the underlinings that convinced Parry that Homer was an oral poet. He found this book in a bookstore on Haste Avenue in Berkeley, see, but he didn't have the money to buy it, so he went home to borrow some money from a friend. When he went back to the store the book was gone! Bundy regretted this for the rest of his short life. I wonder who bought it, eh?"

"Aha, yes, good story," said Hajji.

"I guess Parry was a bit of a wild man," said Birch, signaling to the bartender for still another.

"He was very romantic, yes," Hajji agreed. "You know he used to dress up in Montenegran garb and he always carried a gun. He thought he was going to be robbed. There were bandits in the hills of Bosnia those days."

"Not like today, eh?"

"So that's why he carried a pistol wherever he went," Hajji laughed.

"Of course you didn't know Parry?"

"Do I look that old? No, but I knew his son," said Hajji.

"Well tell me, how did Milman Parry die? Was it suicide like everybody says, or what? And how old was he when he died?"

"He was thirty-four years old. The year was 1933. Everybody thought it was suicide of course. What would you think? He was staying at a hotel in Los Angeles while visiting his wife's family. He opened his suitcase to get out a shirt, dropped the suitcase, and the gun fell out and discharged. The bullet struck him in the chest and killed him instantly."

"Very romantic," Birch mused.

"I understand you lost one of your own people here in a

similar incident last summer … Wally Wills—at the bottom of the stairs at his country estate? Suffering from AIDS, I heard. Or was it a suicide-murder? Something about a second body?"

"Oh my God, no, nothing like that," Birch protested. "Nothing's as it seems. Hardly a similar case. Where did you hear that anyway?"

Birch's eyes traced across the crowd and he again saw Jack Devries, but now in conversation with a heavyset woman who just then swiveled around. Oh shit, it was Dean Karla Marsh.

"Yes, well I think everyone heard about it," Hajji said. "As for the Parry family, violence seems to have followed it everywhere. His son, Adam, you know, was killed in a motorcycle accident."

"I guess I heard that. I met Adam Parry once, in New Haven. He was a Homerist too, and a good one," said Birch.

"Sure, Adam had just flown to Strasbourg with his girlfriend Anne Amory," said Hajji. "He had a rented motorcycle waiting for him. The two of them zoomed off. Before Parry reached the corner he tried to pass a truck. Some kind of bar was sticking out from the truck and both he and the woman were beheaded!"

"Ouch! How old?"

"Mid-forties."

"Uh-huh. Awful. You know I once had a class from Anne Amory, the woman you're talking about," Birch said.

"No! Is that possible?"

"Absolutely, Anne Amory. She was a tough cookie all right," said Birch, watching Devries and Marsh, "even for those days."

Sally Brown came up to Devries and Karla Marsh. Now the three were talking. He thought he saw Sally move her chin in his direction.

"Yeah, I knew about Adam Parry and I knew Anne Amory," Birch said, "but I never heard this stuff about the motorcycle and the beheading."

"Incredible but true," said Hajji and he licked his mouth with a large tongue. "And Adam's son, Milman's grandson—he also died in a bizarre fashion."

"Really?"

"He had bought this house in southern France, near Tarbes, you see."

"Uh-huh."

"He wanted to relax out there, to be away from it all. He had just married a beautiful French girl."

"I can imagine."

"Then he tried to change a bulb in the basement. He was standing in a pool of water."

"No!"

"They found him the next day stiff as a board, still clinging to the socket," said Hajji.

"Son of a bitch! Well I guess philology is a rough game all right." Birch drained the Scotch. "Are there still more Parrys to carry on the line?"

"Gone. The name is extinct, though there are relatives on the female side."

"I'm sorry to hear it, Professor Hajji, and I'm also sorry that I have to go."

"So soon?"

"I'm sorry too," Birch said and shook his hand.

73. Life plays tricks

Birch made a beeline through the crowd, saying Hi this time to the dark-haired waiter, but the boy didn't recognize him, when to his surprise he saw Evelyn Cornel, of all people, standing alone beneath a fifteen-foot high hideous painting of an eighteenth century lady of fashion. Her full robes flowed like impassioned water from a pert pink bosom as she raised one arm to a pink hat bound in a scarlet band.

"She looks just like you," Birch whispered behind Evelyn's ear, moving close to her.

Eddy Cornel's wife turned and for an instant she seemed terrified.

"Sorry, I didn't mean to scare you. What are you doing here?"

Her beautiful face was sharpened somehow, different.

"Eddy is at the conference—he thought he'd come ... he misses the university life, you know ..."

"So do we all. I didn't know oral epic was his preference. Where is he?"

"I don't know. He's here."

"So, how've you been?"

She was as if steel and Birch a magnet and he realized that he desired her but there was certainly no point in anything like that. Birch was angry with himself for his desire as she fell against him. He put her head against his shoulder so he could touch the back of her neck and try to calm her down.

"So, how does the Jim Dine look?" Birch asked.

"It looks fine." She raised her head.

"I barely know you, and you are married to Eddy," Birch said.

"Sure, I am married to Eddy."

"How did that happen, if you don't mind my asking?"

"You mean Eddy? I met him at Wally's. We went to my house. I got pregnant. It was easy."

"Ah, but now he has steady work and the old life is gone?"

Her eyes were actually swollen. Birch thought of his own mother who had often wept.

"If I can help you—let me know. Any time," Birch said.

"Thanks."

"We were all friends of Wally, eh?"

Birch was buzzy from the Scotch.

"Think she really looked like that?" Eddy Cornel asked, coming up from behind and nodding to the painting. On his pinkie flashed Wally's ruby ring. He beamed and smiled and showed his white teeth.

"I didn't know you were into this stuff, Cornel," said Birch.

"Hell Ray, I take it where I can get it."

Birch looked back at Evelyn but she stared blankly at the lady in the pink bonnet.

74. Et tu, Brute?

"**H**ey, I saw Jack Devries in the crowd," Eddy said, thumbing in the direction of the staircase that led to the second floor and the exhibit of ancient Greek art.

"Yeah, I saw him too, Eddy."

"I thought you and Wally had sacked his ass?"

Birch looked where Eddy pointed. Devries was talking to three young women. Devries gestured expansively.

"Yeah—hey excuse me guys, I just remembered something," said Birch, winked at Eddy, and touched Evelyn on the shoulder. He walked straight and somewhat unsteadily toward Devries and his admirers.

"Hi Jack," Birch said when he got close.

Devries stopped talking and narrowed his eyes.

"Ladies, this is Professor Raymond Birch," Devries said studiously.

"You don't need to introduce us," said Charlotte something or other, the one who had had her tubes tied so she could get on with the important work, who had warned him about the impending blackmail.

"Sure—Hi Charlotte, and sorry to barge in like this, but

Jack—I know there's been trouble between us but, uh, this is an emergency. I think we should talk about it."

"What emergency?"

"Jack, please come with me outside for a moment. I'm really sorry, ladies."

The women looked at one another nervously. One pushed away a lock of oily hair.

"It's cold outside, Raymond," said Devries.

"Please Jack, it will only take a minute." Birch took him by the elbow and squeezed hard. "It's about our friend the late Wally Wills," Birch whispered.

Jack went pale as the blood in his tiny veins drained away.

"What about Wally?"

Of course it was a long shot, but Birch didn't see where was the harm in putting the squeeze on Jack Devries for a change, who was squeezing Birch very hard.

Birch hurried Jack down the broad polished granite steps that led from the museum foyer, through thick glass doors, into a biting wind. He half-pulled, half-pushed him across the quad to the wooded path along the shore of the lake, beyond the student union, all the way ignoring Jack's whining complaints.

"What about Wally Wills?" Jack kept saying.

"It's been a good while now since Wally died, old bean," Birch answered at last when there was no one around, "but I thought you'd like to know that the police have never lost interest in this affair." Birch lied. "And frankly, it looks to me like what with this Eric Salton fellow they found dead under the floorboards, and Wally with a bump on his head—I think you see my point. You've done me a couple of favors in the past so I thought I'd do you one—what with your name popping up and I thought you might like to talk about it before this thing gets out of hand. Let's put this whole renewal mess aside, Jack, Sally's changed vote and all that—and think about murder and how you fit in."

"Go to hell, Birch, and let go of my arm!"

Jack's skin was carmine in the brisk air, but Birch had caught his attention all right.

"So you're living with Angela now?"

"I help with the groceries. Is that any of your business?"

The cold wind had turned the lake from blue to black. Still, mallards and pintails swam indifferently off the shore or perched on logs half in the water and half on the land.

"You want to sit down on a log or something, Jack? The problem is that we found your name and phone number in Wally's wallet, something we've never had a chance to talk about. It was so odd that you knew just where Audrey's chair was, next to the bed, and everybody thought you guys weren't speaking. Two plus two, Jack. Facts and explanations."

"That's Angela's phone number!"

"Uh-huh, Oh, really. But you and Wally were seeing each other, huh?"

Devries looked at Birch with undisguised hatred. But in the academy such stares are common.

"It's just a question of time, Devries. There were people at Wally's that night, and they've asked me, you know, for leads in their continuing investigation, etcetera. I've been meaning to have a chat with you about this for a long time. It's ongoing! Frankly Jack, from the beginning you've been hanging around the edges of Wally's death like a *mal odeur*. What if they called you in?"

Birch hated himself for behaving in this way, for bullying this foolish young man who only sought his own preservation. Did he owe it to Wally? What were his motives exactly?

"So Wally knew a lot of people, big deal."

"Sure, but what was going on between you and Wally is what I'm asking, Jack. After a little sex maybe that night, huh, maybe you quarreled, there were bad feelings about ancient crimes. How does this Eric Salton fit in? I mean he's a stranger, from out of town. Maybe you came in on them—Wally bought Salton an airline ticket so maybe he owed him. We should have talked about all this a long time ago, Jack, so excuse me for waiting so long to bring it up. Certainly Salton went back to Wally's and, you know, maybe you came in on them, jealous rage and so forth. I'm just speculating! The place was a wreck—it's an easy place to get hurt in, I mean no railings on the stairs and none on the loft. I bet you liked to sit in the big black captain's chair, hey Jack?"

Birch was breathing hard. He had Devries on the run and it was time to finish him off.

"Go to hell, Birch."

"Jack, there's evidence, that's the whole point," Birch lied again. "The neighbors saw, Jack."

"What neighbors?"

"You came in on them—there was a fight, somebody got hurt. Maybe it wasn't murder but maybe it was. I think we need to get this in the open, Jack, that's the main thing."

"You really don't get it, do you?"

"I think I do, Jack."

"No—" Jack said in a low voice. "I *loved* Wally. I loved him very much and he loved me ... we were always lovers, yes ... I don't know anything about this Eric ... I never saw him in my life ... it was only a front he put on, conspiring with you to get rid of me ... Wally told me everything ... you never had a chance to pull it off, but the gambit set us in the clear, do you see at last? ... you think I like living like this? ... Wally said he would always take care of me no matter what and I know he meant it."

Birch sighed.

"Sure, Wally was a caring guy."

Birch was shaken by Jack's revelation and racing to see what it might mean.

"OK, I was there that night, I don't mind saying it. But Wally was totally OK when I left. *I swear it.* I mean he was drunk and coked but he was OK. When I phoned him in the afternoon he could barely talk and I thought that something was wrong—that's why I went over ... he'd been having some kind of party but he was alone when I got there ... I *loved* Wally ... I'll talk to the police if you want, I don't care. Why haven't they contacted me?"

"Uh-huh."

"I didn't kill him. We went upstairs but right afterwards I left. He was lying on the bed upstairs when I left."

"Uh-huh."

"I wish Wally were alive. I can't believe he's dead! I even talk to him. I told Angela everything ... you can ask her ... she *told* me to keep quiet ... Ask Angela."

"Oh I'll do that," Birch said.

"I saw Vergil Rawlins at the window of his house up the street when I drove away—watching. What about him? Did anyone ever question him? I *loved* Wally Wills."

Birch fell silent. A drake followed his hen in the shallows, dodging lazily between the woven brush in the icy water.

"And Brutus loved Caesar," he said, feeling the loss of his friend.

75. Some people can tell

Birch crossed the boulevard and got into his truck and pulled out into traffic. Wally had deceived him about Devries then. What had been Wally's real intentions? Did he just like to see people move? There was a deep crime in Wally's behavior, yet Birch had loved him too. Certainly Birch had used Wally to justify his own vices.

Birch picked up a tape from the pile scattered on the seat and shoved it into the cassette and turned on the player, thinking it was his favorite Juke Boy Bonner tape with LIFE IS A NIGHTMARE but out came instead the voice of a ghost ... the voice of Wally Wills.

Birch shot out the tape and read the label *ART AS INVESTMENT, WBA RADIO*—Oh, one of the tapes he had taken out of Wally's Lexus before he returned it to the leasing agency. He pushed the tape back in and listened. It was a talk show and a woman caller was asking about a Salvador Dali print she had bought in California.

"... Oh yes, my dear..." Wally interrupted with a sigh. "I think the skullduggery began after the date of your purchase. It's probably OK."

Then the radio host took a call from a woman with a strong German accent who had bought a Chagall lithograph in Switzerland in 1953 and the signature on the neck of the figure disturbed her.

"If I were you, my dear, I would bring it to me immediately at the University Museum. I can always spot a fake," Wally proclaimed.

"Oh I hope it isn't a fake," she shrieked.

"So do we both, my dear," Wally said. "But if you have an eye, and if you have an enthusiasm, hopefully, you will buy wisely. May God bless you."

The radio host said something about the federal secretary of education recommending a requirement in art history for high school graduates.

"I couldn't be happier about this," Wally said—"and add Latin and Greek and we would have a really intelligent and democratic people. I think one reason why people spell less well is because of course they have no fundamentals and that's why they *live* less well too. They don't have the content that art can give to their lives."

The moderator took a call from somebody who wanted to know the difference between signed and unsigned works of art.

"Unsigned works," Wally pronounced "—well, we may mean that in two different ways. I *love* unsigned works—I *collect* unsigned works because to me it is the great surprise to look at the work, to appreciate it, to develop an eye and to appreciate the painting just because it is a painting without a signature—here I think is the best kind of collector ... After all, there are still connoisseurs ... the thrill of an unsigned work is that it is a work of art that you might want to *investigate* ..."

Another telephone caller thought that he owned an unsigned Delacroix. Wally laughed and used words like "atelier" and spoke in a broad Boston accent, saying "ahrt" for "art." Another caller wanted to know where art was *really* headed for in modern times. Wally spoke of Adam Smith and inner tempo and desperate times and delight.

"Yes, art is a mystery, just as life. We lead our lives and each paints his own canvas, but there is no signature and what it really means no one can ever say."

"You mean that art is a mystery?" the caller said.

"Art is a mystery—and so is life. And no one knows the meaning of either."

"Not even God?" said the caller.

"Not even God!" Wally said.

"Not an ounce of shame," Birch snapped and shot out the tape as driving with his left hand he scrambled with his right hand in the glove compartment where he was sure he had stashed, somewhere, a big bomber loaded with Tijuana red.

76. A stranger in his own land

It was dark and Birch was high as a kite when he pulled into his drive and started down the path to his house. At first he saw the shadow near the large bush to the right of the path and then another from behind the large oak to the left of the path. Then something muffled in his ears, though it was a dark night. The sky opened up in a shower of light and for a second Birch thought he had died, at last, and entered the pure white light of the spirit forever. What's the loss in that?

But he smelled the rich grass. An enormous weight across his chest kept him from moving, and everything was stuck in a plasma so that he couldn't get his breath. Now there was an aureole around the light which wasn't the light he saw before but a pale earthly imitation, doleful really, and some kind of voice in the distance was talking, and there was something loose in his mouth.

"I don't think you're getting the point," the voice was

saying.

"Uh-huh," Birch heard himself agreeing.

"Don't play games with me."

Oh—Vergil Rawlins, the greatest drug czar in many counties. Had he grown four extra arms?

"Wally said you were an asshole," said Birch. "But for a second I thought you were the dean."

"Dean who?"

"The gal who murdered Wally Wills."

"What are you talking about?"

"I'm sorry Vergil, but the explanation is likely to run into three syllables."

The light wobbled and disappeared and then came on again inside Birch's head and he smelled the sweet scent of blood. His own.

"Thanks Vergil, I needed that. You're really good at that."

"You piss me off Birch. You treat me like shit but you can't."

"You killed Wally, didn't you? I was on the way out to your place to explain all this in person."

"You're full of shit."

"Come on Vergil, the cops are on to you."

"You're crazy. He's been dead for months."

"They're just taking their time preparing the case. They found the cocaine. They know all about you. You were watching the house when Devries left. He's willing to testify. Do you think Wally fell down the stairs? Would you mind taking this knee out of my eye? I got a call from Lieutenant Little of the Townsend police only yesterday. The lab reports are in—coked to the gills. You're going down, Rawlins. I'd say it's only a matter of days ... or even hours."

"You're insane! All that happened a long time ago," said the disembodied voice.

If Birch could get a breath, everything would be better, but to the enormous weight on his chest was added an excruciating pain in his brain. Hadn't he just been talking to Jack Devries, about the same matters?

"... treat me with some respect ..."

"Huh?"

"What did you tell them?" his voice seemed lower, which Birch took as a bad sign.

"I'm sure we could discuss this in comfort. Like at the bottom of a well."

"Keep him down," Vergil said to somebody. "What did you tell the police?"

"Why don't you ask them? You were there and they know about it. He owed you big dollars, you got in an argument—that's why you're here, isn't that right? Wally owed and you were tired of waiting. You killed the stud in the basement too, the kid from Burlington—sound like a musical?—you killed Wally when he wouldn't pay and you killed the boy too. It's only a question of time, Rawlins."

"You told this to the police?"

"The way I see it this guy Tom and his buddy Eric Salton got him fucked up pretty good, then cleared out sometime in midday, like they said, and a little later Jack Devries, alarmed about Wally's health, breezed in for some service. Jack and I have been over this pretty thoroughly. After he left, you came down to discuss accounts. That's when the killing started. For God's sake, Rawlins, I'm a professor!"

Vergil reached around the light and pushed something cold into Birch's nose.

"Think what you want, professor, but I didn't kill Wally Wills and I don't know anything about it. You're right—I saw Devries leave the house. I did go to Wally's and, sure, he was in a state. We did have words but he was going to get the money—he had a certain business deal. See it from my side Birch. I *owe* people and now the waiting is over."

Birch tried to move his hands, thinking he could get to his pocket and the Smith and Wesson, but they didn't seem to be working.

"I guess this is the sort of trouble you're asking for when you live in a house with no neighbors, huh Rawlins?"

"You're an ass Birch. How're your feathered friends?"

"I agree you've got the advantage and come to think of it your claims seem fair, now that you've explained the details. But you're going to have to give me a little time."

"You're selling Wally's house, aren't you? I saw a sign up ... there's going to be money there ..."

"Sure, well Wally was behind a thousand miles. They were about to foreclose. But look I'll give you a call in the morning and we can talk about this whole matter. When you get right down to it, money doesn't mean a thing to me. To me, it's always the life of the mind."

"And the hands—in someone else's pockets?"

"Reality is my sandwich, Rawlins."

"Try eating this one then, Professor Birch!"

Birch saw the white light again. Then the weight was gone from his chest. After awhile he tried to stand up but kept pitching to the left onto the grass, so he kept down close to the ground where there was no place to fall. In this fashion Birch made his way to the wooden screen door of the back of the house where he scratched like a dog until he remembered there was no one to let him in.

77. Life goes on

On the next morning Birch came around and the first thing he noticed was that he was not feeling very well. He would explain to his colleagues how he had run into a door and then turned around and run into it four more times in the middle of the night. Of course there was his otherwise profligate and unconventional behavior to be taken into consideration.

In any event, they would use it against him.

Birch was also going to have to see a dentist and probably tell the police everything, that he was being blackmailed by a dope dealer and that his house had been broken into and his pets murdered. Of course there was the matter of the pot garden in his basement. And the matter of what had actually happened to Wally's art and furniture, sold to friends at rock-bottom rates, or still resting under burlap in Birch's garage. Not that any of it was worth a nickel, even if the Fodamew Gallery thought otherwise. As far as Birch could see, the Townsend police could hardly keep a dog from shitting on the lawn!

"I'm contemplating murder, again," Birch said aloud, depressed by his enthusiasm. He might as well take out Jack Devries while he was at it, and Angela Bellamy, and, why not, Karla Marsh. Make a clean fucking sweep.

Birch got up, showered, and turned on the TV to the Today Show, a special story about sexual misdemeanors in high places. While watching the show, Birch ate a breakfast of Muesli with sliced banana, but his stomach was jittery. The guest on the show looked like Birch's son, whom he rarely saw any more. They had grown apart. But he always sent him a little something, a token on birthdays and Christmas.

The phone rang. A voice at the other end came from a small girl far away, laughing eerily. Perhaps she was not standing up to the receiver, Birch thought, and, Oh, it must be that cute little girl who lived down the street and always waved to him when he passed.

"Hellooo ..." he crooned.

But she was still talking and, No it was certainly not the girl down the street. With a chill Birch realized that he couldn't understand a single word that the girl was saying. Then the phone clicked off.

He put it out of his mind and went into the kitchen and made a cup of coffee. He sat back down at the table and drank it. The coffee made him feel better, but sleepy like coffee always did, so he went back into the bedroom and lay down and fell asleep.

When he awoke it was past noon and he was hungry again so Birch went back into the kitchen and put a frozen micro-wave pizza in the micro-wave. He turned on the TV but he had to hurry because he had a big lecture at 2:00. He had taped a Brian de Palma movie on HBO about a woman who was murdered by an electric drill and he watched this movie for awhile while waiting for the pizza to cook, then flicked it off with the remote control and sorted through the soap operas, looking for the one that had the man with the eye patch. But he couldn't find it.

When the pizza was ready, Birch opened a bock beer, got down a bag of potato chips and a jar of hot Santa Fe peppers from the fridge, and ate. He glanced at his watch. It was 1:00 and he really had to get going.

"Say, Professor Birch," someone shouted from the front row, when he came into the lecture hall, "what happened to your face?"

Birch touched the Smith and Wesson in his jacket pocket. He thought of shooting into the ceiling to make a strong impression. All he needed was a little real cash to buy off Rawlins and then, well, get on with his life. The hell with it. He was sick of the whole thing. He deserved some of the loot no doubt ... no cops, no mess—what was the problem?

"I cut myself shaving," Birch said to the students and went on to explain in a booming voice to the audience of five hundred how, as a typical hero of oral song, Achilles was an absolutist who wished that all his companions were dead so that only he and his buddy Patroclus were left alive. Then the two of them could by themselves burn down the city of Troy and kill every man in it, rape every woman, and throw the children from the walls. "Perhaps, even, dine on the flesh of man-killing Hector, son of Priam. For that's the way it was in those days," he concluded.

---

78. Doing the best you can

Birch had never noticed the shop COINS AND STAMPS FROM AROUND THE WORLD, only a quarter of a mile down County Z from Wally's place, but it occurred to him as he drove past the shop that afternoon that he might possibly discover the value of the six or seven old fashioned bills enclosed in plastic that he had gotten with Wally's effects from the coroner. Why not check it out?

Just before closing time, he took them into the shop and spread them across the glass counter top. A squat bald man in a soiled white shirt and striped navy pants pulled tightly over his thighs held up an eye-glass and inspected the currencies through their plastic covers.

"They worth anything?" Birch inquired.

The man put down the bills and placed the eyeglass on the counter.

"Where'd you get these?"

"Well—I inherited them."

"Hmmm, I see. You know there was a fellow in town here—a professor at the university, big fat fellow—he used to collect things like these. I think he just recently died of AIDS or something. He had the best collection of mint condition old paper currencies I've ever seen. These are just as good—in fact he had one just like this one. They're extremely valuable, if that's what you want to know. Do you want to sell them?"

Birch didn't like this conversation at all.

"Well, I'm not sure. I mean I inherited them. I have kind of a sentimental attachment to them. How much are they worth, would you say? Ballpark, I mean."

"Oh, a great deal. But I don't deal in paper. Only in coins. I couldn't really tell you for sure. Do you want to sell them?"

"I thought you said you didn't buy things like this?"

"That's true, but there's an auction house down in Detroit—I mean if you do want to sell them—that raises the best prices in general on things like this. They draw an international crowd and, you know, people with serious money. HORNING'S, a few miles outside of town on the interstate. You want the address?"

"I don't see how it can hurt!"

The man on the phone from Horning's told Birch that he'd be glad to look over the bills and that, as luck would have it, they were just about to finalize a major auction of coins and currencies. He would Fedex a circular to Birch and other information about the sale.

Birch was pleasantly surprised when he got the Fedex on the next day to see that on that very Saturday Horning's would also be holding an auction of Indian artifacts, right down his alley. With a kind of hunger Birch went through their catalog, lingering over the description of a Blackfoot beaded elkskin war shirt with ermine drops and matching leggings that had belonged to the Sioux chief William Spotted Crow of Pine Ridge. With the shirt came photographs of William Spotted Crow wearing it, and also a classic hand-tinted pose showing the shirt in great detail. The probable sale price—$75,000!

"Shit, but what's that to me?" he said aloud.

Of course his idea had been to raise maybe $10,000 to stave off Vergil Rawlins, but Birch didn't really see a contradiction because Indian artifacts weren't exactly like cocaine shoved up your ass or anything and certainly he wasn't getting any younger. Birch began to wonder if there might be some way he could get Vergil Rawlins out of his life and at the same time get some good stuff down at the sale. Of course the shirt ... that was out of the question. Not a rational plan, but a plan nonetheless.

"OK, play it by ear," he advised himself.

79. The finest that money can buy

On Sunday he took the obscure turn-off ten miles outside Detroit, crossed back over the tollway, then took a sharp left that led him onto the frontage road. He drove past rows of neat factories and at last found the Quonset hut and the big sign HORNING'S. He parked in front. He got out and locked the doors of his truck. A stiff wind blew dry leaves across the nearly empty lot. Birch had purposely arrived two hours before the auction so as to give himself plenty of time to consign the currencies and then look over the lots in the Indian auction. He could get squared away and maybe sound out the auctioneer about what the currencies would bring and how soon would he have his money.

He opened the heavy metal doors by pushing against the transverse bar with his back and went inside through a spare foyer to the auction hall set up at one end of the hut, separated from the rest of the interior space by offices. At the end of an aisle that led through the offices, in the inner recesses of the dark metal building, were bedsteads and dressers and antique cars. Rows of brown-enameled metal folding chairs were set up in the cordoned area just inside the door, a few of them already occupied. At the front of the rows of chairs was the auctioneer's lectern and behind that long tables covered with items for the auction.

In a glance Birch took in the Indian baskets and cowboy chaps and boxes of books on Indians and war clubs and beaded moccasins and modern southwestern and prehistoric pottery and to the right of the lectern in long rows of movable partitions were kitschy paintings and prints of Navajo medicine men making sand paintings, buffalo dancers, pueblos with Indian maids carrying vases on picturesque heads, cowboys standing in high mountain valleys brushing their pokes, Hopi Kachinas, deer scratching their ears with their hind feet, squaws with papooses mounted in beaded slatted carriers, buffalo hunters fighting Indians on the high plains from behind fallen horses, and war chiefs with eagle-feathers in their hair. There were also pictures of shields portraying visions induced through pain and starvation, pow-wow dancers, mystical maidens descending on ghostly teepees, stallions fighting, voyageurs in long canoes, and the Indian dead devoured by vultures. To the left of the lectern, set up in high glass cases, were the good stuff—quilled legging strips and silver jewelry and antique pottery and guns. All this, brought together, was a delight to behold.

Birch was walking past the glass windows of the offices when he noticed the very Blackfoot war shirt hanging on the back wall along with beaded vests and a Crow martingale and Winnebago and Chippewa bandoleer bags. He ignored the chill he got and turned the corner at the end of the windows and peered over the counter.

"Hi," he said to the receptionist, who was fooling around with a computer. "I had an appointment with a Mr. Measles? I need to consign some antique currencies."

The receptionist was small and pretty with dark hair and almond eyes. Birch wondered if maybe she was the daughter of whoever owned this place. She did seem high quality, but he was easily impressed. She said she'd be right back. She wended through empty desks and disappeared into an office, then emerged immediately with a man wearing a bedraggled pin-striped suit with dark bags under his eyes. The man wore thick black-rimmed glasses.

"Hello, I'm Mr. Measles," he said. His clear youthful voice reminded Birch of the lawyer Ron Fettman.

"I spoke to you on the phone about a consignment of antique currencies?"

"Oh yes, let's see," said the man.

Birch took out of his inner coat pocket the handful of bills encased in plastic and placed them on the counter.

"Someone told me they are valuable but I sort of wondered how valuable, if you could, you know, give me a ballpark figure."

"You have an inventory?"

Birch took from his inner coat pocket a folded list he had prepared that described as best he could the bills' condition and date and the name of the engraver and printer, which he'd looked up in reference volumes he'd taken from Wally's.

"Oh these are fine, these are fine," said Mr. Measles. "These are very nice pieces, very nice. Oh this one—" he picked up a bill whose centerpiece showed an Indian in full headdress—"this is wonderful—this should bring a very high price. We don't get bills of this quality very often, I can tell you."

For a second the man's enthusiasm made Birch regret his whole plan. Maybe he should just keep the collection and go ahead with his instinct to kill Vergil Rawlins and then make a run for it? But that was not a rational plan either.

"I guess it sort of goes with your Indian auction," Birch said and tried to laugh.

"Yes, yes, that's a good point," Mr. Measles said and looked Birch in the eye.

"I collect Indian stuff too, you see," Birch said.

"Oh do you? Indian artifacts? Well, maybe you'd like to stay for our auction? Well, all this looks very fine, as I say. You are—uh, Mr. Raymond Birch, I spoke to you on the phone?"

"That's right."

"You will need to fill out this contract and then we will be all set. The currency auction is two weeks hence."

"Oh, I got here just in time, eh?"

"We'll even print up a special flyer."

Birch filled out the contract which was in quintuplicate so he had to press down hard with the Horning's Auction House black retractable ball-point pen.

"You're from up north, then," said Mr. Measles watching him write his address. "You know just recently we had somebody else from your town with another outstanding collection."

"Indian artifacts, you mean? Yes, there are quite a few collectors up there. What was the name?"

"No, not Indian artifacts, I meant old paper currencies, like yours. And it was a woman. With your contribution and hers, Mr. Birch, we will have one of the strongest auctions this year."

"Really?"

"Yes, really. Wonderful examples—like yours, but many more of course. She had fractional currencies, rare silver certificates,

Bank notes, Confederate issues, National currency notes—a little bit of everything and everything in absolutely mint condition. You know mostly only men collect old money for some reason—I don't know why—but this young woman said she had been collecting them all her life, since she was a child."

"I suppose she needed the money, huh?"

Mr. Measles looked at Birch as if he had just farted.

"Do you remember her name?" Birch went on.

"Oh, well we never divulge such information, Mr. Birch, as I'm sure you'll understand. Now if you will please just sign here, Mr. Birch, then everything will be in perfect order. I'm sure you'll enjoy today's auction. We at Horning's are proud of offering the finest material to discriminating collectors and buyers, always."

80. A close call

The conversation with Measles had thrown off Birch's focus and just before the auction was about to open he realized that he had never got from Mr.Measles an estimate of the value of the currencies, the most important thing, which had a critical bearing on how deep he was prepared to go in the Indian auction. He found a seat in the third row of folding chairs, now mostly filled with potential buyers. A man seated next to Birch looked at him with sympathy.

The best thing would be to leave immediately, Birch thought, but instead he remained seated, and soon enough the large eager crowd was bidding on a military-marked tack-studded Indian-used Colt single-action .45 revolver in a tack-studded worn holster with a quilled and beaded belt attached. The bidding started at

$7,000 and quickly went to $12,000, then $15,000 and sold for $32,500.

"Wow," Birch said aloud.

"That was nice," the man next to him said.

Birch watched the items fly by, twenty, then a hundred and thirty items. Up came a matched pair of quilled possible bags. Very sweet. The bidding started at $8,000 then jumped by $1,000 increments to $17,000. Feeling crazy, Birch raised his hand at $18,000 and for a minute the bidding stopped dead. The man nodded at Birch and asked once for a higher bid—once, then twice, and a shock of fear went through Birch. Shit, he was going to get them. Then a phone bid came in at $20,000 and the bidding broke away again until the bags sold for $38,000 over the phone. The audience burst out in applause, but Birch was covered in sweat.

"Who *are* these people?" Birch complained to the man on his other side, whose immense gut was enswaddled by a concho belt with big nuggets of turquoise. The man wore an enormous Zuni bolo tie in the form of an Apache Yei dancer.

"They got more money than me," the man snorted and took out a cigar and began to chew on the end. "When the sonsofbitches from New York and Santa Fe get in the act, there isn't a goddam thing you can do and that's a fact," he said.

Birch put his head between his knees to get his circulation back. Then he straightened up and took a deep breath.

Everything was going to be just fine.

81. Someone to talk to

The leaves twinkled in the trees outside the window. He had meant to close his eyes for a moment but when he opened them the dusky mists had poured around the leaves which now merged with the gray of the downcast sky. Birch decided to make the call.

He went into the library and found Eddy Cornel's number still posted on his bulletin board along with the numbers of Ron Fettman and Audrie Winters and Harvey Vanderpool and Vergil Rawlins and Sally Brown and all the others who had recently obtruded into his life.

Evelyn Cornel answered the phone.

"*La belle* Evelyn, it's Raymond Birch."

"Raymond, Hello. Where are you?"

Her voice was far away. Was it Evelyn who had been phoning him all this time?

"I'm home. How's Eddy and the baby?"

"We're fine."

"Is Eddy there?"

"No, he's at work. What's up?"

"Ah, glad you asked. Well you know, Evelyn, I never really had a chance to thank you for all that you did after Wally's death."

"What did I do?"

"No, I mean the way you helped clean out his place and all that."

"It was our pleasure."

"You know I always wondered how you found out so fast about Wally's death ..."

"Oh, I think that old woman phoned Eddy, what's her name, Audrie Winter. Or maybe it was her sister. Is the house sold yet?"

"Almost. Not quite enough to pay off the bills but I think they'll settle."

"Oh good. Did you sell off Wally's art? You know Eddy was tremendously happy to get Wally's pinkie ring."

"Well, he earned it."

"And we were both glad to get the picture."

"You mean the Jim Dine?"

"It *is* grotesque, but Eddy always loved that picture and I guess it is worth a lot of money. It must have reminded Wally of his mother."

"Yeah. What did you do with it?"

"We have it in the living room over the couch. You know that Eddy loved Wally. Eddy was like a mother to Wally—taking care of him and everything."

"I hope it's OK that I'm phoning—"

"Of course it's OK. Why not? You know Wally always said that our son was in Wally's will, but you never found a will, is that right?"

"I'm sorry about that, Evelyn."

"What about the rest of his art?"

"Well, I sold some, but I still have some too. Actually Evelyn, now that you mention it—would you be interested in another piece? I think I've squeezed the high-rollers and I don't have room for all that stuff in my house. Frankly Wally's taste wasn't exactly mine."

"Well, we might conceivably be interested in maybe buying another painting. Our house is so bare and, anyway, I guess it would bring Wally closer to us. Also, you know Eddy's birthday is coming up and it could be a kind of surprise," said Evelyn Cornel.

"Well there are still a few pieces left. For example, there is that funny picture of this sort of fat guy on a couch with somebody looking at him from a portrait on the wall."

"Oh yes, I know that picture. Do you think you could sell it to me?"

"Hmmm ..."

"The thing is, Raymond, I could give it to Eddy for his birthday, see what I mean? He hasn't been the same since Wally died."

"How so?"

"He's different. Sometimes he's very angry. It frightens me."

"So you think getting hold of some of Wally's art is going to cheer him up?"

"Yes. I can pay, you know."

"Well, as a matter of fact I have to drive south on Friday on business and I could easily swing along the lake in your neck of the woods. I prefer that route anyway. I could bring the picture then if you want. It would be good to talk to you about some other things too," Birch said.

"That would be perfect, Raymond. I'd really like to see you. What time?"

"Late morning?"

82. A man and a woman

Birch had to give a talk at the University of Chicago on Friday night at 5:00 P.M. on his publication of a new inscription from the Greek island of Thera, but by setting out early in the morning he could easily get to Eddy Cornel's by 11:00, drop the painting, then have a leisurely afternoon before showing up in Chicago by 4:00 P.M. It was better this way—that he put the matter to Evelyn in person.

Following Evelyn's instructions he easily found the house in an old but respectable working-class neighborhood in the modest-sized provincial lakeside town of Paducah where Eddy Cornel had moved after being fired for sexual harassment. It was a two-story frame house painted a chocolate brown and set up high from the street, crowded between similar bungalow-style houses. Birch guessed that you had to keep your shades pulled down in a neighborhood like this!

The sky was overcast, leaden, and the street crowded with cars. Birch saw the address up from the street. He drove around the block but did not find a place. He drove past the house again and headed up the street for two blocks until he found a parking place, though his truck hung over the edge of someone's driveway.

He opened the back of his truck and took out the painting wrapped in an old rug and checked the glass to see if it had cracked on the road, but it was OK. The painting was not large and it was easy to carry.

He walked up the sidewalk to the house and up the cement steps onto a porch whose screens were bashed in on either side. Paint was peeling in long streamers from the siding and the screen door hung permanently ajar. Birch pushed the button at the side of the heavy oak front door. At first he heard nothing, then footsteps as if someone was walking in stocking feet. He wondered if Eddy would be at home—but then the painting would not be much of a surprise.

Evelyn opened the door. She wore black wool trousers and a black turtleneck. For a second Birch thought it was someone else, whom he had known a long time ago, a woman he had loved. She was very pretty and a strand of hair fell across one eye.

"Hi—just on time," she said. "Oh you brought the picture. Come in."

Birch followed her into a narrow entrance hall off which opened an elongated rectangular room. The house, built in the twenties, was trimmed in varnished oak. A wood stove stood at the far end beneath high narrow windows that looked out directly to the house next door, six feet away. A large crack in the long white plaster wall opposite the windows facing the street disappeared behind the enormous painting of the pink headless lady hung over a beat-up couch. A gray square carpet covered the floor. Children's plastic toys were scattered around. No curtains, but yellowed shades, half-drawn.

"Shush," Evelyn said, turning with her finger to her mouth. "Abbie is sleeping."

"Aha. How old is he now?"

"Fourteen months."

"Just a little guy. Well, here's the picture."

Birch unwrapped it and placed it on the couch for display.

"It's weird. I think this guy in the portrait on the wall is Wally's dad—you know that? I found a picture of some old guy under a stack of magazines out in Wally's garage—it was framed, you know, and it looked like Wally wanted to hide it, but I'm sure it was his father. He looked just like this guy on the wall in this painting!"

"Like his father was watching him. I wonder who painted it?"

"Oh probably some friend," Birch said. "Wally had a lot of artist friends and they were always making pictures of him. Wally loved to have his picture all over the walls. So look, that would be Wally on the couch—depressed by the guy looking at him."

"Sure," Evelyn smiled. "Anyway, I think Eddy will like it. You know how close he and Wally were even after we got married."

"Wally was quite a guy."

She had made up her face with light lipstick and wore a pleasant perfume.

"How much do I owe you?" she asked awkwardly.

"You don't owe me a thing. I'm glad to get rid of it. It's not my style."

"Oh let me give you a little something."

"Forget it."

"Not even $50?"

There were no lights on in the room and it seemed like late afternoon.

"How about a cup of coffee?" Birch said.

They laughed at the same time.

"If you put in a dash of Jack Daniels I promise not to notice," Birch added.

She laughed again. "I'm sorry, but I don't have any. I don't keep liquor in the house."

"I see. Well, everybody knows that you reformed Eddy, Evelyn. I was amazed at the change in him after he met you. When I first knew Eddy—he was pretty far out. I never imagined Eddy could change."

She seemed ill at ease.

"Well look, you sit down and I'll get the coffee."

Birch followed her into the dining room off the living room, bare except for a square white-painted wooden kitchen table and three chairs. He pulled up a chair but one leg fell off with a clatter and rolled across the broken varnish of the oak wood floor.

"Gosh I'm sorry," she apologized and bent down to pick up the leg. "I've been meaning to fix it but I haven't had a chance."

From a back room a child cried, then stopped.

"That's Abbie. He's kind of sick."

"What's the matter?"

"I don't know, one of those childhood diseases. I looked in Dr. Spock but couldn't find quite the right thing."

Birch took the pieces of the chair from her and placed them in the corner of the room. He pulled back another chair.

"That one's OK," she said and went into the kitchen.

Birch immediately got up and followed. The kitchen had never been remodeled and still had its original high plyboard paneled cupboards painted white, badly chipped. The walls and the baseboards were an ugly matte pink and the counter a fifties job. The faucet drip-dripped into a sink filled with dirty dishes. There was a small refrigerator covered with canisters in the corner of the room. Another door led down to a pantry or into a backyard.

"Nice color scheme," Birch said.

Evelyn laughed.

"I know, isn't it awful? I just hate it. I've been trying to get Eddy to repaint but he doesn't get home until late from work and then he's too tired to do anything. He hates his job. I don't think he'll ever get over what happened to him at the U. I'm working half-time myself."

"What do you do?"

"I'm working at a Border's bookstore in a mall. I shelve books. The people are real nice but it doesn't pay much. Of course I have to pay day-care for Abbie, too." She rinsed out a tea-kettle and placed it on the miniature stove. "We need a new stove—the oven doesn't work so I can never make bread or anything like that. Being married isn't what I imagined it was going to be like, Professor Birch!"

"Of course."

"But you're not married, are you?"

"Not any more."

"Why? I mean, it's none of my business."

"The usual reasons. Infidelity and mutual antipathy."

She seemed offended.

"And what about your children? Don't you have three?"

"Ah yes, well my oldest son Brian—you said you went on a date with him—he's a bicycle courier in New York City."

"Is that a disappointment to you?"

"Not at all. Maybe he will get rich and famous. I guess we all want that."

"Not me. I just want to be a normal person with a normal life."

She stood with her back to the counter. The electric unit had heated up and the kettle rocked slightly on top of it. The gray light of the dark day framed her black hair and her features were in shadow.

"Well, looks like you've succeeded," Birch said. She held her arms crossed tightly over her chest.

"So Eddy's not happy with his job, huh?"

"It's all these Baptists! He's supposed to teach them English composition. If they ever heard a word about what happened at the U, he'd be fired in a second. I'm amazed that they haven't heard anything."

"Usually Karla sends around a fact sheet."

"I didn't know you were such a right-winger, Raymond."

"Some guy—a visiting scholar from Cambridge—he thought I was a Republican. Thirty years I been making bombs, and now I'm a Republican!"

She laughed.

"Anyway, it's touch and go, eh?" Birch said.

"Touch and go is right."

"But aren't Eddy's folks glad that Eddy straightened around, got married and is leading a steady life—all that? Aren't they well fixed?"

"I guess. But you know they didn't really know that much about Eddy. I mean Wally for example—they liked him but ... they thought he was a good influence!"

Birch guffawed.

"It's just that they never imagined what was going on."

"Uh-huh."

The water steamed from the kettle. Evelyn tore off a paper towel from a roll mounted on the side of the cupboards and folded it into a square and opened the square to make a filter which she placed in a red plastic funnel. She filled the funnel with Hills Brothers coffee, put the funnel on top of a mug, and poured the hot water through the grounds. She transferred the funnel to a second mug and poured in more water.

"Milk or sugar?"

"No, I'm drinking black," Birch said.

"Me too."

"Let's go in the other room."

They went into the dining room and sat down at the white table. A privet hedge, long neglected, grew outside the windows. A mist or a cold rain drifted past the window.

83. The innocence of a child

"**S**o do you own this house Evelyn, or what?"

"Yeah, we bought it just before Abbie was born. Eddy's Dad gave us the down but even so we can barely make the payments."

"Still, it's nice to have your own place."

Evelyn looked into her coffee.

"You don't seem very happy, Evelyn," Birch said and remembered what had passed between them in the museum after the epic conference.

She looked up. She was going to cry. Women in pain gave Birch a funny feeling. He wanted to calm them down and make a difference in their lives, an instinct that had gotten him into very serious trouble in his life. He reached down anyway and took hold of Evelyn's foot and slipped off her black flat shoe and began to massage her toes through her stocking.

"That feels good," she said.

"Your feet are cold."

"It's always cold in this house."

"So you and Eddy are having problems, eh?"

Her pleading eyes were dark, an animal's eyes.

"Raymond, it isn't what I thought. I feel like I'm trapped, like I'm going nowhere."

Birch let go of her foot and picked up his coffee and took a deep drink and she tucked her shoeless foot behind her calf.

"But you're young, Evelyn. Good coffee by the way."

They sat in silence and between sips of coffee glanced at each other and Birch steeled himself.

"Evelyn—"

"What?"

"You know, Wally's death, and that super weird thing with this dead guy in Wally's basement."

"I couldn't believe that!"

"Nobody could believe it. And nobody can make sense of it, either."

"What do the police think?"

"I don't think they think anything. They're just waiting around hoping something will happen. Officially they don't think anything. Both men—Wally and the kid—died from falls."

"That is so weird."

"You know it turns out there were other people there that night. I hope you don't mind my talking about this?"

"No, not at all."

"There was this guy named Jack Devries, a little squirt that Wills and I had been putting the screws on—I thought he and Wally were enemies but it turns out they were carrying on—"

"That's typical. Wally always wanted everything both ways."

"Sure. Anyway Devries was there sometime that afternoon and this kid Eric Salton wasn't there when Jack was because he was with his friend Tom who had been at Wally's the night before. And now it looks like this Vergil Rawlins was at Wally's too. He seems to have broken into my house, and killed my parrots! He's made threats against me."

Evelyn acted as if she'd been touched by an electric wire.

"He killed your parrots?"

"Sure! I think Rawlins was trying to prove how dangerous he could be so that I would somehow find the money Wally owed him. I have been cavalier with Wally's property and I should have kept records. You know this weird guy showed up from the West coast named John Carson—the guy Wally always said was his brother, then it turned out he wasn't—at least that's what Wally thought—and this guy, who is a lawyer, now claims that he really *is* Wally's half-brother after all, but Wally never knew it. You'd think we were living in some fucking two-bit novel."

"I'm not sure."

"Maybe this guy Carson even has some claim on Wally's property for all I know, but anyway he says that Wally owed him big money too."

"That was Wally all right."

"Of course in the end, with no bona fide heirs, the meager profits from Wally's estate will go to the state, you realize."

"You really haven't kept records?"

Birch laughed abruptly and waited for her to say something but she was silent.

"Let's not think about that right now Evelyn. The fact is that probably only I know all the angles of who was at Wally's and all that because I sort of stumbled on these things or squeezed them out of the woodwork and from time to time I really do wonder just what the hell is going on."

"I've been wondering that for years."

"Sure. But look, everybody says that Wally was seriously toasted that night, but still alive, including the infamous Vergil Rawlins, and my guess is that this drifter Eric Salton found dead in Wally's basement hadn't even got to Wally's until late at night, because nobody seems to have seen him there earlier that day— Tom Allen, Eric Salton's friend, thought he had left town in the afternoon. Rawlins and Devries admitted they were there that night but deny seeing Salton."

"Uh-huh."

"Of course they could be lying, but my idea is that the dying took place late Monday night. Obviously Eric had come back at some point and Wally must have been alive when he did come and I don't think they killed each other."

"Why not? Maybe Wally put him down the cellar to hide him."

"Sure, but for a second let's think about a couple of other things. For example, I mean Wally was a bullshitter all right. Who would deny it? He deceived me for twenty years. On the other hand, one fourth of what he said was, you know, sort of based in fact. Even the lies he told about his family, that his father owned this big mill—in fact his father worked in a mill as some kind of janitor, I guess."

"The man in the picture?"

"I suppose. And his mother was supposed to be a math professor! She was a waitress."

"That belongs to the three-fourths total shit, you mean."

"Right. I mean it was a complete fabrication. Well I guess she had to add up receipts, huh?"

"I see."

"You know what always sort of bothered me was this thing about Wally's collection of old paper currencies."

He watched her face but she didn't blink, not a flicker.

"Like, you know, we never found all of these currencies which everybody kept talking about except for a few which the police found in a drawer in the washstand and which I got from the coroner along with the pinkie ring and Wally's keys and wallet. It turns out that those bills were probably the most valuable thing Wally owned. In any event they were not the whole collection, that's for sure. You know he had that humongous big set of books on old currencies on the shelves next to the stairs. See, there had to be a larger collection."

"Maybe he sold it?"

"I thought about that because Wally was always collecting

stuff and then selling it off. Once he had a big collection of stoneware—he gave it away to the Historical Society to perpetuate his name for as long as the sun circles the earth. Also, he once had some Japanese prints—he gave those to a museum in Chicago. That was it—when Wally got rid of things, it was to further his name in some way. But nothing ever came out about these currencies, see? They disappeared without a trace."

"Do you think maybe that other guy who was there—Tom whatever his name was—maybe he took them? Or maybe Wally gave them to Vergil Rawlins to pay off his debt?"

"That's what Rawlins told me—that Wally was going to sell them and that he had set up some deal on the East coast and apparently he had told his so-called brother Johnny Carson the same thing. Carson came all the way out here from the coast just to look for the collection! Me and Carson even got in a big fight out at Wally's."

"A fight!"

Evelyn raised her brows and opened her eyes.

"I guess that's a little silly all right, but I've been nervous, I admit it," Birch said. "And then this Rawlins waylaid me in my own backyard."

"What do you mean?"

"He and some other guy beat the shit out of me."

Her eyes examined the abrasions still visible on Birch's face.

"Why?" she touched the back of his hand.

"Because I'm in charge of Wally's affairs and because Wally owed him money. Somebody's leaning on him and I think he's desperate, frankly."

"I'm sorry."

"It's not your fault—and I'm getting used to it. But look, Wally was in serious financial trouble. The bank was on his back and it looks as if he was going to sell off the one painting that had real value—the Jim Dine—to this local art dealer, a guy name Fodamew. And why did he leave part of the currency collection in the washstand where the police found it?"

"Maybe this Tom guy or if it was Vergil Rawlins—whoever, just didn't find those bills and just took the ones in the safe?"

"Good point. That could be right. But you know I really doubt that any of these guys could have known about this safe. I knew Wally for twenty years and was in that closet plenty of times but I never heard a word about this safe. It seems to me that the big collection must have been there all right, just like Eddy said, but when Eddy looked, when we were at Wally's that morning, the safe was open and empty. And Vergil Rawlins—what would he want with a bunch of old bills? He wouldn't have the faintest idea what to do with them. Rawlins was one of the first to mention these currencies to me and why should he draw attention to them if he had latched onto them? None of this adds up."

"Oh no! Do you think Eddy might have taken them from the safe?"

"Well, going over all this, I wondered that too—you know, that somehow Eddy might have put them in his pocket or something on that day when we went into Wally's. I guess it's possible, but that doesn't seem right either—I mean Sally Brown was in the bathroom with Eddy when he was looking for the safe and that is a pretty small room. Also, it's not likely that he could have concealed them in his shirt or pocket without somebody noticing. The way I see it, Evelyn, the safe really was empty when Eddy looked in there, just like he said."

"Excuse me," she said and stood up and went through the kitchen into a back room. Birch wondered if he was supposed to follow her. Of course, the child was sleeping there.

84. A normal life

She came back into the room, a grim look on her face and tears in her eyes. Her breath was short.

"Sorry about that. I needed to check on Abbie," she said and sat back down. "So anyway, you think Eddy's in the clear?"

"That's the way I see it. Unless maybe, just supposing, Eddy was there that night too—at Wally's. See what I mean?"

"Not really. Do you want more coffee?"

"No thanks."

"Then how about a cigarette?"

"I thought you'd never ask."

"Eddy doesn't like me to smoke in the house but I do anyway, sometimes."

Again she went into the kitchen and came back and placed a pack of Marlboros on the table and a paper of matches and sat down. Birch managed to get two cigarettes out of the pack. He offered her one and took one himself, then lit a match and both cigarettes. He took a long drag and suddenly felt dizzy. He thought he was going to fall down onto the floor.

"I don't smoke much any more Evelyn," he moaned, "but when I do—you know, I notice it."

A red cardinal came from nowhere and perched on the privet hedge outside the window and arched its handsome crest.

"Excuse me, Raymond, I have to get an ashtray."

She went back into the kitchen and returned with an ashtray and put it on the table and dipped her ash into it. So did Birch. Then he stood up and went into the living room. He came back into the dining room.

"Then, you know, like I said on the phone, about how you and Eddy found out about Wally's death—I mean Eddy said that Audrie Winter's daughter Mimi Esperanto told him. But Mimi Esperanto doesn't *know* Eddy it turns out. And Audrie didn't find out until pretty late in the game."

She was silent.

"So anyway Evelyn, you see where all this is leading."

"Where?"

"Have you ever heard of Horning's Auction House?"

Her shoulders slumped forward and pinched her small breasts. Her head fell onto her chest as if she had been struck on the crown of the head. She had dropped her cigarette in the ashtray and a stream of smoke spun crazily toward the cracked plaster ceiling.

"Yes," she said.

"Of course! You see it's the weirdest coincidence, but I have business with Horning's too. That's how I found out—by accident! So Eddy was there that night, wasn't he Evelyn?"

Her face gathered together, her lips drew into a thin line. She covered her face and whimpered like a puppy far from home.

"Tell me, Evelyn."

"No, it wasn't Eddy. It was me."

"What do you mean?"

"I thought you knew anyway—I thought you knew all along—for some reason."

"Knew what?"

"Everything! I had a dream—you were standing over me and whispering in my ear. You must think I'm crazy but I thought you knew all along. I thought you were just pretending."

"Tell me."

"How can I?"

She dropped her hands from her face. Her complexion had changed and a network of fine veins inscribed the flesh pulled against her high cheekbones. Her face glistened.

"Don't you see, Ray? Eddy's *gay*—That was the irony of his getting fired the way he did. It was a cover-up as much as anything—he didn't care about the women and that's why they plotted against him. It was a revenge thing with him—sleeping with women. I thought it was, you know, because he had never found just the right one. I was just one of the women he was screwing—but I got pregnant. I was sure I could change him. *Nobody* can change Eddy Cornel. After we were married he went on seeing Wally. I accepted it because—I didn't know what to do about it. You know he had his own key to Wally's place? He went whenever he wanted and when we quarreled—which was often—off he'd go to Wally's and sometimes he wouldn't come back for days. He'd go off and leave me alone—me and Abbie, alone."

"Sure."

"Eddy said he was sick of me and sick of Abbie. He hated his job and he hated the straight life. He was going to leave me and go and live with Wally again."

"Uh-huh."

"That Monday night we got in an enormous fight and he hit me really hard. I was desperate—I didn't know what to do. He left in a fury. I waited an hour and then I followed him."

"You have two cars?"

"If you can call it that. I still have that old VW bug I had when I was a student. I knew he was going to Wally's and that's where I went. I wanted to have it out once and for all with him and with Wally too. For me—for Abbie."

"You took Abbie with you?"

"I left him with my mother across town. It was late when I got there, maybe 1:00 in the morning. I parked the car up the street so no one would notice. I went down Goldbug Walk until I saw Eddy's car on the apron. I went back up the walk and down to the lake and followed along the edge of the lake until I got to the deck. I could see them through the glass doors. They were doing coke over the white table. I marched straight in and started shouting. 'Is this what it's all for, Eddy? You never loved me even a little, did you?' Things like that. I wanted to embarrass him ... I wanted Eddy to ... come back ..."

"Of course."

"Eddy was furious that I had followed him. He was extremely high and had been drinking hard. The place was a shambles. There had obviously been a big party going on. Eddy grabbed me by the shoulders and pushed me down on the couch and Wally just laughed. Eddy said he was sick and tired of me and that he wanted me to know just what he and Wally did together and what Wally could do for him that I could never do. He hit me. I couldn't believe this was happening! Eddy went back to Wally and ... then they did it right in front of me."

"Uh-huh."

"I was terrified. I didn't know what to do. Eddy's mouth was sort of fallen open and his eyes were half-closed and unfocused. It went on and on. Eddy said 'Give her a lick,' things like that, and Wally said, 'Whore, whore!' Eddy said, 'Don't make so much noise, you might wake up Evelyn' … What did I do to deserve that such things should happen to me?"

Birch lit another cigarette.

"I'm sorry to be telling you this," she said.

"It's OK."

" 'There's a real lover for you,' Eddy says, looking over to me. He meant Wally. Wally got up—he could barely get to his feet because he was so drunk—and he went over to the table and got some cocaine on his finger from a plate and he rubbed the cocaine all over Eddy's penis. Then he started in again. Afterward he rubbed his gums with his fingers and Eddy was saying, 'That taste good, Wally?' and Wally called Eddy a cow. He said his mother never gave him enough milk!"

Evelyn was breathing in spasms.

"So that was it, huh," asked Birch.

Evelyn straightened her shoulders and searched Birch's eyes.

"Can you imagine what I was feeling? Wally got up and went back to the table and for a second I thought he was going to fall over. He got some more cocaine and went to the counter and poured a big glass of Vodka which he drank like it was water. Then Eddy went over and took the bottle of vodka and started drinking it like it was nothing. Then Eddy said to Wally, 'You gotta work tomorrow, eh?' I couldn't believe any of this was happening."

Evelyn got up and went into a back room and came back with a box of kleenex. She blew her nose and wiped the tears from her face.

85. The sex was bad enough

"**W**hat next?" asked Birch and knocked off the ash from his cigarette into the ashtray.

"I'll tell you what next. After Eddy drank the vodka he threw the bottle in the trash piled in the corner of the room and then he sort of howled and staggered into the bathroom. In spite of everything, I don't know, I wanted to help him so I got up and went in after him. He was kneeling on the floor with his arms around the toilet bowl. Then he got up and pulled down his pants and sat on the bowl and then he fell off the toilet and rolled over on his side and held the bowl in his arms. He was throwing up everywhere. I don't think he even knew I was there. He went past me like I was invisible, and then he went upstairs. I heard him fall down on the mattress up there. All I wanted was to have a reasonable discussion about what was going on in our life. That's why I went there in the first place."

"What was Wally doing?"

"I don't know, I guess he was sitting at the table by the windows. He looked real weird, I mean his eyes were real small—like a pig's and fiery. I guess then he got up and went right past me and sat down on the couch. There were bad smells and furniture thrown everywhere and empty beer cans and filthy clothes. He was looking for something and after awhile he picked up this old red telephone—it was buried beneath a bunch of paper, the old-fashioned dial kind … and he dialed some number."

"Who did he phone?"

"I have no idea. They didn't answer."

"What time was it?"

"Maybe 2:30 in the morning—it was real late. Then after awhile he hung up and went back to the kitchen and opened the refrigerator. He just acted like I wasn't there. I can't remember—maybe I was talking to him, pleading with him, but he just ignored me, naturally. He took out a tin of Libby's tomato juice and poured an inch of juice into this dirty glass and then an inch of vodka on top of it and went back over to the table and sat down again and started drinking. He seemed to perk up a little bit. It was like the first time he even noticed I was in the room and he says, 'How you doin Evelyn? I'm glad you could come … we're having a little party … we don't usually have people like you to our parties but we're glad you could come … do you want a drink?' … something like that. Then he went back in the kitchen to make another Bloody Mary, but this time he goes over to the couch in front of the fireplace and puts the glass down on the coffee table and lies back on the couch. I think he must have forgotten I was there. I was screaming at him, I guess, but after awhile he got up and started going through these papers scattered everywhere. Finally he found the remote control to the TV and he turned on the TV. It was nearly three in the morning!"

"What was on?"

"Oh, I don't know … he kept flipping the channels. And then he lights up a cigarette, I remember, and settles back on the couch. He kept saying he was going to chew another asshole in Karl Marx! I thought he was insane."

"Sure."

"I couldn't really understand him because he was muttering but suddenly I wasn't afraid of *any* of this any more and I just went over and turned off the TV and he says 'What'd you do that for?' I guess he had vomited on his T-shirt because there was tomato juice all over it."

"Sure."

"It was this that I was trying to protect us from, me and Abe."

"Right."

"Wally just looked at me and I'm sure I was screaming at him again and I told him that all this had to end. You know, Ray, he had promised me before that it would end—he really had."

"What did Wally say?"

"He didn't say anything. He laughed at me."

"Sure."

"I felt like *I* was the one going crazy. I told him I was going to *kill* him if all this didn't stop and if he didn't leave Eddy alone once and for all. He laughed again. I told him that I wanted back the $350 that Eddy had loaned him—Wally said that if he didn't pay it back he would give us some or other painting—the sex with Eddy was bad enough but at least I knew what was going on and where Eddy was … but really, Ray, when Eddy gave him our money it destroyed me. We didn't need his stupid painting. We don't have any money. Eddy was taking the food out of our mouths and putting cocaine in Wally's nose. Can you understand what I'm saying?"

"All right."

"It really wasn't the sex … I told Eddy never to give Wally money for *anything* but he did it anyway and then they just went out and did this, do you understand? Wally would say he'd pay it back but he never did."

"Of course."

"Wally started in laughing so hard when I asked him for the money back he sort of rolled to his feet and threw back his head. I remember he was barefoot—his feet were so disgusting, fat and with black bristles on the toes—'Oh sweet Evelyn,' he says, 'why don't I just write you a check?' I was a big joke to him. Anyway we were shouting at each other and somehow we were in the kitchen—I mean there was trash everywhere, it looked like a bomb had hit the place. That's when I saw this guy on the floor."

She looked out the window. The cigarette had burned down to the filter and the long ash fell onto the table top and her hand was trembling, her eyes focused at something in another room or another world.

"What guy?"

"What?"

"You said you saw somebody."

"That's right. It was the boy—he was lying on the kitchen floor, sort of curled up behind the partition. It was dark there. I think I was screaming. Wally said he was a friend. There was a little pool of blood coming out of this boy's mouth."

"Uh-huh."

"I just wanted to be a normal person with a normal life."

"What did you do?"

"I asked Wally who he was and he acted as if nothing was wrong. He said he was a friend. Wally was completely out of it. I tried to move the boy. I knew he was dead. I didn't have to touch him but I did touch him. I was a para-medical one summer, Ray, and I felt for his pulse."

"Wally didn't know he was there?"

"I don't know. He must have. He said, 'Oh Eddy and Eric were having a little disagreement.' "

"A fight?"

" 'I broke them up …' he says. 'Eric, is he all right?' he says. 'No, Wally, he's not all right. Can you call a doctor?' He says, 'He doesn't need a doctor.' I said, 'Sure—he's dead!' "

"What happened then?"

" 'Oh, I thought he was just sleeping,' Wally says. Then he stepped past me like nothing was wrong and poured another drink of vodka and tomato juice. 'He's not sleeping,' I said—"

"You think he fell from the loft?"

"He was under it—there was no railing on the loft. I don't even want to think about it."

"There was some kind of fight, you said. Wally broke them up and Salton fell, you think?"

"I was really scared! I ran up the stairs. I wanted to wake up Eddy and get him out of there but Wally starts in after me. I was scrambling up the stairs and I knocked off one of the paintings— some kind of drawing of a fence or something. It fell and smashed on the stairs and, you know, sort of slid down."

"Uh-huh."

Evelyn lit another cigarette and Birch lit one too. "I never liked Marlboros much," Birch said, "but they're better than Virginia Slims."

Evelyn looked at Birch as if he too were insane.

"I can't believe you just said that."

"You mean at a time like this? but—look, Wally was chasing you up the stairs and you knocked down a painting—"

"That was the only thing Wally really cared about. He didn't care about people. People were things to him."

"Let's not think about that right now, Evelyn."

"Like I say he was sort of lumbering after me and he had this funny look on his face. He seemed puzzled or confused. I thought he was going to grab me and that's when I—there was some kind of a pot or something on the landing. I don't know what it was, like an orange pot, a sort of papier-mâché thing. I picked it up and let him have it! I hit him as hard as I could. He fell backwards. He made a huge crash as he went down the stairs."

"Wow."

"I was terrified. I ran down after him. He was lying at the bottom of the stairs. Somehow he had turned over. He was still alive—like he was trying to breathe but he couldn't. He was jerking around. I tried to turn him over to help him breathe but I couldn't. He was too fat. At first his eyes were closed but he opened them and was making these horrible squealing sounds. He was thrashing around with his hands and legs like he was trying to get hold of something but his tongue was sticking out. There was blood coming from his mouth. There was nothing I could do. His face was purple. He was staring at me—reaching. He was like a balloon swelling up to explode!"

Birch dipped the ash from his cigarette.

"Then he stiffened—you know, like a fish when you're cutting its head off with a big knife. My father used to make me do that—cut off the heads of catfish when they were still alive. I knew he was dying."

"Why didn't you phone an ambulance?"

Evelyn gave Birch a gentle look and stopped trembling and was calm.

"Ray—there was cocaine all over this house and a corpse in the kitchen!"

"Right."

"He died even as I watched him. He could not have been saved. Maybe now Eddy would go straight and be with me—and Abbie."

86. The jig is up

"**Y**ou know Wally always said that he had left $200,000 to Abbie. Eddy always said that the will was in a safe in the bathroom. Once he showed the safe to me. I went to the bathroom and looked. The door to the safe was open. I pulled everything out of it. There wasn't any will but there was a bunch of old paper money in plastic folders. They were mine by rights."

"Wally was dead you mean?"

"He was still sort of quivering when I came back into the room. Snakes do that, kind of move around until the sun goes down."

Evelyn was silent while she crushed out the stub of her cigarette.

"I see," said Birch after awhile.

"I wanted to see if Abbie was in the will, you see, so we could get the money and get out … of here. That's why I looked in the safe."

"So that's it."

Evelyn wiped under her nose with her index finger and rubbed her eyes.

"Yes. That's how Wally died. Then there were two dead bodies in Wally's house, you see. Do I have two black eyes now?" she asked.

"What do you mean?"

"I mean from the mascara. Has it run all over the place?"

Birch held the peak of her chin with his finger and looked closely at her in the low light.

"I guess they are a mess, Evelyn."

"That always happens when I cry."

"But what about Eric Salton? And what about Eddy?"

"It was so strange. When I saw that Wally was dead, I became completely calm. I knew about the trap door because once I went down there with Eddy when the furnace wasn't working. I raised up the door and dragged the boy to it and pushed him down the stairs."

"Why? I mean what was the point?"

"I wanted to clean up the house, I mean straighten things up, and then get Eddy out to the car and just get away. But then I went to drag Wally to the hole and I couldn't budge him—not a little! I thought I could kind of slither him down and around the stairs but he got wedged under an old-fashioned chair. I heard Eddy moving around upstairs. I shut the trapdoor and pushed the couch over on top of it and went up the stairs to see if Eddie was awake. I picked up the painting off the landing and hung it back up. Eddy was sitting on the edge of the futon but his eyes were only half open—he seemed like in a trance. He sort of hung onto me and somehow I got him down the stairs and around Wally and we got out to the car."

"But he knows what happened?"

"Not to this day! The next morning he couldn't remember a thing. Nothing! We went right past Wally at the bottom of the stairs. Maybe he wasn't dead even then—I think he moved a little. I became totally frightened. I got Eddy in the back seat of my car. Then I got in his car and drove it a couple of blocks away and parked it on the street and walked back to Wally's. Eddy was completely out of it. That's how I drove him back. When we came over to help clean up that day—Eddy drove his car back then."

"Eddy doesn't know what happened?"

"He thinks Wally fell down the stairs after we left. That's it. Eddy did remember that this Eric Salton had come back that night to have sex with Wally but Eddy thinks that he left right after that. I don't know about the fight or how Eric Salton fell off the loft. I didn't want to question Eddy too closely. We made up the story about Mimi Esperanto phoning about Wally's death. When we came over to your place, you see—I wanted to go back to the house because I was afraid there was something there, that I might have left something."

"Uh-huh."

"You can have me now if you want," Evelyn said matter-of-factly.

"What do you mean?"

"You can fuck me if you want. It's OK. You want to. I can see that."

Birch's heart beat fast. He spoke very softly.

"Maybe I do, Evelyn, but I better not. Now is not a good time for that. Maybe some other time."

Evelyn glared.

"What are you going to do, then?" she said.

"About what?"

"Are you going to tell the police?"

"That you murdered Wally Wills?"

"That's the law, isn't it?"

"And what abut Eric Salton? Did you murder him too?"

Her eyes swelled with tears.

"I told you what happened, Ray."

"OK, anyway, what good would the police do?"

"It might be a relief. I thought you knew all along, like I say. I've been crazy with fear. I was happy when you phoned because I wanted to get it out in the open."

"Look Evelyn, as for the police—they're just going to come in and cause a lot of trouble and make a lot of people unhappy. In spite of what you say—Wally had been behaving bizarrely. He phoned up his so-called brother in California that weekend and left this weird message on his machine. He was out of control—drinking and carrying on when he was supposed to be working. The jig was up for Wally Wills, so don't feel so bad. He was in deep with Vergil Rawlins. The bank was on him. He owed money to this Johnny Carson. There was a weird note in his wallet—a suicide note really. Wally was supposed to be writing a book for Harcourt-Brace but I don't think he had a thing on paper. They gave him a big advance, I don't know, but I think I know where it went. I see you hated him, but don't you think that Wally set up his own death? I mean you barely hit him. Wally was big—a mountain. You're small and that papier-mâché pot—I think it was a prop in that Plautus play they put on. I don't see how you could have hit him very hard."

She was silent.

"Let's put this behind us. Wally had plans and he had his life and now it is over. We are alive so let us go on and put the past behind us."

He liked the feel of her breasts and he liked the way she smelled.

"So what will you do now?" he asked.

"Take the money from Horning's and go, I guess … Leave Eddy. But half of what I get is yours, Ray. Let us say, for the painting."

Birch laughed.

"Forget it—I consigned the bills the police found in the washstand to the same auction as you! Looks like we're in this together, Evelyn."

She turned her face.

"How much do you think yours are worth?" she asked.

"The way I see it Wally had culled them from the rest—those were the bills he was going to sell, along with the Jim Dine, to bail himself out. Then he lost his nerve, when he saw that they really were going. Wally loved art and he loved money. In those beautiful bills was his whole life, his twin and vile passions."

"So unlike our own."

"You take your money, I'll take mine. Don't look back. Wally would have wanted that."

She smiled broadly.

"If we hurry, we can be done before Abbie wakes," she said, taking Birch's hand.

The cardinal had returned to the privet hedge and tugged angrily at something stuck in it. Then the brilliant bird gave up his effort, raised a fine scarlet head, and gave forth a long and lovely song.

87. Goodbye, my sweet

When Birch got back from Chicago he parked in front of his house instead of behind beside the garage because he wanted to pick up his mail from the rural mailbox. He went in the front door and turned on the light next to the couch. He sat down. Outside the window he thought he saw a form in the darkness. He removed his revolver from his pocket. He thought he would go into the yard, but instead checked the lock on the front and back doors and returned to the living room.

He had dropped the mail on the floor. He picked up the bunch of catalogs from *Beans* and *Sierra Design* and *Landsend* and then a long business looking thing with an L.A. postmark on it and a return address JOHN CARSON, ATTORNEY AT LAW. Birch scanned the dense prose of the three page legal document. Apparently he was being sued for malfeasance in the administration of the estate of Wally Wills. The plaintiff John Carson was laying claim to all proceeds of the estate and requiring an exact inventory of all properties and moneys received for said properties to be delivered by such and such a date etc. etc.

Birch put the letter down on the stack of catalogs. There was a letter from FLEISHACKER, DORPFELD, AND FETTMAN. Thank God he had good connections in the legal community! Birch flipped through the thick letter—a long catalog, a log of time spent on phones, in cars, in the office etc., and remittance due $19,384.64.

"With friends like that!"

The phone rang.

"Hi, it's Marylou Stieglitz. Raymond—you know I asked you about that plate. Really, I do need to have it."

"I forgot all about it, Marylou. I've been so busy."

"It's really, you know, to remember Wally by. It's special."

"I'll phone Harvey Vanderpool."

"I don't see what right he had to those plates anyhow. They're valuable, you know, by the famous potter Don Wright."

"OK, I'll phone."

He put down the phone and then saw the letter from the OFFICE OF THE DEAN. He knew what it was before he opened it:

> *Dear Professor Birch:*
>
> *A complaint has been lodged against you by disinterested parties with regard to various facts of your personal life in contravention of 11479&a of the Academic Code of Ethical conduct. I need to advise you that prima facie you are guilty of violating prescriptions. A hearing on the matter will be held at 8:00 A.M. on Monday morning in the office of Dean Karla Marsh. Personal counsel is not allowed. You should be advised that the complaint is extremely serious and dismissal with cause a possible outcome of this hearing.*
>
> *Yours sincerely,*
>
> *Karla Marsh, Dean of the College*

The phone rang again and he picked it up— a distant hum but no voice. He put it down in the cradle but immediately it rang again.

"Oh Raymond, I've been very lonely," said the voice loud and clear.

"Audrie—I'm sorry. I thought it was someone else."

"Well, who did you think it was?"

"I don't know. I keep getting weird calls."

"I wish I'd get some weird calls. Nobody ever phones me now that Wally's gone! But if Mohammed won't go to the mountain, then the mountain must go to Mohammed."

"I've been neglecting you. It's shameful," Birch said.

"I thought you were going to visit me on Sundays? I need some friendship in my life, you know."

"No one can replace Wally, Audrie."

"Oh please Ray, don't say that …"

She was crying.

"I'll try to be better."

"Oh but try, please Ray, to visit me," she pleaded.

"Good-bye Audrie."

Birch went over to the mantle and began to take down his artifacts. He wrapped them carefully in cloths and laid them in a large pile on the oriental carpet on the floor. He rolled up the carpet and carried it through the front door and the darkness and placed it in the camper of his truck. Then he went back in the house. He went upstairs and began to take down the artifacts from those walls too. He rolled them in another carpet and took that out to the truck. He gathered what remained in a third carpet and put that in the truck and went back in the house when the phone rang.

"I've had it Birch. Just thought you'd like to know."

"So have I."

The line went limp.

He hurried up the stairs, turned around the railing, went into the upper bedroom and carelessly picked up his jacket off the bed so that the Smith and Wesson slipped from the pocket, struck the hardwood floor butt-first, and discharged a bullet directly into his heart. He was actually conscious for a second, and recognized what had happened before he fell.

Birch adjusted his eyes to face the moment he always knew would come.

88. The garden party of death

Birch locked the doors, got in the camper and drove to the Forest Hills cemetery and parked in the general vicinity of Wally's Wills' grave, though he couldn't remember exactly where it was. When the dawn first broke through the edge of the trees beyond the railroad track he started the truck and drove to the International House of Pancakes. He had a large helping of flapjacks and two cups of coffee. He got back in his truck and got on the interstate heading south. He blended into the heavy traffic heading for the outskirts of town.

By noon he had crossed the great river. That night he slept in a rest stop on the interstate in the back of the truck. He had his Indian pipe, and when he woke in the night he inadvertently touched its silken stem.

The rising sun woke him and for a second he couldn't remember where he was. He crawled stiffly from the truck and went into the public toilet at the rest site and pissed in the urinal and splashed cold water on his face. When the room was empty, he wrapped the .38 in a paper towel and dropped it into the white-enameled trash cylinder with a push down aluminum door. Then he got back in the truck.

He lay the Indian pipe on the seat next to him and started the engine and soon was purring down the on-ramp onto the interstate. The sun was directly behind and shining in the rear-view mirror so that for a second he was blinded. He flipped on the radio and was listening to the morning report on hog prices and grain commodities when an enormous crow swerved ten feet off the hood of the truck and, back-flapping, disappeared into the sky.

Birch settled back and turned on the air-conditioning and the cruise control. It was going to be a hard drive. He needed all the comfort he could get.